DEEP WITHIN THE SHADOWS

TERESA J. REASOR

Contact Information: **teresareasor@msn.com**
Cover Art by Tracy Stewart
Edited by Faith Freewoman

Teresa J. Reasor
PO Box 124
Corbin, KY 40702

Publishing History: First Edition 2015
ISBN: 13: 978-1-940047-04-1
ISBN: 10: 1-940047-04-8

DEDICATION

For my wonderful friend and cover artist Tracy Stewart. You are always so supportive and I love you for it.

TABLE OF CONTENTS

PROLOGUE

A HUNGRY SCREAM echoed in the distance behind him. Willy jerked, a strangled gasp tearing from him. His heartbeat leapt high in his throat as he pushed his shuffling jog into a run. Sweat ran in rivulets down his face. After the cool of the basement he'd just left, he was baking alive in the hot, still humidity.

Damn that security guard for kicking him out. He wasn't botherin' nothin'. Fucking jerk. Luckily Willy knew where Gerry was staying. They'd split up weeks ago, hoping to throw the shadows off, but it hadn't worked. They just kept coming, night after night. And now the daytime creatures were on the prowl, there was no place left to hide.

God, he was so tired.

Another angry cry sounded from a block away. They were getting closer. If he could get far enough ahead, he might find somewhere to hole up until daylight. Somewhere no light could enter. A basement, crawlspace, anything. He'd even take the bottom of a dumpster if he could find one empty enough for him to squeeze into.

He careened around the corner of Kentucky Street and slipped into a dim alley. The sour smell of his own sweat mingled with the odor of rotting garbage from the dumpster behind one of the restaurants. His feet hit a flat sheet of corrugated cardboard and his right foot slid forward before the other could catch up. His left knee hit the ground with all his weight, and he cried out.

"Jesus, oh Jesus." He was hurt. Something had cut into his knee.

Pushing up with one hand, he felt something gooey squish between his fingers. He swore and slung his hand to get it off as he staggered to his feet. Hugging the brick wall of the building, he settled back into the deepest pool of darkness he could find. He wiped his filthy hand on his pants and probed the knee with the other one. A triangle of glass stuck out of his flesh, and he could feel blood welling up around it. He jerked the shard free, and a whimper leaked from him. He slung the piece of glass away with a sob.

They'd smell the blood and track him. He didn't know how they did it, but the *things* always seemed to know where he was. Oh God, if only he and Willy hadn't tried to kidnap that girl. She had something to do with *them*. He just knew it. They'd shown up right after he and Willy killed the guy she was with. The burns she gave him had finally healed, but now he had a cut that would probably rot his leg off.

He hobbled forward a foot or two, the pain making him lightheaded, and he gagged at the coppery scent of his own blood.

How long had it been since he'd eaten? Two days. He'd been afraid to leave the basement. Until the asshole guard had tossed him out. If he could just reach Gerry's motel room. Gerry would have some food. Maybe some weed. They could wait out the night in the dark together.

Another scream came from the end of the alley, almost

right behind him, and he nearly jumped of his skin. From the wide, yellowish-white pool of the streetlight, a dark gray figure rose. Its arms hung down nearly three quarters of its form. Strangely elongated fingers repeatedly flexed in a grabbing motion, like a crab's claw, as if hoping to pluck him from his hiding place. Though it had no eyes, and Willy hid twenty feet away in the deepest shadows cast by the three-story brick building, it homed in on where he stood with unerring precision. The creature opened its mouth like a black pit and screamed. The sound, a blend of a baboon-like cry and an ear-ringing roar, reverberated with frustration and rage.

Willy's fear shook him to his bones. His knee ached like an abscessed tooth. His mouth tasted pasty and dry, and his bladder felt uncomfortably full.

The shadow paced back and forth, searching for the light it needed to reach him. Willy stumbled further down the alley, hugging the building. The rough bricks picked at his clothing and scraped his arm, his hand, as he attempted to stay out of the anemic light cast from the windows above him.

His head jerked up at the rumble of an engine approaching. A silver car swung into the street directly in front of him, the bright headlights pinning him against the wall. Willy opened his mouth. "No-o-o-o-o!" The scream of denial worked its way up his throat. Almost from beneath his feet, a shadow leaped from the ground with inhuman speed.

Willy half turned to run. A slicing pain caught him just beneath his ribs and he was shoved against the wall and lifted. His legs cycled weakly. A suffocating fullness invaded his chest. His heart seized. The pain stole his breath and limited his scream to a choked gurgle. His bladder released and the warm urine ran down his legs to wet his pants all the way to his socks.

As the creature squeezed his heart to bursting, Willy's last thought was one of relief. His two-month hell was over.

CHAPTER 1

JULIET TEMPLETON SCANNED the patrons lined up at the bar waiting for drinks. Her hands flew as she packed ice into a glass and measured vodka in a jigger and dumped it in. She reached for the orange juice and tipped the jug.

"Have I told you this vampire-biker-chick look suits you?" Justin's warm, moist breath brushed her neck. She flinched away, resisting the urge to elbow him in the gut. Orange juice splashed onto the counter. For weeks, since he'd been hired to bartend, he'd pushed for a date. He was doing it again tonight. With his shaggy mop of dark hair, clean-shaven, angular jaw, and hazel eyes, he could pass for Hayden Christensen's cousin. Even with the Goth makeup turning his skin pale, he exuded sex appeal. Had her feelings not been deadened to it—to him—to every man, since—

"Look Justin. I don't date anyone I work with. It causes too many complications. Move on to someone else."

His smile wavered but didn't quite die. "Maybe I'll have to quit my job, then."

She shook her head. *I'm not worth the sacrifice. I'm trouble you don't need.* She slid the drink to the waiting customer and picked up his money.

A woman slinked up to the bar, her tight black strapless dress hugging her generous curves like a sausage casing. With

5

arrogance and grace, she raised her hand in a demanding gesture. Juliet took a deep breath. She didn't have the patience to deal with Justin and her, too. She nodded toward the customer. "Can you get her order? I need to ring this up." She waved the money in her hand.

With a wry grin, Justin strolled down the workspace behind the bar, his shoes squeaking on the rubber mat.

Juliet heaved a gusty sigh. Maybe he'd hook up with Ms. Sausage and quit pressuring her. Hell, maybe they'd find true love together. She could only hope.

Her feet ached, as did her back, from nearly ten hours behind the bar. Even her facial muscles felt tired from smiling at customers. She just wanted to finish her shift and go home to a long, long bath and an empty bed.

She returned to the task at hand. The heavy metal beat from the stage pounded against her ears, drowning out the beep of the cash register as she keyed in the order. The base drum thumped in time with the headache throbbing behind her eyes. Jesus! She rubbed her temples. The rock bands Hector hired were usually more than loud enough, but for the last two weeks, The Skull's music had been falling just short of an assault.

She scanned the dance floor where a strobe light captured the dancers' stop-action gyrations. Not couples, but the group, the collective. They moved as one. She paused a moment, attempting to guess which were human and which had something to hide. The smoke machine backstage provided an eerie atmospheric backdrop for the band and the audience. Since they were already painted and garbed in Goth style, the special effects lent the patrons the look of extras on a *Day of the*

Dead movie set.

The bar was the new happening hangout in Superstition, Kentucky. Business was booming. Tips were good. Unless you knew what to look for, it was difficult to sort the real from the imagined. Management strenuously encouraged the employees to dress a part. And the clientele.

Since the college had taken root, the sleepy little town of Superstition had begun to attract an interesting demographic. Very interesting.

The counter was sticky from orange juice she slopped while trying to fix a screwdriver and also avoid Justin's latest pseudo-amorous efforts. She wiped her workstation with a damp sponge, tossed it in the sink, and turned her attention to the next drink order, a Primal Scream. The lead singer accompanied the order with a shrill demonstration. Juliet winced.

From the stage, a spotlight swept across the crowd and paused on the bar. Blinking against the harsh glare, she snatched up a bottle of Kahlua from the packed shelves. Its sweet scent momentarily dulled the flowery smell of her last customer's cologne. The mirror behind the bar captured a brief glimpse of her pale face and exaggerated eye makeup.

A movement, a form, stealthy, fast, and gray, rose behind her in the glass. Cold feathered her skin and crawled across her scalp. The shape sprouted two very long arm-like appendages that looped around her. With a startled yelp, she twisted around to face the threat. The spotlight swung away.

Juliet blinked, blinded by the change in light. Her vision cleared.

Nothing. Nothing was there.

Her heart thudded in her ears. A reactive tremor shook

her. What the hell had happened? The sharp edge of the cash register dug into her hip, and she pushed away from it, her legs spongy.

Chill bumps prickled her forearms. She rubbed them away while she scanned the area behind the bar. What had it been?

She peered beneath the counter. Nothing but stacked supplies lined the shelves.

Could it have been some weird reflection, a shadow created by the spotlight? Or maybe smoke from the smoke machine? She studied the gray mist that twined and writhed along the floor around the band and dancers. It crept around the tables.

Yeah, it had to be the smoke.

Jesus—she needed a day off.

One of the few customers at the bar not painted with the heavy Goth makeup beckoned. All right, it was time to shake this off. She tilted up her chin, straightened her shoulders and consciously banked her nerves. She'd deal with this shit later.

The guy's well-trimmed hair and Armani business suit shouted money. He looked as out of place as a movie star at a car wash. What was he doing with this crowd?

Fighting the urge to search the narrow space once more, Juliet sauntered over to take his order.

The band erupted into a grand finale at the end of the number, their volume increasing. Unable to read the customer's lips, she leaned across the bar. "What can I get you?" she shouted above the din.

His gaze homed in for several seconds on her breasts, which were plumped up by her leather bustier. When he leaned close, she caught a subtle whiff of Polo cologne. "What time do you get off?" he asked.

"Sorry, house rule. We don't date the customers."

"Meet me for coffee after you get off, and I won't be a customer."

How many times had she heard that line? She leaned back, taking in the guy's dark blond hair and darker brows.

Déjà vu overwhelmed her. Tanner Newton's face came to mind. *Never again.* She'd learned her lesson.

She shook her head. "Sorry."

As she withdrew, he grasped her wrist, his features taut.

Mr. Money wasn't used to being turned down. Was he going to be trouble? She met his narrowed gaze with outward calm, though her stomach muscles tightened. After the earlier fright, her nerves stretched taut.

If only Tanner had been a jerk like this guy.

The man shrugged and released her. He flashed her a smile. "Guinness."

The single word released the tension in her shoulders, but did nothing to alleviate the pain her memories had stirred. The guy even drank the same brand of beer as Tanner.

On autopilot, she reached for a glass to fill the order. She tilted the glass, pulled the lever to draw the beer, built the dark ale and set it in front of him. In the flashing crimson lights from the dance floor, it looked like blood.

CHAPTER 2

M IRANDA TEMPLETON SCANNED the open floor space of the library reading area. Couches and chairs were set in nooks and crannies with small end tables and lights. The pillows were plumped, the vacuum cleaner run. Everything was in its place. "You can finish up tomorrow, Vivian," she said.

The work-study student hovered at her elbow, waiting to sort the final few books she'd scanned into the system. "Might as well finish these. It won't take but a minute or two to shelve them." She reached for the books and her shoulder brushed Miranda's.

Miranda shifted away, uncomfortable with being touched. The woman was a non-traditional student, older than most by eight or nine years. She'd started at the beginning of the spring term and was always eager to work, often to the point of pushiness.

"I know how much you like to start the day with an empty desk and everything in order," Vivian chirped. She marched down the aisle into the non-fiction section, the books hugged against her generous bosom.

Miranda reached for a calming breath. Yes, she liked to start the day with everything in place. Her OCD demanded it.

Aubrey McClellan, Superstition's only openly practicing

resident witch, laid a stack of books on the desk.

"Those texts you requested through interlibrary loan are here, Aubrey. I'll get them for you."

"Thanks. I appreciate it."

Miranda slipped back into the office behind the front desk and went to the shelf of reserved books, selecting three and carrying them out to the desk. One was a very old book of spells.

Miranda hadn't called the quarters or cast a circle in years, but sometimes she missed it. That had been one of the most exciting times of her life, during middle school and high school. It had given her and Juliet something to believe in when they had nothing else. It had become their life, and they'd both been forced to walk away from it.

The wave of suspicious hysteria during the nineteen nineties had passed, but they still kept their practice secret from everyone but Aubrey and Sherry Connor, the girl who'd made up the fourth in their tiny coven. It had been a sisterhood. Then Sherry's father, an engineer on the railroad, had been transferred to Florida, reducing them to three. Soon after, circumstances had driven her, and Julia, away from the Craft and Aubrey. She had been too metaphysically perceptive even then, and Miranda and Juliet had too much to hide.

She looked up into Aubrey's clear green gaze. Her auburn hair was still as vibrant as it had been in middle school, and her pale skin glowed like alabaster, her Irish heritage made indisputable by her wide, round face and narrow nose.

"I still read things like this sometimes, when I'm missing it." There. She'd said it. "Let me know if you need anything else."

Aubrey smiled, her cheery face open and inviting. "Thanks. I will." After Aubrey had slipped her checked out books into a canvas bag, a troubled frown cramped her features, and she touched Miranda's wrist briefly. She leaned close. "While I was upstairs—there was something... The second floor, I think. I sensed something up there. It may be time for you to open yourself again. There's trouble headed your way."

Miranda studied her face, the serious concern she read there creating a flutter of tension. Aubrey wasn't one to spread hysteria. She'd come to Miranda in the past when things were going to be particularly difficult. And she'd always been right.

Aubrey also left herself open, so she could sense things. Miranda had pretty much locked herself down good and tight, and had been closed off for so long she wasn't sure she could lower the barriers even if she wanted to.

"Thanks for the warning. I'll be on guard."

Aubrey looped the handles of her bag over the crook of her elbow. "If ever you need me, or just want to visit, my door is always open."

"Thank you, Aubrey."

Miranda watched her walk out and turn left, heading for the side parking lot. Susan, one of the work-study students, came back to the desk from shelving books.

"If you'll wait until Vivian comes back to man the check-out desk, then you can go, Susan."

"Will do, Ms. Templeton."

She studied the student a moment. Her skin looked paler than usual against a tawny mane that fell midway down her back. Half-moon shaped circles discolored the skin beneath her cat-shaped eyes.

"Are you—eating as you should?" Miranda asked, her voice dropping. "You don't want to let yourself get run down."

On a campus filled with the unknown, it only took one slip to throw the whole balance off and draw attention where it wasn't wanted. Finding one of the human students unconscious and suffering a case of instant anemia might send up red flags.

"My boyfriend is picking me up and bringing me—something. I can hold out until then."

Since there weren't many students in the library, Miranda took another moment to assess the girl.

"I'm good, Ms. Templeton," Susan assured her. "It'll only be five or ten minutes more."

"Okay. I trust you to know your limits."

The girl smiled.

With one concern dealt with, and Aubrey's warning still resonating through her, Miranda took the back stairs directly to the third floor and strolled between the heavy wooden bookcases, straightening and adjusting the books. There was a comforting repetition to this task, and she could usually lose herself in it. By the time she finished a circuit of the room, and found nothing, her tension had eased.

She checked both bathrooms, and finding them empty, moved on to the study areas.

The midnight warning chime sounded, and she heard the two students she'd spotted scuffle down the stairs. She glanced over the railing that opened the third floor to the main floor commons area to search for Vivian, and found her at the desk checking out books.

Miranda paused a moment to look across the empty space to the other areas of the library. The structure—a huge, unwieldy rectangle on the outside—had an unexpected grace in the interior. The open space in the center of the library shot upward to the roof, where a multi-paned skylight stretched across the full distance of the first floor. A third quarter moon shone down through the panes, the summer sky clear of clouds.

The offices across the commons were locked down tight and dark except for the security lights that burned here and there. She'd closed and secured the technology center herself half an hour earlier.

The sound of the front door opening downstairs drew her attention. At the same time Susan and another student were leaving, Caleb Faulkner wandered in. Spotting her near the third floor railing, he tilted his head back to look up at her.

"Hey, Mandy."

His deep, masculine voice with its husky undertone echoed in the open space and triggered a sharp pang of longing. What would it be like to hear that voice whisper in her ear while they made love? Why did she want someone she could never—? She cut off the thought. She could, if she allowed herself to set aside all her baggage and just reach for it. Every time she looked into Caleb's eyes, she knew he was waiting for her to do it.

"I'll be right down. I have to check the second floor and make sure everyone's gone."

He nodded. She descended the stairs to the second floor, straightened the study area, placed a couple of magazines tossed on a table back in the appropriate rack, and did a quick walk-through between the shelves to make sure there were no lingerers.

She knocked on the men's restroom door and heard thumps and heavy breathing, so she paused at the threshold.

Surely they weren't... Yes, they were. She could see the tangle of feet and clothes about their ankles. She spoke loud enough to startle them. "I'm going to count to ten, and the clothes better be back on and you'd better be out of there by then, or I'm calling security." For at least two seconds silence reigned, then the hasty scramble was easy to hear.

She leaned back against the wall just outside the door and waited for them to show themselves.

When they did, the cocky, unapologetic smile on Robert Hoag's face sparked her anger. He was a junior, an honor student, and the apple of Dean Jackson's eye. His blonde Adonis looks assured he had more than his fair share of female attention, and his place on the tennis team did as well. That in itself wasn't enough to dislike him. It was his arrogant, uncaring behavior toward the girls that troubled her.

Miranda snapped, "Wipe that grin off your face. This isn't funny."

His face turned sullen.

As soon as Miranda saw the girl, her heart sank. Nora Donavan was an A+ student too, but didn't have the protection Dean Jackson afforded the boy she'd hooked up with. Her cheeks were flushed a bright pink, and she kept her eyes lowered in embarrassment while rubbing her hands up and down her crossed arms.

"Let me tell you what's going to happen because of this situation," Miranda said, her tone quiet.

"You," she pointed at Robert, "Mr. Hoag, have put Miss Donavan in a precarious position, and from the smirk you were wearing as you came out of the bathroom, I doubt very much that you give a damn. I also know that if you had any real affection or respect for the woman you're with, you would be more interested in protecting her, cherishing her, and finding a more appropriate place to show your affection than a bathroom stall. A deduction you should have reached quite easily with your well-known IQ."

Robert did have the grace to flush, although Miranda detected more anger than embarrassment.

Nora glanced in his direction and started to speak, but Miranda raised a hand. "I know your grades are just as good as his. But you're a year younger, and haven't cemented your ties to any particular instructor who might lend you their support.

"What will happen, Nora, if disciplinary action is taken, is you'll bear the brunt of it all. The rumors will certainly get around, and the jokes will start, which will enhance Mr. Hoag's reputation while it splinters yours.

"I realize this is the twenty-first century, and things are supposed to be equal despite your genders, but this is still rural Kentucky, and things aren't equal or fair when it comes to life in academia. Right or wrong, that's just the way it is. This is unacceptable behavior, and grounds for expulsion."

"Are you going to write us up?" Robert asked, and while he hid his agitation very well, it was still there.

Miranda raised a brow and gave him her best Librarian Stare until he looked away. "It is college procedure that I do just that, Mr. Hoag."

The situation was finally beginning to sink in with him,

and more than a hint of worry crimped his blonde brows. "I do care about Nora, Ms. Templeton. I don't want to see her get into trouble or be embarrassed. It was just a spur of the moment thing. And we didn't—there was just kissing going on."

Sly devil. He'd keyed in on her protectiveness toward Nora and was using it to try and get off the hook.

Just kissing. With their clothes down around their ankles? She narrowed her eyes at him, then turned her attention to Nora. "Was that all that was happening, Nora?"

The girl barely lifted her eyes. "Yes, Ms. Templeton."

"If anything like this happens again—"

"It won't, Ms. Templeton," Nora said with a sideways look in Robert's direction.

"Good. I'd hate to have to suspend use of the library for both of you for four or five weeks. It might be detrimental to your grades. The midnight tone has already gone, and I suggest you leave. Be sure to walk Nora to her dorm, Mr. Hoag. It's late."

"Yes, Ms. Templeton."

The two walked sedately across the commons area of the floor, then walked faster when they reached the stairs.

Miranda waited for the tense aftereffect of disappointment and anger at the two brilliant students to dissipate. He should have more respect for her, and she should have more respect for herself. But maybe some of what she had said would stick with them.

They'd both have brilliant careers if they could control their hormones. And if Robert lost some of his arrogant, entitled attitude.

With a sigh, she walked across the hall, pushed open the women's bathroom door, and took two steps into the room. She paused by the sink and looked in the mirror. She didn't look much older than those two students, but she felt ancient in experience.

A tingling sensation brushed along the back of her neck, like icy fingertips. She shivered and, breath catching, jerked around to look behind her. The room was empty. She could see every stall easily from where she stood. She was just feeling uneasy because of Aubrey's warning. The thought did nothing to calm the panicked beat of her heart or ease the anxious tightness from her muscles. Rushing out, she escaped the room and the sensation.

Once outside and in the commons area of the floor, she paused a moment to listen. The only sound was the distant beep of the bar code reader downstairs as books were checked in or out of the system.

She was tempted to reach out and see what she sensed. It had been a long time since she'd used the skill. But, no. She'd left that part of her life behind. Did she really want to open herself again? Or was she afraid of what she might discover?

She was allowing a few vague words of warning to spook her. Straightening her shoulders, she strode decisively to the switch for the overhead lights and flipped it off. The large security lights held the dark at bay in the central part of the floor, but cast deep shadows between the stacks.

She caught another glimpse of Caleb from over the second floor safety glass railing; he seemed to be waiting patiently for her to finish. The eagerness to see him, be with him, tugged at her. If only her mother hadn't brought Clay Maddox into their lives, she and Caleb might have had a chance. Regret twisted inside her, and she turned away from the railing to continue closing down the library for the night.

A strange rustling sound caught her attention. She turned the switch back on and walked toward the end of one of the shelves. The halogen streetlights cast illumination through the eight tall windows equally spaced across the west exterior wall. Air ruffled the hair at her temples. Her tension dissipated. She sauntered forward and stopped when she found one of the windows opened six inches at the bottom. Someone must have opened it to sneak a smoke. But why hadn't she noticed it before?

Tiptoeing, she pulled the pane down and fastened the window. She heard the rustle again, this time from two rows to the right. Uneasiness crept across her nerve endings, leaving behind goose bumps.

If someone was playing a prank and trying to scare her, she'd suspend them from using the library for a month. Anger pushed aside some of her fear, and she marched forward. A movement, dark gray and quick, streaked across the end row of books, lit by the streetlights. Was that someone's shadow as they rushed away? She spun around the corner intent on cutting them off and collided with a tall, muscular body. With a startled yelp, she staggered back.

Strong hands caught her before she could fall. "Jesus, I'm sorry, Mandy," Caleb said. "I just got worried about you being in the dark by yourself. You've been up here for quite a while."

Miranda placed her hand over her chest, where her heart still tried to beat its way free. She leaned against him in relief, relishing the warmth and safety she found in his embrace.

Realizing what she was doing, she straightened, though the momentary fright lingered, and so did her shakiness. "Thanks. There was an issue with a couple of students, and then I had to close a window."

Caleb frowned and ran a soothing hand down her back. "Are you all right?"

She fought to get her breathing under control. "I'm fine. You just startled me."

She led the way back down the aisle to the stairs and flipped off the lights again.

Caleb's hand rested against her waist. "I don't like you being here until midnight every night with just a couple of other people."

"The security guard's in the building. He checks the offices at the back of the building, and then patrols the library commons after we're gone. I have to be sure no students are left behind. What if one was still here and startled him? He might shoot them by accident."

"I understand why you do it. I just don't like that you're doing it alone."

The doing it alone part had started out as a means to face her fears. Now she clung to it as a reminder of how far she'd come. "I've done this for seven years now, Caleb." They descended the stairs to the main floor of the library.

"And just because nothing's happened in the past, doesn't mean it can't."

She understood his concerns. And after her scare upstairs… Maybe it was time she let go of that particular demon, or rather her attempt to conquer it. "Okay. From now on, I'll take one of the others with me while I check each floor."

If his grin held just a touch of relief, she ignored it.

"Got your car fixed." Caleb leaned against the checkout desk, his lean, lanky frame at ease, yet—not. Since returning from Afghanistan, he seemed poised for action even while lounging against something. He focused on her with eyes blue as a slice of sky, his sun-bleached hair curling along the back of his neck and over his ears, casually flipping her key ring around his finger.

Miranda swallowed, though her mouth had gone dry. "What was the problem?"

"I had to replace the fuel and air filters. It's good you get your oil changed at regular intervals, but you have to have the filters and hoses looked at now and then, too."

"I'll try to be better about getting things checked. How much do I owe you?" She opened the cabinet beneath the desk and retrieved her purse.

"We can settle up tomorrow. Walk down to The Dish and eat a piece of pie with me. They don't close until one."

Was it fear or excitement that had her heart drumming at her wrists and throat? She bit her lip. "It's awfully late."

Caleb rested his fingertips atop her clenched hand on the counter. A sensation of warmth spread from the point of contact to her wrist. She glanced up into those blue, blue eyes.

"It's just pie, Mandy."

This was Caleb. The boy who'd looked out for her all the way through high school. He was no longer the sweet young boy from down the street—he was a man. A good man, who had done and seen too much. She wasn't very good at saying no to him. But she needed to be. To get closer meant he might find out all the things she needed desperately to hide.

"All right," she said before she had a chance to think herself out of it. As Caleb smiled, panic spread like wings beneath her rib cage. "It's just pie," she repeated. Was she reminding him or reassuring herself?

"All done," Vivian said as she returned. "Hello." The smile she offered Caleb seemed overly bright and flirtatious. Her golden brown hair swung forward around her face and curved beneath her chin becomingly. With her lush figure, she was very attractive to the opposite sex. Miranda had noticed some of the male students' interest focused on her.

She studied Caleb's dismissive attitude as he nodded at Vivian and offered her a brief smile.

"All set?" he asked, looking back at Miranda. He slid the car keys across the countertop.

How could she stand around watching for a reason to be jealous and refuse to seal the deal herself? "Yes, I'm ready." She really wanted to be. She grasped the keys and swung her purse strap over her shoulder. "Before we leave, we'll make sure you get to your car safely, Vivian."

"Thanks, but I'll be fine. My car's just outside the back door. It isn't like the big city of Superstition, Kentucky is a hotbed of crime or anything."

"You can't ever be too careful," Miranda said. A brief flash of memory made her flinch. To hide her reaction, she bent to gather the two books she'd reserved for herself from beneath the counter.

She moved around the checkout desk and went to the front door to flip the lock. The three of them ambled toward the back entrance. Along the way, she hit the wall switches, turning off the lights. Dim nightlights flared on, and shadows settled between the rows of shelves. A florescent bulb hummed overhead as they ambled past the back conference and rest rooms.

"Darn, the streetlight's out again," Miranda said as they walked out the back door. "I'll have to call the city utility company tomorrow and get them to repair it."

"We're safe with Caleb here," Vivian said. "I'll see you tomorrow. Good night." She strolled away from the awning-covered back stoop and across the dark parking lot to her car.

"Good night," Miranda called, and Caleb's voice blended with hers on the word night. She turned to lock the door, conscious of his warm, waiting presence beside her.

Vivian's headlights flashed on, leaving blue-white spots dancing in Miranda's vision before the car pulled away.

Her small Honda, parked beneath the dead streetlight, sat alone in the lot. "I'll put these in the trunk," she said, shifting her books.

As Miranda approached the car, she paused at the leap of anxiety jangling her nerves. Every night it was the same. And every night she forced herself to face it.

Caleb was waiting for her, protective, strong. He wouldn't allow anything to leap out of the night to hurt her. She hit the keypad, and the locking mechanism released. The back panel rose an inch. She caught the rough edge of the trunk with her fingertips and flipped it up. Light spilled out.

A gray mass rose from the opening, its maw wide open, hurtling at her face.

CHAPTER 3

D ETECTIVE CHASE ROBINSON paused by the back door of the police station and watched as two patrolmen, Williams and Carmichael, wrestled a handcuffed Gerald Abbott from the back seat of their unmarked police car. Once outside the vehicle the man's struggles increased, panic edging his features with white. Chase hit the button to automatically open the door just as the officers staggered through the back entrance with Abbott. The creative line of expletives that spewed from Abbott's mouth questioned the two officers' heritage and sexual orientation, and offered explicit instructions on how they could pleasure themselves.

"Thanks for the advice, but I'm a happily married man," Williams said through gritted teeth while dragging the guy forward.

Chase grinned and stood back to let them pass.

Why wouldn't Abbott give it a rest? He'd been caught.

"Where do you want this?" Carmichael panted.

"Interview room two," Chase said.

The men manhandled Abbott down the hall and through a narrow doorway to the right. Chase paused at his desk in the open-floored squad room and secured his gun in his desk drawer, then collected a file.

When he entered the interrogation room, Carmichael was

holding Abbott's head pressed to the top of the metal table bolted to the floor, and his arms pinned behind him.

Chase tossed the folder on the table. He unlocked one of Abbott's handcuffs and quickly fed it through a ring in the center of the tabletop and snapped it closed around his wrist again. Bright red burn scars discolored the man's hands and wrists.

The moment Carmichael and Williams released him, Abbott lunged forward.

Chase jerked back, and missed being head-butted by inches.

Secured and unable to fight without harming himself, Abbott shouted, "Fucking assholes."

Williams grabbed him by the back of the shirt and jerked his ass down onto a steel-legged chair.

"Thanks for bringing him in," Chase said as the patrol officers shuffled out.

"Our pleasure," Carmichael said. Williams nodded and closed the door.

Chase shucked his Kevlar vest and draped it over the back of a chair. He moved the seat closer to the table and sat down.

He took a moment to study the man across from him. Dark circles ringed mud brown eyes sunk into a gaunt, pale face. Blotchy beard stubble shadowed the lower half of his jaw. His clothes, wrinkled and stained, hung off his bony frame. His hands looked bright red, and as grungy as the rest of him.

Abbott had fought them the entire time, from capture to transport and all the way into the building. Now the fight had drained from him, and he slumped into his seat like a bag of dirty laundry. A rancid smell hung around him like a force field.

"You're going away on drug and weapons charges, as well as resisting arrest, but there's more," Chase said. "We have an eye witness who will identify you as the killer of Tanner Newton. And I can almost guarantee the DA's going to push for the death penalty."

"I'm a dead man anyway. Do whatever you like," Abbott said. He slumped and rested his forehead on the table.

Chase studied the greasy brown strands glued to Abbott's scalp. After the earlier fight, he had expected more. *What the fuck was up with this guy?*

Chase opened the file and slid a couple of photographs across the table. "Last night around midnight we responded to a report of a dead body in an alleyway off Bodin Avenue. This is who we found."

Abbott remained unresponsive for a minute, then two. He lifted his head as if it were almost too heavy to move, and glanced at the photos. He flinched and jerked his face away. His throat worked as he swallowed.

"We know Willy Porter was your partner in the Tanner Newton killing. We don't know how Willy was killed yet, but it seems he pissed someone off real bad."

"That's his problem," Abbott said. His tone lacked the hard edge his words needed. His body language broadcasted defensiveness and exhaustion.

"Why did you go after Tanner Newton?"

"Newton's death was an accident. We weren't after him, we wanted the girl."

Chase's brows rose. "Why?"

Abbott rested his head on the desk again. "It don't matter

no more. They're going to get to me sooner or later." He remained that way for several moments, then struggled to sit back up. "We were supposed to just shoot her dead, but Willy and I got the idea how we could make some money off of her first. So we planned how we'd take her, dope her up, and set her up in the life."

"After you'd had your own fun?" Chase asked.

"Well, yeah. I mean—have you seen that chick? She's a real looker, and I bet she can give good head, too."

Chase had never met Juliet Templeton, but he had seen photographs of her and the injuries she'd sustained fighting off the two. He thought he'd heard it all, but the idea of the two drug-addicted thugs laying hands on the woman and inviting other men to the party made his gorge rise. He swallowed back the flood of acid and cleared his throat.

"So who wanted you to shoot Juliet Templeton, and why did they choose you two?"

"We've done some things for money in the past. We ain't never killed nobody, but we done other things. I don't know why they wanted the woman dead, but—" He started to make a placating gesture but his hand was jerked back by the cuff. "Look, when you're hooked, you'll do a whole lot of things to get the next hit you wouldn't think about when you're straight."

Abbot sighed and cleared his throat. "I been clean over a month now, and my mind's clear," he continued. "I know what we wanted to do to that woman was wrong. So wrong I can't believe we even talked about it. And I can't believe we thought we could pull it off. We didn't count on Newton being so good with his fists, or that Templeton bitch being able to light Willy's clothes on fire."

"How the hell did she do that?" Chase hadn't read anything in the report about that. Had there been evidence of an accelerant at the scene?

"I don't know, man. Me and Willy were whaling on Newton, and Willy's pants caught on fire, and he started rolling around on the ground screaming. Once I got the fire put out, we took off. He had blisters all over his legs."

Tears ran down Abbott's face, and Chase wondered if it was because he'd been caught, or because he was actually experiencing a moment's remorse.

"Newton was never supposed to die. The person just wanted Juliet Templeton dead."

"Why?"

"I don't know, man. They promised me and Willy five thousand dollars. Sent us twenty-five hundred as a deposit, and we was supposed to get the rest after. We spent half of it on cocaine the first two weeks, and then when we realized we was going through the money pretty quick, we decided we'd better kill her fast so we could get the rest. Then we had the bright idea that as long as the girl disappeared, the client wouldn't care when she died."

"Who promised you the money?"

"I don't know. Weed Keller brought us the envelope with the instructions."

Weed Keller had been shot two weeks ago. The case was still open and unsolved. And now they'd have to look in a different direction, because he might have been killed for an entirely different reason than what they'd first suspected.

Though Superstition was a middle-sized community,

drugs were becoming a more and more common problem. And with drugs came the other issues of overdoses and killings over drug turf and drug deals gone bad. And just the stupidity and mayhem associated with people getting high and losing touch with reality. So far those issues were still relatively small. But they did happen.

"Weed Keller is dead, Abbott."

"Yeah, I heard." Abbott's head made a hollow thump as he rested it on the table. "He was the only one who knew who hired us."

"Who's after you?"

The man turned his bloodshot gaze to Chase's face. "You wouldn't believe me if I told you."

Chase leaned forward and rested his forearms on the table. "Try me."

Abbott's eyes bounced blindly, jerkily around the room. He bit his lip hard, his yellowed teeth leaving reddened indents in his skin. "It isn't a person, man. It's a thing, and there's more than one of them."

What the fuck? Chase studied the man through narrowed eyes. Abbott had just said he was clean. His pupils were normal, his speech wasn't slurred, and he seemed lucid.

Was he trying for an insanity defense? Fuck that.

"I told you you wouldn't believe me." His eyes teared up and, unable to raise his hands, bent his head to rub his face against his grungy shirtsleeve. "I ain't crazy."

Chase studied the bloodshot sclera that turned the whites of Abbott's eyes pink, the dark rings like bruises that encircled them, the trembling exhaustion of his movements. The guy hadn't been sleeping or eating from the look of him. He'd put up a crazed fight when Chase dragged him from the cheap hotel with Carmichael and Williams's help. His eyes had darted around the parking lot as though a bogeyman lurked behind every car. The guy was terrified.

"All right. What is it you're afraid of?"

THE GRAY SHADOW form boiled up out of the car trunk and snapped at Miranda. Instinct kicked in and Caleb dove in from the side, slamming the trunk lid down in the midst of the oily gray mist. An unearthly scream rent the air. He rolled off the car, landing crouched in front of Miranda, his arms wide, and poised for battle.

Jerking around, he grasped her arm and dragged her away from the car. "Run, baby! *Run!!*"

Miranda stumbled into a lope. Caleb clamped an arm around her waist and half-ran, half-carried her around the corner. Midway up the block, he darted into the dark alcove of an apartment entrance. Through the dingy glass in the door, a dull light shone like an amber theatre gel. His arms tightened around her and he touched her lips for silence. He waited, listening. Was it coming? His heart raced. *Jesus, what the hell was that?*

Miranda trembled against him, her muscles tense. After several moments she asked, "What was it?" Her voice ricocheted off the narrow space, a hoarse whisper.

"I don't know." It. Not him. So she'd seen it too. He wasn't hallucinating. He drew a deep, relieved breath. "It wasn't a person."

"No." She pressed into him. "It tried to bite me." A shudder ran through her and she burrowed her face into his shoulder.

Her hair brushed his chin and he savored the fresh apple scent of her shampoo. Her breasts pressed into his ribs. Despite the fear-laced adrenaline racing through his veins, it aroused him in an instant.

But it had taken him weeks to get her to relax with him enough to go out. Even joining him for a piece of pie seemed major. He needed to take things slow. And he had to deal with this weird shit first.

"Stay here." He peeled her away, and, pressing her back into the deepest recesses of the doorway, took a cautious step away.

"Caleb." She gripped his arm, her fingers digging in.

"I'm just going to look out and see if anything's out there." When she continued to hold on, he covered her fingers with his own. "Some time soon, I'd like to spend the night with you, Mandy, but not hiding in a doorway."

She caught her breath. "Oh...Caleb."

Rejection wasn't what he heard in her voice. Sadness? Despair? If only he could see her face. Should he read hope in how slowly she released him? He knew she cared for him.

"Please be careful," she said.

"I will." Edging out onto the sidewalk, he looked one way, then the other. The street appeared empty, save for the occasional car passing by. The muggy air captured and held the smell of exhaust. The evenly spaced streetlights cast gray-green shadows on the sidewalks. A couple exited a doorway and strolled by across the street.

"It looks clear, Mandy." Caleb offered her a hand and

smiled when she took it.

Her gaze darted about as she emerged slowly from the alcove. Caleb slipped his arm around her waist. "I think we need to get off the street. Stay close."

"What do you think it was?" she asked.

"I don't know. Let's wait and talk about it once we're inside The Dish." He urged her up the street. Every nerve in his body was clamoring with the fight or flight instinct.

The Dish's sign flashed bright neon pink only fifty feet away, the café nestled back onto a corner lot. A drive on one side made room for the handicapped ramp and access to the back parking lot. As they reached the well-lit parking slots out front on the street, Caleb heaved a sigh of relief. "Stay close, Mandy." He scanned the area around them.

A Ford Taurus pulled up to the café, and a slightly built silver-haired woman climbed out. She threw up a hand in a dainty wave.

Miranda waved back in acknowledgement. "That's Mrs. Farley. She comes to the library every Saturday."

Mrs. Farley's silvery hair gleamed beneath the row of overhead lights outside of the diner. "Why, Miranda. I don't think I've ever seen you out this late," she said, her attention focused on Caleb with avid curiosity.

Caleb felt Mandy tense with her effort to pull herself together. "I just closed the library, and we thought we'd have a piece of pie before we called it a night."

Mrs. Farley started up the stairs to the front door. "I had a craving for something sweet, and though I'm not really supposed to indulge, I couldn't go to sleep. I hope Evelyn has some blueberry pie left. I just love it with vanilla ice cream."

Caleb reached around Mrs. Farley and opened the door to allow the older woman to precede them into the restaurant. The dinner specials were listed on a white board to the left, as was the selection of the restaurant's justly famous pies. Mrs. Farley perched on one of the bar stools in front of the counter and a waitress approached her.

Isolated in the back booth, Miranda continued to shiver. Caleb moved to sit beside her and rested an arm along the back of the seat, sharing his warmth. Her eyes lifted to his face for a moment, and color touched her pale cheeks. "Thank you."

Sherry, the lone waitress who worked the late shift, approached the booth. Her blond hair was twisted up at the crown of her head and held in place with a pencil. Her jeans and top looked a little wilted behind the apron she wore. Though exhaustion weighted her movements, she smiled. "Hey, Caleb. Hey, Miranda. What can I get you?"

Caleb waited for Miranda to answer. "Some water and a piece of peach pie if you have it, Sherry," she said.

"We still have some." She focused on Caleb.

"Strawberry-rhubarb with ice cream for me and a cup of coffee."

"Coming right up."

Caleb turned to assess Miranda's condition as soon as Sherry walked away. "Better?" he asked.

"I think I'm starting to calm down."

"Good."

"What do you think it was?"

He shook his head. "I don't know. All I saw was something gray exploding up and out of the trunk. It wasn't there when I had the car at the garage, Mandy. I checked your spare tire to make sure it was okay, and I'd have seen it then." Had he let it in when he opened the trunk? Was it there because of him?

"It was going to bite me, Caleb."

"That's sure what it looked like."

"Why do you think it was there?"

"I don't know. But you can't go back to your car tonight. After we've eaten, I'll walk over to the garage to get my Harley and give you a ride home."

She nodded. He'd visualized her riding behind him on the motorcycle more than once, but never thought she'd agree. Why had it taken fear to drive her toward him?

"How long have we known each other, Mandy?"

"Since kindergarten."

"Do you trust me?"

"Of course."

This wasn't the time to bring it up, but this barrier she'd erected between them since he returned home from deployment was driving him crazy. He turned her face toward him so he could look into her eyes. "I mean really trust me?"

She studied his features. "Why are you asking?"

"You know how you've acted since I got back from Afghanistan."

She tried to turn her face away, but he held her chin.

She grasped his hand and held it. "It isn't about you. There are things about me you don't know. It's about me, Caleb."

"I know I've changed a lot since high school. We both have but—"

She shook her head in an adamant gesture. "It's not you. You're still the same protective, caring, wonderful friend you've always been."

But he wanted more now, and she knew it.

She bit her lip and swallowed. "I can't give you what you need. I can't give anyone—"

"Here's your pie, guys," Sherry said as she slid the plates onto the table in front of them and placed their drinks within easy reach.

Miranda was the first one to respond. "Thanks, Sherry."

"Let me know if I can get you anything else."

Caleb swallowed back feelings of disappointment and hurt. *I can't give anyone—What had she meant by that? Why couldn't she? He wasn't giving up. He'd just rushed her at a time she didn't need any other pressure.*

Miranda's fingers dug into his arm and her voice wobbled as she whispered, "Caleb—"

He followed her gaze to the door. On the other side of the glass, a gray shadow slithered back and forth, as if seeking a way in. Clutching a takeout bag, Mrs. Farley pushed open the door. Caleb jumped to his feet. The elderly woman walked into and right out the other side of the gray mist.

CHAPTER 4

C HASE SAT AT his desk and read over what Abbott had said again.

The guy had to be insane. Gray shadow creatures that could tear out your insides. He had to have injected some powerful stuff for him to dream up that crap. Chase's mouth tightened. Dammit. If he were this guy's lawyer he'd plead diminished capacity.

But Abbott wasn't on drugs. He didn't look or act drugged. But something was certainly going on.

Chase thumbed through his in-box for the coroner's report on Porter. He and Abbott were partners, or at least they had been until recently. More than likely, they'd both ingested the same drugs.

A large manila envelope captured his attention and he tore it open. Good, he'd look this over and see what the hell was going on. Fifteen minutes later he sat back in his seat. What the hell? He read over the section again. It couldn't be right.

"Jesus, Chase. You need to put in your contacts, man. You look like a freaking vampire," Detective Brian Underwood said as he and his partner Hollis Garr sauntered into the office.

The scent of coffee wafted to Chase, and he focused in on the Styrofoam cup Underwood held in his broad hand. He'd made a trip down the street to the Mugz Coffee Shop rather than chance the pot in the squad room. Maybe he was smarter than he looked.

The remark about the vampire reminded him he hadn't put in his contacts. Because of his pale eye color, sunlight forced him to wear sunglasses. At night, with less light to bother him, his sensitivity wasn't an issue, so he seldom used them. "You need to get some new material, Underwood. Your current routine is getting boring."

Hollis Garr, Underwood's partner, laughed.

"Do you scare small children, Robinson?" Underwood asked.

"No." Chase glanced up at Underwood's belly. "Do you?"

Garr stretched his feet out on the bottom drawer of his desk and laced his hands over his belt buckle. The pair was an odd couple. Garr was a seasoned detective with twenty-five years' experience. His thinning gray hair hugged his narrow head, and with his rangy build and steady, hazel gaze, he projected competence and patience.

Underwood, on the other hand, had just made detective the year before. He always seemed to have a sugar-laced drink in his hand, and the extra tire he carried around his waist proved it. His suits were always pressed and clean, and he never had a hair out of place, but all his energy went into his appearance, and little went into his investigative techniques. Garr was the brains behind the partnership, and Chase hadn't quite figured out where Underwood came into the equation.

"I'd give it a rest, Brian," Garr said. "Chase has been around the block a time or two. He's worked in departments bigger than this in Detroit. If the guys he drags in here don't get under his skin, what makes you think you can?"

Chase aimed a hard, unsmiling look he usually reserved for violent perpetrators at Underwood. "Why do you want to?"

Underwood looked away. "Just joking with you, Robinson."

"Sure."

"Why did you move here from Detroit? I mean it's not exactly exciting. You'd have seen a lot more action there," Underwood said.

More action. The man wanted more dead bodies. Chase had seen more than he ever wanted to in Detroit. He'd worked streets where drive-bys were a way of life. He'd take the three or four homicides a year here over the thirty or forty he'd worked there any day.

"I'd had enough of big city crime and decided to come back to Superstition to be close to my mom and sisters."

"You used to live here?"

"Yeah, about fourteen years ago. I came back during holidays when the workload eased up to visit family." But it never had, and he'd missed many Thanksgivings and a few Christmases because of it.

"Where's Pfister?" Garr asked.

Chase eased back in his seat. Garr was a good detective and an okay guy. There was no reason for him to slight him because he had a dickhead for a partner. "One of his kids had a bike accident earlier and hurt his leg. He's with his wife at the hospital. Timothy may need surgery."

Garr's wrinkles increased as he frowned. "That sucks. Do you need some help?"

"Thanks for asking, but no. I've got this tied up. I'm just going over my notes so I can write up the report."

"Good. You've been after Abbott and Porter for two months, haven't you?"

"Yeah, ever since Howard retired and passed the case on to me. After Tanner Newton was killed, they went underground for a while. But they resurfaced two weeks ago. We got a tip where Porter was, but by the time we found him he was dead. When we recovered his phone, we were able to track Abbott."

"Did Abbott kill Porter?" Garr asked.

"No. The two separated and have been on their own for weeks. Pfister and I have been tracking them both. Almost caught Abbott a couple of times. We're not sure exactly who killed Porter or how. The coroner's report has some strange anomalies."

"What do you mean?" Underwood asked.

"The coroner said he'd never seen anything like it, but it looked as if Porter's heart had been crushed inside his chest, but there were no external signs of trauma. His heart was pulverized."

Garr jerked back in surprise. "Jesus. Were there any drugs in his system?"

"None."

Underwood pulled his desk chair closer and sat down. He held the cup between his hands. "Does the coroner have any idea how that could have happened?"

"No. He said he knew it wasn't possible, but otherwise he would swear someone had reached inside Porter's chest cavity and squeezed his heart to a pulp."

"Hope this is an isolated case. It doesn't sound like something we want to run into again," Garr said.

Chase nodded. He scanned the notes he'd taken during

Abbott's interview again. The things Abbott had told him couldn't be true. But he could tell the guy really believed every word he'd told him. And he was terrified. The man had been so long without sleep he nearly passed out during the interview in the middle of a sentence. If the guy was going for an insanity defense, he'd gotten off to a good start.

From his observation, he'd have to testify the man was frightened, exhausted, but he wasn't disoriented, or experiencing hallucinations.

Unless he was. He had to get a warrant for the lab to draw some of Abbott's blood.

✧   ✧   ✧

MALE VOICES RUMBLED in from the back entrance, then were cut off as the door closed behind the cleaning crew. Juliet scanned the empty space one more time. The scent of bleach lingered and blended with the smell of stale perfume, booze, and a sweeter odor. In the three years she'd worked at Steampunk Alley she hadn't quite been able to identify the scent. Maybe years of spilled liquor mixed with the pineapple, cherries, and other fruit added to some of the tropical drinks they served. Maybe it had seeped into the floors.

The space looked shabby with the house lights up. The walls could use a fresh coat of paint, and the stained wood baseboards a touch-up as well. She glimpsed her reflection in the mirror behind the bar and grimaced. Smeared mascara ringed one eye, and now she'd taken the feather fascinator out, her hair looked like a flock of sparrows had nested in it. She hissed an oath and reached for her bag under the register.

She scraped her hair back and secured it with a black ponytail holder. Wetting a dishtowel, she wiped the smeared Goth makeup off her face.

A rhythmic squeak came from down the hall the cleaning crew had just vacated and Hank, the bouncer, appeared. His muscle-bound body moved with the grace of a ballet dancer as he shadowboxed his way across the empty floor. "I've done the walk-through, Juliet."

"Thanks. The service already picked up the deposit, so we're good to go." She tossed the stained cloth into the wash bin and grabbed her bag from the counter.

"Need a ride?" Hank asked as they reached the door.

Riding would be taking the easy way out. "No, I'll be fine. The walk helps me unwind."

"The ride would too," Hank said. "It's dangerous walking this late at night."

"I've got my pepper spray and my track shoes on." And the nine-millimeter she'd purchased after the first attack. She lifted one foot, pointing to the sharp-toed boots she'd changed into now she'd finished working.

Hank studied the keys in his hand. "You need to be more careful, Juliet. Even guys have to keep an eye out in this neighborhood. You shouldn't purposely put yourself at risk."

She wasn't doing that...or was she? By forcing herself to walk past the place where it had happened, she punished herself. And at the very least she deserved that punishment.

"Look—I know you feel responsible for things...you didn't really have any control over," Hank said.

"You're wrong. I don't feel responsible. I don't take responsibility for anyone but myself." She flipped her ponytail over her shoulder.

Swallowing against the knot of tears lodged in her throat, Juliet shoved open the door. "Lock up for me, will you? I've got things to do."

Outside, humidity slapped her like a wet towel.

She jogged clumsily along the shadowed edge of the parking lot and darted around the corner of the building. Damn Hank and his good intentions. Pain gnawed at her with jagged teeth. She fought off tears.

At the slight scrape of the door opening, Juliet shrank back against the building. After a brief pause, the sound of Hank's footsteps receded, and a few moments later a car engine fired. Cones of light stabbed the shadowed depths of the parking lot, and then swung toward the exit.

Juliet leaned back against the building. Hank's kindness had brought her emotions bubbling to the surface, and she needed a moment to settle herself. The humidity made her feel like she was breathing soup. Perspiration misted her face and neck and already trickled down from her hairline. The leather bustier seemed to shrink in the heat and squeeze her ribs like a vise.

Hank's taillights disappeared around the corner.

She had to get a move on. Hiking her purse strap back up on her shoulder, she moved out from behind the edge of the building. A gray-black hand snaked out and grabbed her arm. A scream ripped from her throat. Her whole body jolted. She jerked her arm free and staggered back.

"Relax. I'm only here to talk with you." The well-dressed jerk who'd asked her out for coffee emerged from the shadows.

"Jesus H. Christ. What the hell do you think you're doing? You scared the shit out of me."

"Like I said, I'm only here to talk." Pushing his suit coat back, he shoved his hands in his pockets. The dim glow from the streetlight cut across his features, hollowing his eyes and giving his face a skeletal appearance.

Chill bumps rose on Juliet's skin and, despite the heat, she folded her arms against her waist. Shoving aside the itchy foreboding, she said, "Well, talk fast. I've been on my feet for ten hours, and I've got somewhere to be."

"Got a hot date, huh?" he said, his tone snide.

Juliet gritted her teeth against equal parts of anxiety and anger. "Yeah, with my pillow. In case you haven't noticed it's one in the morning."

"That didn't keep you from being out with my brother Tanner at this time of night."

His brother?

Tanner was his brother. This had to be Samuel Newton. Tanner had spoken of his brother Sam. He had the same jawline. The same green eyes. No wonder he reminded her of him.

Tears burned her eyes and she looked away. "What do you want?"

"I want to know why those guys were after you. You told the police Tanner was killed trying to protect you. Were you coming on to them and got in over your head?"

Juliet absorbed the emotional punch without giving him a reaction, though the pain of it echoed through her. At one time it might have been true, but not during or after Tanner. "You were here tonight. Did it look like I was coming on to anyone during my shift?"

"You don't have to come on to them when you're dressed

like that." He nodded toward the leather bustier and the way her breasts pressed up against the blouse she wore beneath it.

Juliet swallowed a sharp retort. "I dress this way because it's required by my manager. I suppose if I'd been raped that night, it would have been my fault as well. I'm damned no matter what I say, so I don't see any point in saying anything." She hitched her bag more firmly over her shoulder, and pivoting on one foot, strode away.

He fell into step with her. "They've caught the men. Or at least one of them. The other one was killed," He said.

"Good."

"That means you'll be testifying about what happened that night. A jury is going to look at your job, your background, how you look, and they're not going to believe one word that comes out of your mouth."

Rage rushed up to burn her cheeks and nearly choked her. Juliet reached in her bag for her phone. "You have exactly two seconds to get out of my face or I'm calling the police."

"Did you try to call them that night?"

"Go call your snitch at the police department and find out. Or better yet, use the Internet to look it up. 911 calls are public record. You can listen to every word I said to the police, while I did CPR to try to keep Tanner alive. Now, *leave me alone!*"

Tears ran down her cheeks as she marched away from him, which just made her madder. Where was the hard-edged woman she'd been for so long? Tanner's death had ripped away something inside her and left her vulnerable to all of this in ways she hadn't been in years.

She'd tried harder with him than any other man. Tried to

feel something, tried to love him. And the more she tried, the more she became convinced she was never going to be normal.

But she'd truly cared about him, cared for him. And now her feelings were going to be perverted in court because of the way she looked, the way she made a living. Her past. She brushed aside the tears. *Fuck 'em. Fuck 'em all.*

The man rushed up behind her, and she jerked to one side, defensive, expecting a blow that didn't come.

"I want to give you a job. I want to help you clean up your act so you'll project a more sympathetic image."

"You narrow-minded prick. Because I work tending bar I'm automatically a whore to you. Because I dress like this," she ran a hand down her midriff, "I'm a slut. I don't need your handouts. I don't want your handouts. Leave me alone."

He clenched his fists and his eyes glittered in the reflective brightness of the nearby streetlight. For a moment she thought he might punch her. "Don't you want justice for my brother? He saved your life. You owe him."

Exhaustion weighted her limbs. "There is no justice. Tanner is dead. No matter what they do to the man who killed him, it will never bring him back. It will never end this." She turned away and staggered a little on her spike heels. The bag slipped off her shoulder and she caught the strap and shoved it back up.

"You really cared about him, didn't you?"

She paused just outside the yellow pool projected from the overhead lamp and looked up into the light. "He was the sweetest, most decent man I've ever known."

She looked over her shoulder at him. His eyes widened and his mouth fell open as he focused on something ahead of her. She pivoted and couldn't inhale as a gray mist filled her mouth and throat, her vision. Cotton rammed down her throat, and she gagged. She shook free of the purse and clawed at her neck, her mouth. Her feet left the ground, and she hung, suspended, the weight of her boots dragging at her legs.

A yell, masculine, like a growl came from behind her. Something bulky, hard, struck her from behind and tore her free of the suffocating grip. Asphalt ripped at her cheek, her hands when she hit the ground hard, unable to catch herself. Blessed blackness rolled over her.

CHAPTER 5

THE DINER'S DOOR closed behind Mrs. Farley. Caleb stared at the gray apparition pacing outside. Why hadn't it rushed inside the brightly lit diner when the door opened?

"It didn't hurt her. Why did it let her pass?" Miranda asked.

Caleb shook his head and knotted his fists on the top of the Formica table. "I don't know. Maybe it's waiting for us to come out."

A group of rowdy college students came up the ramp, their loud voices carrying through the thick glass of the restaurant windows. The students passed through the creature as if it were no more than a patch of mist, and the figure dissipated.

He tensed. What just happened? Why had it disappeared at that particular moment?

Miranda looked up at him, her face pasty white. "It's gone. Should we leave?"

He didn't like the idea of either of them going outside just yet. He needed more info about the creature first. Did these things have to have light to appear? Did they live in the shadows? And were they after him or her? Or both?

The only way to find out was for him to take a step outside the restaurant and see what happened. But if he suggested doing it now, she'd panic. He had to calm her first. Help some of her fear leach away so she'd be ready to focus on things ahead.

"Since we seem to be the only two people who are seeing something, what is it you're seeing, Mandy?"

"It's grayish-black, like a shadow. It has no eyes but does have a mouth. It screamed, Caleb."

"I heard it too. Why don't we both just eat our pie and relax for a moment?" He forced himself to take a bite of his strawberry rhubarb. Though the ice cream had melted, the combination of sweet and tangy cut through the metallic taste of adrenaline that lined his mouth.

Miranda picked at her pie and he offered her a smile of encouragement.

"While you're in combat, you have to take advantage of calm where you can find it." He held up a small bite of his pie. "Want a bite of mine?" he asked.

"No." She shook her head. "Thank you."

Any other man would be put off by that prim, proper little schoolmarm thing she did. He smiled and caught her studying him.

"What are you smiling at?" she asked.

"You. You still have your Miss Goody Two-Shoes thing down."

Her cheeks flushed berry red, chasing away the pallor from her earlier fright. "I'm not a Goody Two-Shoes. I can't believe you even said that. It sounds so juvenile."

Caleb chuckled, though it sounded a little forced even to him.

She poked him with her elbow. "Stop trying to rile me."

"But I like getting you worked up, Mandy. When you get

riled, I sometimes feel the real you is finally breaking out."

Her lips pursed tight and her eyes darkened. "This *is* the real me, Caleb. If you're interested in someone who's a risk taker, you'll have to hunt up my sister."

"I've loved you since kindergarten. I know who you are. I wouldn't change one hair on your head."

He caught a quick look of longing before she could suppress it. But she chose not to acknowledge what he'd said about love and jumped ahead. "Then what are you talking about?"

"I'm talking about when Brian Underwood tried to kick my ass in high school and everyone else turned a blind eye. But you came out swinging." She could do that again if she needed to.

"Actually I just held on to his hair for dear life and screamed bloody murder."

Caleb laughed. "You were a sight, going all ninja on him."

"Ninja?" She laughed.

"You snuck up on him. No one thought shy little Miranda Templeton would leap on his back and attack."

"Well, I was tired of his bullying. He'd knocked Donald Lester down earlier that day and hurt his arm. Brian claimed it was an accident, but he shoved Donald into the lockers on purpose. I saw him. Because he was some big football jock, they gave him a free pass on everything."

"He didn't get a pass after that. All the guys started banding together in packs to protect each other. You shamed them into action. When he pushed, we pushed back."

Caleb grew solemn. "What I'm getting at, is you need to get your ninja on now, sweetheart. You need to be calm and focused. Because we don't know what we're facing."

✧   ✧   ✧

DID SHE EVEN have any ninja left? Miranda balled her fist and held it against the sick pain in her midriff. She'd used it up in one fell swoop. What happened to her sister was her fault. Had her actions set Juliet on the path she'd chosen? Had their giving up the Craft had anything to do with it? Or was it because of what had taken place before?

She glanced up at him. "I'm calm now, but why are you bringing all this up now?"

"I want to go outside and see if it comes back," Caleb said. "We can't stay here all night. We need to know if it's just a shared hallucination, or if this thing is real." His sky blue eyes settled on her face, calm, steady.

What would she do if something happened to him? When he went to boot camp after high school, they lost touch for a while. His absence had left a void in her life. Through his grandmother she'd sent cards at birthdays and Christmas. But when he deployed to Iraq and Afghanistan, they'd begun to email, and email had slowly morphed into calling, and calling into Skyping. The closer they got, the more difficult the worry for his safety had become. To lose him now, to never see him again, hear his voice—

How could she feel this way about him and continue to push him away? But if he got close, she'd be tempted to tell him. Not only about Clay but *everything*. She was tempted already. It would change everything for him, for her.

"I don't want you to."

"We have to see if it's gone. If it comes after me again, I

can run back inside."

"It tried to bite me. Would have, if you hadn't slammed the trunk."

"But it followed us both, honey."

These endearments had to stop. Every time he called her honey, nerves fluttered in her stomach and her heart leapt. He made her want things.

"I'll jog over to the garage and get my Harley and take you home."

He started to slide free of the booth, Miranda grabbed his arm. "Caleb—"

His lips covered hers, soft, gentle, warm, the strawberry flavor of the pie he'd barely touched on his lips. She wanted to hold him close. Keep him safe. *Don't go!*

When he raised his head, she drew a shaky breath. "Please be careful."

"Roger that." He slipped away from her, paid for their pie and drinks, then strode to the door. When he reached it, he paused to look back at her and smiled.

What if something appeared when he was halfway there? Where would he go? How would he get away? She rose to stop him, but he had already opened the door and was on his way out. Her heart leapt into her throat, making it impossible for her to call to him. The group of students who'd entered a few minutes after them broke into laughter, filling the room with sound.

Caleb walked through the door into the night and jogged down the ramp and across the parking lot. Nothing appeared.

"Hey, Ms. Templeton." One of the girls at the table spoke.

Miranda dragged her gaze from Caleb's athletic figure,

now disappearing around the corner in the direction of his shop, and forced a smile. She focused on the dark-haired girl, a student she recognized. The girl was popular, friendly, and always polite. "Hello, Sylvia."

"Is something wrong?" Sylvia asked. The other five students quieted.

"No. Not at all." She shook her head.

"Do you need a ride somewhere?" Sylvia asked. "The Dish is getting ready to close."

"No. My friend just went to get his motorcycle so he can take me home."

All six of the students' identical expressions of surprise made her smile. Staid Ms. Templeton riding on a motorcycle was pretty much a stretch.

"He'll be right back." *Please let him be right back. Please let him be okay.* She returned to her seat to cover the fact that she was trembling. Maybe this *was* just a shared delusion. But how could two sane, responsible people share a hallucination? And why could they see the creatures when no one else seemed to?

What made *them* different from the other people in the restaurant?

She looked at her reflection in the napkin dispenser. She and Caleb had something important in common. Had it triggered this creature? Was it here to punish them? Or had someone sent it after one of them?

All of this smelled of magic. And she'd left hers behind. Could she reach for it again? And would it do any good at all against such a creature?

And how the hell was she supposed to use it with Caleb watching?

✧   ✧   ✧

CALEB JOGGED AROUND the corner. He scanned the street ahead, his eyes moving warily from one cluster of shadows to the next. So far so good. When he reached the block where his garage was located, he broke from a jog into a run. The night-lights cast a golden glow over the interior of the office and the three mechanic's bays. Nothing moved.

He scrambled for the key, shoved it into the lock, and entered the shop. He raised the garage doors and muscled the bike outside, then lowered the door. In seconds, he'd secured the garage, gathered his helmet and a spare, and straddled the Harley. He shoved the spare helmet down on the back seat support, and then fired up the engine.

CHAPTER 6

J ULIET WOKE TO an odor that burned her nose and stole her breath. It smelled like someone had lit a match, but concentrated to the point of suffocation. What was that smell? Had she instinctively triggered a fire while being choked? She coughed and fought her way clear of the darkness. What had happened? Her thoughts seemed muddled and slow, and breathing through her damaged throat was an agony of effort.

Gray. Her heart gave one hard thump. Some-one...some*thing* had been choking her. And Samuel had helped her. It had to be him. No one else had been there. She forced her eyes open. She yelped in fear as a gray creature came into focus. It lunged against the circle of light only six inches from her face. She jerked further back into the shadow cast by the nearby storefront.

She rolled away onto her knees. The world spun, and she closed her eyes to stop the sickening rotation. She opened them and forced herself to look at the thing. It was like a shadow, but it had bulk, and it had no eyes. Fear hit her like a slap, and tears streaked down her face. This couldn't be happening. She was dreaming.

Samuel. Where was he? She looked across the uneven disk projected onto the ground by the streetlight. He was lying on his back, his head turned away. Was he still alive?

Juliet staggered to her feet, almost too dizzy to stand. Every inch of her body hurt, her throat and chest the most. Every breath was an agony. The creature inside the circle of light lunged and snapped. She stumbled away from it. It bounced back, as if the darkness formed an invisible, impenetrable wall between them.

Samuel lay on his back, his arms outstretched. As she got closer to him, she could see his chest rising and falling in a steady rhythm, but his skin looked gray. He was fading fast.

Black spots danced in front of her eyes, and she fell to her knees beside him and braced her hands on the concrete, her scraped palms sending sparks of pain up her arms. She gripped Samuel's arm and shook him. "Samuel Newton, wake up." Her voice was less than a whisper, not enough to drag him from unconsciousness. His arm stayed limp, and he remained unresponsive.

Juliet looked around for her purse and flinched as soon as she moved her head. She was hurt, really hurt, and so was Samuel. She needed to call for help. Her bag was just out of reach behind the creature. The thing paced back and forth, its focus riveted on her every move. Without any eyes, how did it know where she was? What was that thing? And why was it after her?

She glanced back at Samuel. He'd helped her, just as Tanner had. What if he died, too, because of her? She couldn't be responsible for another man's death. "Please don't die," she mouthed.

If she called EMS now, she'd never be able to speak loudly enough to give them her location. They'd lose precious time trying to locate them or think it was a prank call.

She tried to ignore the demented screams of the creature and focused on pushing away the pain and dizziness that threatened to swamp her. With an effort she centered herself and lowered her shields. A surge of energy flowed into her, embracing her like a long-lost friend. She gathered it to her, and immediately the pain in her chest and throat eased a small bit. While she waited for her head to clear, she spiraled the energy down into her hands.

Earth to center and support him, water to cradle him in a womb of protection, air to blow each healing breath into his lungs, and fire to heat and ease his pain and suffering. Her efforts drained some of the energy from the creature, and it became almost transparent. She stretched her hands over Samuel. After five minutes he began to groan, and his eyes fluttered open. She broke off the healing, afraid he would feel what she was doing.

As could happen when using energy to heal someone else, it had somewhat relieved the agony in her throat and chest, and her dizziness had ceased. She ran her hands over his pockets until she found a flat shape large enough to be a cell phone and jerked it free of his jacket pocket. What was she going to tell them? A gray creature trapped in a circle of light had attacked them? They'd have to see it for themselves. Otherwise they'd cart her off to the psych ward.

She dialed 911. When she spoke, she sounded as if she were speaking through broken glass...and felt like it, too. "A man is unconscious at the corner of Seventeenth Street and Stoker. I—we've been attacked. I need an ambulance."

She gave the dispatcher all the information she had and then stayed on the phone. Five minutes seemed an eternity as she waited and watched the creature's attempts to escape. Would it stay there until morning? Would daylight set it free? If it escaped, would it be able to find her again?

She glanced at her purse, lying just out of reach. Though she no longer had a car, she still had her license and other identification in it. The creature had shown no interest in the bag, just her. As she looked into its horrible, blank gray face, she shuddered. Its face split into a dark, empty maw. It shrieked again, the sound wild with rage. Her fear wound tighter, and she covered her ears.

Dear God, what was it?

What would it have done to her if Samuel hadn't intervened?

An ambulance came around the corner, siren blaring, lights flashing. They'd see it, too, and maybe call the police. With a sense of relief, she turned to glare at the creature. The glow of the streetlight reflected off the empty sidewalk. It was gone.

✧   ✧   ✧

MIRANDA STOOD AT the door and kept watch for Caleb. The students had departed fifteen minutes before, and with no distractions, every minute stretched to at least five.

She'd spent the time drawing some power to her, which had felt so unbelievably good she almost cried. It had been so long. But she wasn't sure she'd be able control it—maybe it was like riding a bicycle, and once you learned you never really lost the ability.

But her magic might not work against the entity they'd seen outside. And what then?

She'd left all this behind as a kind of atonement, determined to live as normal a life as possible. But normal wasn't what she'd gotten. She'd been alone so long. Closed off from everyone. When she contacted Caleb after his grandmother had died eighteen months ago, she hadn't had any thought of starting up a long distance relationship with him. And when he continued to email and skype, she hadn't had the heart to shut him down.

He'd been alone, too. His only living relative gone. He'd needed her.

And now she'd put him in danger.

Ted, the busboy, ran a steam cleaner over the linoleum floors, making them shine like glass. Sherry sat on one of the stools refilling ketchup bottles and saltshakers. The clatter of dishes being stacked came from the kitchen.

The purr of an engine vibrated through the thick plate glass windows before Caleb came into sight, and Miranda allowed herself a sigh of relief.

"Looks like your ride is here." Sherry rose to unlock the door for her. "I might take your picture on that Harley and post it on Facebook," she threatened with a tired smile.

Miranda laughed. "The students were stunned when I told them I was going to ride on it."

"I'm glad to see you kicking back with Caleb. You couldn't ask for a nicer guy."

"Yes, he is. Thanks for letting me stay until he got here. There was an issue with my car, and he had to walk to the station to get his motorcycle."

"No problem. We wouldn't have let you stand out on the sidewalk and wait for him in the dark. You hold onto that man real tight." Shelly opened the door for her.

Miranda smiled. "I will." She scanned the restaurant parking lot. Nothing moved. She stepped outside.

Caleb rolled to a stop at the base of the ramp. Clutching her purse, Miranda hustled down the incline. A gray outline flickered out of the corner of her eye, and she broke into a run.

"Run, Mandy," Caleb barked, his attention directed just over her shoulder, his features rigid with anxiety. She had barely swung her leg over the side of the motorcycle and gripped his waist when he spun the motorcycle around.

She turned to look behind her, and for a second Miranda was face-to-face with the entity. It struck out at her, and she raised a partial energy shield to try to block it. It wasn't enough. An icy spear of pain lanced through her shoulder and arm, and she cried out. Caleb gunned the motorcycle and shot out of the parking lot.

Miranda's right arm hung useless at her side, but she clung to Caleb's waist with the other and pressed close against his back. The faster Caleb drove, the more rapidly the overhead streetlights flickered past like out-of-control strobe lights. Nausea struck her, and she swallowed and closed her eyes against it.

CHAPTER 7

JULIET JERKED WHEN she heard the soft pad and squeak of footsteps out in the hall. Every nerve in her body seemed to be stuck on high alert. She clung to the blanket a nurse had given her and clenched her teeth against their need to chatter. The hospital bed's metal headboard pressed against the back of her head, and she yanked at the pillow behind her. As the adrenaline started to drain from her system, exhaustion took its place, and every bump and scrape she'd sustained during the attack grated along her nerve endings. She hated to think how bad the injuries must have been before she channeled the energy to help heal Samuel during those five minutes before the EMTs arrived.

Never again would she walk home alone after work. She'd almost cost Samuel Newton his life. He'd sustained major bruising to one whole side of his body, and it would take weeks for him to recover. Just imagining it turned her stomach, and knowing she had once again been the cause of someone's pain, this time because of sheer stubbornness, made it worse.

She was such a fuckup! Always causing trouble. Always responsible for people getting hurt. She and Miranda had never been the same since...She flinched away from the memory. They had lost each other that night.

She closed her eyes and rested her head back against the wall behind her. A vision of the creature's gaping maw snapping at her face popped into her head and her eyes flew open again. As she scanned the room, sweat gathered under her arms and along her hairline, and the tremor in her hands worsened. The noises in the hall got louder. Could it follow her here? Could it get inside the hospital?

She covered her face with her hands, and even the delicate pressure of her own touch hurt, and her cheek burned where she'd skinned it on the concrete. She touched the sticky salve they'd put on the abrasion. Her palms had stung, too, at first, but they no longer burned.

A dull throb lurked at the base of her skull. Jesus, she'd been suspended in the air like a marionette. Her throat, still raw from whatever had been forced into her mouth, made swallowing difficult. Adrenaline had kept the pain of her own injuries at bay, but not any longer.

"Juliet?" The nurse who'd brought the blanket stood at the door.

"Yes," her voice was just shy of a whisper.

"A police officer is here to speak with you about what happened."

If she told him the truth he'd have her thrown into a padded room.

Her thoughts froze as Brian Underwood sauntered into the room. He was bigger than he'd been in high school, and a ring of fat around his middle perched atop his belt like an inner tube. But his features hadn't changed. He still had the same shaggy brown hair. The same big hands. Her fingers knotted the rough binding at the hem of the cotton blanket and she stared at him.

"Hello, Juliet." He paused to pull a straight-backed chair from the corner toward the bed.

The closer he came, the harder she had to fight to keep up her facade and not cower beneath the blanket the way she wanted to. As he paused next to the bed, a flash of memory made her stomach lurch. He'd stood over her, his fists bloody, his features contorted with hate. He'd called her Miranda. Bile rose into the back of her throat. She covered her mouth with the edge of the blanket.

"I just need to ask you some questions," he said, as he sat on the chair. His hazel eyes studied her, his face bland. "I already have some information from the ambulance attendants. I just want to double-check the facts. You called nine-one-one to report Samuel Newton had collapsed and was unconscious."

There was something surreal about being interviewed by someone who had beaten her bloody and gotten away with it.

She began to shake. Her bottom lip began to quiver. "I don't want to talk to you." She had to force her voice past her swollen throat.

"Look, Juliet, I have a job to do, and you have the information I need to do it. Just answer my questions and I'll get out of here."

"I want you to go. Now." Anger started to offset her fear.

Brian's expression morphed into the sulky, threatening one she recognized from high school. "Don't give me a hard time, Juliet. Just tell me what the fuck happened."

"Fuck you." Just saying the words felt good, even if the hoarseness of her voice stole some of the power from them. "I don't have to say shit to you. Get out of my room."

Brian stood up and loomed over the bed.

If he laid a hand on her she was going to scratch his eyes out. Or worse, she'd set him on fire and damn the consequences. She tensed, ready to defend herself. He didn't have a bathroom stall door to knock her out with before he beat her this time. She wasn't taking any of his shit again.

At a quick tap at the door, Brian twisted around, and she caught her breath, half with relief, half with regret. An older man with gray hair stuck his head around the door, and seeing, Brian, meandered in. "Hello, Miss Templeton. My name is Detective Garr, and I'm Detective Underwood's partner."

It must suck to be him.

He offered his hand, and after a brief hesitation she clasped it.

"I've been in to see Mr. Newton," Garr said.

She dragged air into her lungs and gripped her hands together around her blanket-covered knees. "Is he okay?"

"It's going to take him some time to heal, but he'll be fine as long as he doesn't try to get up and walk out of here."

She nodded.

Garr angled toward the door. "I'll let Detective Underwood continue with his questioning."

Brian shrugged. "We haven't really started. Why don't you go ahead, and I'll take notes?"

Garr frowned, but nodded and removed a pad from his pocket. "Will you state your full name, Miss Templeton and your address?"

Acutely aware that Brian was not only listening to her answers, but taking notes, she hesitated. Would he try to pay her a visit and get back at her? "Juliet Marie Templeton. Five-four-four Hallow Street."

"Your call came in at one-ten. How long before that do you think the attack happened?

"I don't know. I left work at one. And walked two blocks toward my apartment."

He remained silent for a moment as he wrote something down.

"Where do you work?"

"I tend bar at Steampunk Alley."

Garr focused on the pad in his hand. "Was it there you met Samuel Newton?"

Juliet hated the defensive heat that ran into her cheeks. "I didn't meet him. He was a customer and I waited on him."

Garr eyed her for a moment. "Were you planning to go somewhere after work together?"

"No. He'd come to tell me the men who killed his brother Tanner had been found."

"Why would he come to tell you about Tanner Newton?"

Juliet remained silent for a long moment. "I was with Tanner when he was killed. I identified his killers."

"And Samuel was walking you home?"

"Yeah."

"And this attack happened on the corner of Seventeenth and Stoker Street, not far from where Tanner Newton was killed?"

"Yes."

He raised one brow. "Why didn't Mr. Newton just drive you home?"

"I didn't trust him, and I wouldn't get into his car." As it was, the car would have been a safer option. She looked directly at Brian Underwood for a moment. "No place is safe. Not even a stall in the ladies' room."

Underwood's features tightened, but he kept his eyes on the pad in his hand.

Damn him. He'd left what he had done to her behind. Because he'd never paid for it.

Juliet folded her arms against her and rocked against the freshly hewn pain brought on by just seeing him. She concentrated on the door, praying a nurse would come in and interrupt.

"Mr. Newton wasn't able to tell me much. Did you happen to see the man who attacked you?"

"All I saw was something gray. There was a cloth over my face, something around my throat, and I couldn't breathe, and I was lifted off my feet, then I blacked out."

Garr nodded. "Something gray." He lifted his head and focused on her with his mid-toned brown eyes. "Do you mind if I look at your throat?"

Juliet peeled back the blanket, revealing the pale blue hospital gown. She knew her throat looked like she had been burned. Even the ER doctor had commented on it.

Garr frowned. "Would you mind if another detective comes by to question you, Miss Templeton?"

She shook her head, then flinched when her strained neck muscles twinged, and stopped. "No, I won't mind." Anyone but Brian Underwood.

A nurse pushed open the door and came into the room. "Miss Templeton, I thought you'd like to know since you're her emergency contact on record, your sister has been brought into the ER, too."

✧   ✧   ✧

MIRANDA FLINCHED AWAY from the doctor's probing touch. He looked as confused as she felt. What the hell had it been, and why was it after her?

It *was* after her. She'd had time to think it through while waiting with Caleb for the doctor. The shadow hadn't become visible until after she emerged from The Dish. It hadn't pursued Caleb when he left the diner. But it had come after her.

Chill bumps rose on her skin as fear rushed over her like an icy breeze. She swallowed though her mouth was dry.

Aware of the damage it had done to her with just a glancing blow, she was scared Caleb's instinct to defend would get him killed. He would put himself between her and the shadow, and it would—

"And you say you were struck by something?"

The doctor's question dragged her attention back. "That's what it felt like. It numbed my whole arm."

"I'll be back shortly." The doctor stepped out of the room.

Caleb edged closer to the bed. "You look a little pale. You're sure you're okay?"

Miranda nodded. She clasped Caleb's hand. "You don't have to stay. I'll be fine here on my own."

His brow creased in confusion. "What the hell are you talking about, Mandy?"

How could she get him to leave her here and go? He needed to get as far away from her as he could.

"This thing that hit me isn't after you. But it might try to hurt you if you get between me and it. I couldn't bear that."

His fingers tightened around her hand. "We can't know anything for sure."

"I know for sure." her stomach ached with tension, and she pulled her knees up. "If it had wanted to hurt you, it would have followed you to the garage. It didn't appear again until I came out of the diner. It's after me, and I can tell from looking at you that you know what I'm saying is the truth."

He remained silent for a long moment. His eyes had never looked so blue. "I can't leave you. I won't."

The curtain was jerked back and they both jumped. Seeing her sister clutching a blanket around her shoulders left Miranda speechless for a moment. "Juliet. What are you doing here?"

With one sweep she took in her sister's disheveled appearance. Her hair hung in stringy curls, and she had on almost no makeup. A round scrape marred her cheek, and there was a horrible red burn around her throat. Juliet strode to the bed. Behind her, an older man with gray hair stepped into the cubicle.

"The nurse told me you were here. And that someone hit you while you were on a motorcycle. I told her that couldn't be true. My baby sister would never ride a hog." Juliet's voice sounded edgy around a hoarseness that was almost painful to listen to. Her fingers clutched the hospital blanket around her shoulders, holding it taut.

"Well maybe there are a few things about me you don't know," Miranda said as she met her twin sister's gaze. They might not have spoken in the last few months, but she had no problem reading the emotion in Juliet's face. She was stressed and upset. No matter what issues they had, they always looked out for each other, protected each other. She sensed Juliet needed support. She reached for her, then flinched when she raised her arm.

Juliet pressed a cheek to hers. "That looks damn strange," she commented as she drew back, her attention on Miranda's injury.

"And yours looks like a burned handprint," Miranda commented.

"Weird, huh?" Her studied Miranda's arm again, her frown deepening. "What's the odds we'd both end up in the ER at the same time with strange injuries?"

Miranda started to reply, but her attention snagged on someone in the hall. Was that Brian Underwood just outside the door? Rage flooded her. With her left hand she flipped the blanket aside and gingerly scooted over so she could get up.

Juliet blocked her. "You need to take it easy, sis. The police are here interviewing me about an assault, too."

Looking at each other had always been like looking into a mirror. Though they were identical twins, they were total opposites. At least in personality. She'd always been the straight-as-an-arrow twin, while Juliet had been the rebel. She understood why that had to be. Juliet never had any other choice. But it was Miranda's own temper, her desire to protect Juliet, which could unravel everything for them. She glanced past Juliet to the door again, her eyes narrowing on the man who stood there just out of reach.

"Ms. Templeton?" The gray-haired man who came in with Juliet spoke.

She looked up, and Juliet turned to face him. He had a long, homely face and deadpan eyes, as though he'd seen it all, and none of it good.

"My name is Detective Garr. As your sister said, I'm here investigating her assault. I'd like to take a statement from you about yours as well. The doctor just flagged me down in the hall. Your injuries are similar to Mr. Newton's, the man who was with your sister when she was attacked. Very similar." He held a pad and the stub of a pencil. "Will you state your full name, address, and place of employment, please?"

"Miranda Ann Templeton, 223 King Street, and I'm head librarian at the college library."

Garr wrote down the information. "Just who attacked you?"

What was she supposed to say? "They were behind me, so I didn't get a good look. I got the impression of a gray figure. If Caleb hadn't gunned the motorcycle, I'd have been hurt even worse. As it was, I just received a glancing blow."

Garr's attention shifted to Caleb. "And who are you?"

"Caleb Faulkner. I own Faulkner's Car Repair in town. Mandy had an issue with her vehicle, and I was giving her a ride home."

"And what did you see?"

Miranda tensed. What could he say that wouldn't sound crazy?

Caleb remained silent for a moment, his features creased in thought. "Some—*one* dressed all in gray, their face covered by a gray stocking or some kind of mask. They were fast and came out of nowhere. I didn't see what they hit her with, I was too busy getting us out of there."

Miranda tensed. He hadn't lied. He'd just held back the parts guaranteed to turn this nightmare into insanity. When

Juliet gripped her hand, Miranda fought the urge to look up.

"Juliet, did you speak to your sister after your attack or speak to her tonight at any time?"

"No."

He turned his attention on Miranda.

"No. I haven't spoken to my sister tonight." Or in the last month. What was wrong with them? Why couldn't they be in the same room without memories standing between them?

Garr looked at Juliet. "Your sister's description of her attacker is exactly the same as Mr. Faulkner's."

CHAPTER 8

C HASE STRODE THROUGH the emergency entrance of the Superstition Regional Medical Center. He flashed his badge at the receptionist sitting at a semi-circular registration desk and continued through the automatic doors leading into the emergency room. He paused by the nurse's station. "I'm here to interview an assault victim. The last name is Templeton."

The nurse barely paused long enough to look at his badge. "We have two patients with that last name. They're twins who came into the ER within half an hour of each another. At the moment they're both in exam room four with another detective."

Chase's brows shot up. What were the chances of that? He found Underwood standing out in the hall outside the curtained alcove and frowned. "Why aren't you in there with Garr?"

"It's a small space, and I thought the victims would feel less pressured if they didn't have a room full of badges to contend with."

Fuck me! If Underwood was developing any kind of sensitivity he'd eat his badge. He searched his face. Underwood looked away. Yeah, something else was going on. The rookie detective had screwed up somehow.

Chase pulled the curtain aside and entered the room. The small twelve by twelve compartment was dominated by a large hospital bed, and did, indeed, feel cramped. Two women sat side by side on the bed, their features so identical it was like seeing double. Both had long, dark brown hair, high cheekbones, and flawless skin. Except for the one who had what looked like road rash on her cheek. Both wore blue hospital gowns over their pants. There was one chair in the room unoccupied by the two men in the room. Everyone's attention shifted to him.

Garr motioned toward him. "This is Detective Robinson. If you'll excuse us a moment, I'll get him up to speed."

The two of them went out into the hall. Garr instructed Underwood to stand guard and not to allow any of the victims to leave. He motioned Chase down the hall to a more private room and shut the door. "There's something really hinky going on here. As you could see, the women are twins. Both were attacked within a few minutes of each other, but in different parts of town."

Garr referred to the small notebook he'd been writing in. "The first victim is Tanner Newton's brother, Samuel. Newton is being kept for observation for a couple of days. He's showing bruising over half his body. One of the ER docs said he'd never seen that kind of extreme and widespread bruising from a fall or a beating in his life. One of the Templeton women, Miranda, has a weird bruise on her arm that looks like a lightning bolt. The other twin, Juliet, has a burn around her neck where she said her attacker tried to strangle her."

Caleb scrubbed his short hair. "So this whole thing has to have something to do with the Tanner Newton killing. Juliet

Templeton was with him when he was attacked and beaten to death. What the hell was she doing with Samuel Newton at one in the morning?"

"He was walking her home. She refused to get into the car with him."

"She's afraid to get into the car with him, but she walks home at one in the morning?"

"That's what she said."

"Is Newton conscious?"

"Not yet. They sedated him so he wouldn't move around too much. One of the nurses treating him said he was raving about something gray attacking him. He said it screamed at him, then threw him nearly fifteen feet against a building, like he weighed nothing."

"Jesus!" Abbott had described the same thing. "This is crazy."

Garr frowned, his face as wrinkled as an unmade bed. "Well, when one person describes something crazy, you can ignore it. But when you have four people who haven't had a chance to compare stories describing the same thing— Something is going on here."

"Yeah. And it has something to do with Tanner Newton's murder."

✧ ✧ ✧

"I AIN'T HAD nothin' to eat in two days. Got any food around here?" Gerald whined.

Deputy Bowhan scowled. "This is a jail, not a hotel, Abbott."

Gerald remembered him from a DUI arrest six months

before. The guards weren't friendly, but they were fair to the prisoners. "Some crackers, anything. I'm going to be sick if I don't get something."

"I'll look around the break room and see if I can find something," the other deputy said, though he didn't look happy about it.

Gerald was quick to say, "Thanks, man." He stole a quick glance at the deputy's name tag. Scott.

They stopped before an open cell. "Step in and turn around," Scott instructed.

Gerald cooperated. He was a murderer, and they were taking no chances. He deserved it. The cocaine had made him aggressive. He had killed an innocent man. This is what his life would be like for probably the rest of his days.

The cuffs off, he rubbed his wrists and turned just as the heavy, barred metal door slid closed with a clang. His stomach clenched. Would the shadows be able to find him here?

Panic blasted through his system. If the guards left him alone, would the shadows come for him? He gripped the bars and tracked Bowhan and Scott's path as they ambled away. His neck muscles strained with the need to call them back and beg them not to leave him. Once he could no longer see or hear them he rested his head against the bars. His eyes stung again, the urge to cry almost overwhelming.

The cell light went out, and he backed away from the door. Light slashed diagonally across one end of the cell to bathe the wall opposite the bunk. He retreated as far away from the hall light as he could. With his back against the wall, he slid down and huddled between the metal sink and commode. The smell of the heavy-duty cleaner used to scrub the facilities permeated the air.

He looped his arms around his knees. His stomach ached with the added pressure. He'd gone hungry before, but he'd been high, and the drugs had made it bearable. Sober, it was impossible for him to think of anything but his hunger. He pressed his hand against the ache and rested his head against one knee.

Exhaustion pressed down on him. It had been days since he'd had more than a couple of hours of sleep at a time. Like a bat, he'd slept in complete darkness only to wake every few minutes, his heart racing.

Would being arrested finally end this? Would whoever had sent the monsters be satisfied, knowing he was behind bars? The things he and Willy had done. His eyes stung again. He'd had weeks of sobriety to contemplate it. He should never have tried to kidnap that woman.

"Abbott."

He jerked his head up at the deputy Bowhan's voice, a momentary panic sending his blood rushing through his chest. He hadn't even heard him approach. Had he fallen asleep?

"It's your lucky day. Scott's wife swung by and brought him another supper by mistake. It's yours if you want it."

"Hell, yeah, I want it." He gripped the metal sink and hauled himself to his feet. His mouth had begun to water before he ever reached for the paper bag and plastic water bottle. "Thanks, man."

"Thank Scott next time you see him."

"I will." He was already tearing into the paper bag and taking out the sandwich and potato chips before the Deputy turned and padded back down the hall.

Gerald tossed the empty bag on the blue blanket covering the lower bunk and returned to his seat against the wall. When he took the first bite of the sandwich, he groaned in pleasure. Roast beef, sliced thin, with mayonnaise, lettuce and tomato. He'd never tasted anything so good. The chips were barbecue, salty and sweet. He crammed them into his mouth a handful at a time, scattering greasy crumbs all the way down his clean orange prison uniform.

After three bites of the sandwich and two handfuls of potato chips, his stomach was already feeling better. He forced himself to slow down and savor the food. It might be a while before he got anything but bologna, since the jail was famous for serving the cheap meat and plastic-tasting processed cheese at every meal.

Ten minutes later he licked his fingers and even the inside of the potato chip bag to get the last few crumbs. It was probably the best meal he'd ever had. He cracked the lid on the water bottle and took a deep drink. Now his stomach was full, his weariness returned. Still not trusting the position of his bunk, he leaned his head back against the wall and closed his eyes.

A flicker of color teased his eyelids, turning the inside pink and he opened his eyes a slit. A strange sheen came from the paper bag he'd ripped open. Two long, clear, almost clawlike legs gripped the side of the cot, and the creature attached to the legs dragged itself forward, bag and all. It was a spider, only bigger. He hated spiders.

His heart hammered against his ribs. Bile filled his throat as he pressed back against the wall. He wanted to move, needed to move, but his limbs felt heavy and uncooperative as a numbing paralysis gripped him.

He was dreaming. He was asleep and fucking dreaming. He needed to wake up. *Please let me wake up!*

The paper ripped and the creature shook free. It poised, hunched on the cot, swaying back and forth in a threatening dance.

It was going to jump on him, bite him. Gerald's feet dug at the floor, but the flimsy slip-on house shoes the guards had given him had no traction. He had to scramble onto his knees to get to his feet, and then he hugged the wall.

The spider bunched its eight long legs and leapt. Gerald gasped and threw up an arm, expecting it to land on him. When nothing happened, he lowered the limb to find the thing clinging to the well-lit area opposite the bunk.

An odd rainbow patch of refracted light shone on the floor. As he gazed up at the creature, tiny sections started spilling off it down the wall, and he realized they were smaller spiders. As each took its position, the patches of light connected to a narrow point of shimmering color leading straight to him.

Gerald's throat seized with fear, his heartbeat sluggish and his breath coming in harsh gasps. He pushed his way around the sink and cringed behind it into the corner. His bony elbows burned as they scraped against the cinderblock walls.

A large gray shape rose from the diagonal band of light at the end of the cell.

A scream built in Gerald's chest, but his throat closed around it like a vise. His breath huffed in and out in an asthmatic wheeze. His words "I'm sorry, I'm sorry," were no more than a whisper of thought.

The shadow danced along the fractured light on the floor to that small peak. Only part of its body was visible, the rest lost in the darkness around it.

Gerald dragged air into his lungs. "I'm sorry. I'msorry-I'msorryI'msorry. I never meant to kill him." It was a lie. He'd been high on cocaine, his drug of choice, and he'd been hot to get to the girl so he and Willy could share her. He'd killed Tanner Newton with no more feeling than he'd have had stepping on a roach. "Ain't it enough they're gonna keep me in here for the rest of my life?"

The gray form swayed back and forth, its eyeless face glaring at him, soulless and hungry.

It dissolved like so much smoke. At the disappearance of the reflected light on the floor, Gerald scanned the room for the spiders. They were gone.

Had he been hallucinating? Coming off the cocaine, he'd had some flashbacks that had seemed just as real.

The squeak of shoes on the tile floor preceded Scott's appearance. "You okay, Abbott?"

Gerald's muscles shook when he came out from behind the sink. "Yeah. Thanks for the food. It was real good."

"You're welcome." Scott gave the empty bag on the bunk a pointed look. "Square away your trash and get some sleep." Scott moved on down the aisle.

"Okay." Gerald sank onto the lower bunk and sucked in a shuddering breath. Spying the torn bag next to him, he lashed out, batting it across the cell where it glanced off the wall.

The few moments of terror had drained his remaining strength. He couldn't continue like this. Tears trickled out of the corners of his eyes, and he curled up in the bunk, his back against the wall and his knees drawn up.

They'd be back and he had nowhere to go. He shivered and dragged the heavy wool blanket up over him. It smelled of some kind of detergent.

After the adrenaline rush of terror, it took several minutes for him to relax. His eyes grew heavy. For nearly half an hour he fought the pull of sleep until he could struggle no longer.

He woke with the sensation of choking. Something was lodged in his throat. He looked down at the blanket. A thousand tiny spiders, their bodies glistening like glass, rushed up the blanket, over his arms, his chest. He kicked and batted at them, a scream locked in his chest by the obstruction.

He tried to keep his mouth closed, but the spiders forced their way into his nose. The sensation of them crawling down into his body, eating into his flesh, triggered a seizure of panic. The pain surged, beyond unbearable. Something exploded in his chest. Darkness feathered the outer edges of his vision. Empty blackness closed in around him.

CHAPTER 9

JULIET STUDIED DETECTIVE Robinson as he led her back to the observation room. He was at least six-three or four, and he towered over her in her stocking feet. His fingers had clasped lightly around her upper arm, as though he expected her to make a break for it. She didn't doubt he was looking at them all as suspects in their own assaults. There had to be a reason why they'd all been attacked.

During Tanner's murder investigation, she'd seen how the cops worked. They separated witnesses to keep them from talking or comparing notes. Whenever they started this divide and conquer bullshit, someone was in trouble.

Miranda never did anything to attract blame. Well, she had once, and in that instance Juliet had reaped the chaos in her sister's place. This time neither of them had done a damn thing to deserve being attacked. She was certain of it.

But if there were a way the cops could pin it on one of them, they'd do it. The bird in hand was always worth more than the two hiding in the brush.

Detective Robinson urged her to take a seat on the bed while he pulled forward the chair Brian Underwood had been sitting on half an hour before.

He had a narrow face and short-cropped, blondish-brown hair. The shallow cleft in his chin gave his strong jaw an extra jolt of masculinity, and his brows, darker than his hair, emphasized how pale his eyes were. His gaze seemed to penetrate her outer shell and bore right into her.

"Do you walk home after work often?" he asked.

"Most nights."

"You know you're borrowing trouble with that kind of behavior?"

Juliet kept her face blank.

"Do you walk past the place where Tanner was killed every night?"

She swallowed, though her throat felt dry. "It's on the way."

"You were only a block away from the spot when you and Samuel Newton were attacked."

"So?"

"Why wouldn't you get into the car with him?"

"I didn't know who he was, and once I did…I thought he might want to hurt me."

"Why?"

"His parents blamed me for Tanner's death." She tentatively touched her throat. It ached every time she swallowed.

"Why did he show up tonight?"

Juliet reached for the plastic cup on the bedside table. Detective Robinson rose and quickly poured more water and ice from the plastic pitcher into the container. Beard stubble darkened the lower edge of his jaw. The powerful width of his shoulders blocked out the overhead light as he leaned forward and handed her the cup. She didn't sense any aggression from him, and the momentary anxious tension in her muscles relaxed.

She held a piece of ice in her mouth and let the cold water soothe the pain. When it eased she said, "He wanted to groom me to testify against Gerald Abbott at his brother's murder trial. He didn't think a bartender would project the proper image and wanted to ensure my testimony appeared credible." She kept her tone flat and devoid of bitterness, though it remained in the background, eating away.

Tanner had never treated her with anything but respect. He'd looked beyond the heavy makeup, the leather pants, boots, and bustier she wore at work, and had seen the normal woman beneath. With his boyish charm and wit, he'd whittled away at her shield and wormed his way into her affections.

She'd cared for him, had tried to love him. It had been her own fault she couldn't. No matter how much he tried to convince her, she'd never felt worthy.

"What did you say to Newton?"

"Thanks, but no thanks."

"Why?"

"Just because I tend bar doesn't mean I'm a slut. I don't need him looking down his nose at me or treating me like I'm something he needs to scrape off the bottom of his shoe. He doesn't know anything about me."

"But you've been in trouble before."

"Not since high school."

"You were present when a man was beaten to death, and now his brother is injured."

There was the look she'd been waiting for. The look that said you're a fuckup, and everything is your fault. She'd seen it at home from her mother and stepfather. Even while the bastard was slipping into her room at night to touch her, fuck her, when she was thirteen.

She'd seen it at school every time she'd visited the principal's and counselor's offices. She'd even seen it while she lay beaten and bloody on the bathroom floor at Superstition High.

She'd read it in Principal Underwood's face while EMS loaded her on a gurney. Maybe she'd learn a lesson from having her nose broken, her ribs cracked, a concussion. Having shoe prints mark her hip, her back, where Brian had kicked her.

But Principal Underwood had learned a lesson, too, when she identified her attacker, and Brian's bruised, busted knuckles and bloody football cleats had verified her story.

Her parents had seen an opportunity and threatened a civil suit for damages.

In return for the charges being dropped, Principal Underwood had been more than happy to pay to keep his son out of jail and clear the way for him to become what he was today. A bully with a badge.

In those few minutes Brian had been in her hospital room, she'd seen he hadn't changed. People rarely did.

But she had. Gradually. Tanner had taught her to be more open, and thus more vulnerable. And now he was dead.

Tanner's death was her fault. And she'd been looking over her shoulder, waiting for the men who killed him to catch up to her.

Now, instead of men, something else had taken their place.

The silence stretched. Robinson continued to eye her, waiting for her reply. Despite the pain, Juliet dragged the hard shell she'd spent so many years perfecting around her and kept her features even, expressionless. She could wait all day if need be.

"We have Abbott in custody, and Willy Porter is dead."

Though Samuel Newton had said so, Juliet had been skeptical. Robinson's confirmation lifted a weight from her, but the small feeling only lasted a moment. "How was Porter killed?"

"We're not certain yet. He was found in an alley a few blocks from where Abbott was staying."

"I've been waiting for them to come after me."

"Then why did you continue to walk home at night?"

Because she'd hoped they would come back and she could exact just a little revenge for what they'd done. Though she was completely capable of dealing with them through other means, she'd bought the gun. Shooting someone was permissible. Burning them to a crisp wasn't.

If the police decided she was guilty of something, they'd search her bag and find the gun.

"This is my life. If I gave up, they won," she finally said when it looked as though they were heading for another standoff.

"Abbott said you set Willy Porter's clothes on fire."

She'd expected, if they took Abbott alive, that he might say something about the fire. She felt no remorse at all about lying. "I doused his pants with perfume and set them alight. It was the only weapon I had. It got them off of Tanner."

Robinson finally asked, "Is there anyone you can think of who would want to hurt you and your sister?"

"Only the men who killed Tanner. And Mr. and Mrs. Newton."

"In the weeks before Tanner Newton's death, did you notice anyone following you, or taking a deeper interest in you than before?"

"No. Tanner was there most nights. We often walked to my apartment after work. I never noticed anyone following us until that night."

"Did he mention anyone he might have had a run-in with or had any kind of argument with?"

"No, but his brother might be able to tell you more once he wakes up."

"Did you notice anyone following you tonight?"

"No."

"Describe the attack for me one more time."

Her voice had hoarsened to a whisper. "We were walking east on Stoker, and paused on the corner of Stoker and Seventeenth. I was walking backwards, getting ready to leave Samuel Newton. He looked past me and I knew someone was behind me.

"Something in his face made me turn to look behind me, and suddenly something gray was over my face, in my mouth. Someone gripped my throat and squeezed. He had to be strong, because he lifted me up off my feet. I dropped my bag on the sidewalk. I was scared he was going to choke me to death, and I started trying to kick him. Then I felt like he might snap my neck, but he kept on squeezing until I started to lose consciousness.

"Something hit me from behind. I didn't know what it was at the time, but it had to have been Samuel. I fell to the sidewalk and hit my cheek." She touched the scrape, still swollen and sore on her cheekbone.

"When I came to, I thought for a moment I'd been having

a nightmare." Once again she was flooded with the panicked fear she felt facing the creature inside the circle of light. She'd never forget the rage and hatred in its scream.

"Samuel was unconscious on the sidewalk a few feet away. I went to him." She swallowed as emotion and tears threatened to overwhelm her. "He was still alive, but unconscious. I took his cell phone from his pocket and dialed nine-one-one."

He closed his small notepad and rose to stand over her for a moment. He surprised her when he placed his large hand on her shoulder, the pressure of his fingers light. "Rest your throat. I'll get back to you in a few days."

The tension eased and she relaxed against her pillow.

He'd made it to the door, then turned back. "You never saw your attacker clearly?"

The image was burned into her brain. "No. Just something gray."

✦   ✦   ✦

MIRANDA WAS LYING there, still, awake, her mind too plagued by all she'd experienced to sleep. The nurse's footsteps sounded muffled as she passed, but the squeak of wheels needing to be oiled carried through the door. Why didn't the nurse just spray them with a little W-D 40 so she could sleep?

Now Caleb was asleep in the chair next to her bed, she could allow herself to look at him. Really look at him.

His thick, dark hair needed a trim. It curled along the back of his neck and around his ears in a show of abandon that sharply contrasted with the rest of him. A five o'clock shadow darkened his chin and jaw and lent his features a dangerous masculinity she found hard to resist.

Her attention rested on his well-shaped mouth, and for a moment she relived their brief kiss. He'd kissed her before. Quick brushes against her cheek, forehead, and even her mouth, but nothing like the kiss they'd shared tonight. The instant sensual buzz she'd gotten from the brief contact amped up while she ran her eyes down his long, rangy body slumped, muscular and strong, in the reclining chair. His thigh muscles seemed to test the strength of his jeans' seams, and his forearms and biceps, toned and conditioned in the Marines and from a mechanic's hard, manual labor, bulged. His hands were rough from that same labor, but that didn't bother her.

She'd tried to convince him to go home and get some sleep, but he refused to leave her—leave them. She'd always known he had a stubborn streak a mile wide. He was laid back and content to go along as long as it suited him, but once he'd reached his limit—she might as well have been singing to a wall for all the notice he'd given her suggestions. The air of quiet command when he refused had stopped her in her tracks.

They were such total opposites, and had only childhood memories and his overseas correspondence in common, but she still loved him. She couldn't remember a time when she hadn't. But now her love was intensified by needs she tried hard to suppress.

Since he returned home from Afghanistan, she had been careful to keep their relationship casual, though Caleb had been chipping away relentlessly at the distance she tried to maintain between them. She told herself often what a bad idea it was for them to get involved, but her resistance was slipping.

Giving in to him could only cause them heartache. Sooner or later the past would catch up with her, and he would find out the sweet, innocent young girl he still saw in her no longer existed. Hadn't existed since she was sixteen.

They'd all been in survival mode back then. Caleb's mother had lain around drunk all the time, and his dad out of the picture.

Miranda's stepfather had dominated their every move, and their weak mother had turned a blind eye to his behavior.

Or had she?

Had she sacrificed her daughters as a way to keep him?

She and Juliet would never know for certain. Their mother would never own up to it if she had. But her needs had always been more important than her daughters. Even after he…disappeared…it had been all about how their mother was going to survive, not them.

Miranda turned onto her back and glanced over to check on Juliet. Her sister's gaze met hers across the dimly lit five-foot separation between them. Miranda shoved aside the covers and slipped out of bed, and Juliet folded back the covers so Miranda could slip in beside her.

For a beat or two they remained silent, heads resting on a single pillow. Miranda remembered how they'd lain like this as children and shared everything. Until Clay Maddox, their stepfather, had decided Juliet needed her own room. Had they insisted on staying together, would things have been different? They'd never know.

"I'm not crazy," Juliet said, her voice barely a whisper. Her fingers closed around Miranda's good arm.

Miranda covered the hand with hers with difficulty. Her arm had stiffened and was sore as hell. It hurt to even move it.

"What I saw wasn't a human," Julia continued. "It was

gray, with no eyes, only a wide, empty black mouth. It screamed at me as if it hated me, was hungry for me."

Juliet had always been the braver twin. She had to be. But she was shaking now.

"There's more than one of them. There has to be," Miranda said. "I thought they were only after me."

Some of the tension went out of them both.

"I won't ask, why us? There are too many reasons to count. But why now?"

Miranda shook her head. "I don't know."

They remained silent. "It's because of Tanner's death," Juliet said with a sigh. "It's the only logical reason. But why would they come after you?"

She wouldn't have forgotten. "Clay was evil. I wouldn't be too quick to discount him."

"He's been gone too long, Miranda."

Her fingers tightened over Juliet's. "An eternity wouldn't be long enough."

"Amen to that." Juliet said with feeling.

"They didn't just suddenly appear. Someone has to have sicced them on us. We have to figure out who."

"It wasn't Tanner's brother. He was with me when it attacked. He saved my life."

"His parents?"

"I can't see them sending him to vet me to testify against Abbott and at the same time unleashing these things on me."

"Who else is there?"

Juliet shook her head, then flinched. "I don't know. We'll have to talk to Samuel tomorrow when he's awake. He may know something. I need to thank him for saving me, too."

Miranda hesitated. She dropped her voice to a whisper. "What if it has something to do with what we did in high school?"

It most likely had something to do with the Craft. Not the Wiccan customs they'd always followed, but something darker. After Clay disappeared, they'd backed away from Wicca entirely.

"It's been too long, Miranda. That was nine years ago. If we were meant to reap anything from it, wouldn't it have boomeranged back to us before now? Besides, it wasn't magic that solved the problem."

No, she has solved it the hard way. And caused both of their lives to spiral downhill in a constant loop of fear.

Was there a time limit for bad karma? Surely they'd paid for everything long ago.

"What did you think of Detective Robinson?" Miranda asked.

Juliet's features stilled. "I don't trust him. If he can find a way to blame us for this, he will."

Miranda wasn't surprised Juliet hadn't taken to him. He was all business and a little abrasive. And those eerie eyes, so pale a blue they looked almost colorless.

Juliet sighed "If we told him, he wouldn't believe us. No one will believe us."

"Caleb saw them too. So there are three of us who know they're real.'

"Samuel saw them, too, but he's in no shape to help. If he starts talking about what he really saw they'll think it's just the trauma."

They fell silent for a moment. Juliet rolled over onto her

back and rubbed her forehead. "Do you think because we're twins the creatures can't tell which of us they're supposed to come after?"

If she agreed with that, it would only heap more guilt on Juliet's shoulders. She already had enough of a burden. "Does it really matter? We have to figure out how we're going to get rid of them."

CHAPTER 10

ARLY MORNING SUN glinted off the parallel rows of
windshields. It was ten o'clock, and the hospital parking
lot was close to capacity already. Caleb scanned every shadow
between the cars. Nothing moved. But then they wouldn't
know if anything was there until Miranda and Juliet emerged
into the sunlight.

Trying to keep both of them covered was a fucking nightmare, especially since he didn't know how these shadow
creatures worked. Could they appear in sunlight as easily as
they did under streetlights? They needed to figure out what
they were fighting and how to fight them. He'd bet firearms
wouldn't work. It would be like shooting smoke. But there had
to be a weapon they could use against them.

Jesus, this was crazy!

Oliver Sparks pulled up in the cab Caleb had ordered earlier. Oliver had a fleet of four cabs, and as a second, part-time
job, Caleb did all their maintenance. As a perk, he could catch
a ride whenever he needed, but this was the first time he'd
taken advantage of the offer.

He turned and motioned to the two women sitting in the
lobby behind him. In looks they were very much alike. Even
their facial expressions and mannerisms were very similar. But
there was a hard edge to Juliet which Mandy didn't have. He'd

tried to pinpoint exactly when Juliet cultivated it, and narrowed it down to middle school. It had gotten sharper in high school, especially after she was attacked in the girl's restroom her junior year in high school.

There was something different about her now. There'd been rapier sharpness to her wit, bitterness behind it. Now she'd grown quieter, more introverted.

Had Tanner Newton's death hit her that hard?

She had watched a man die. It changed you. He knew firsthand.

He watched the sisters argue about who would step outside first.

Juliet strode forward, her spike-heeled boots eating up the distance. Dressed in leather pants and a leather corset, she looked like a cross between a hooker and a Comic-Con look-alike of Kate Beckinsale from an *Underworld* movie. She certainly got everyone's head turning in the lobby.

"I'm going first. If something's out there waiting for us—there's no sense in both of us having our asses hanging out there, when one will do." Her voice still sounded as if it were slowly traveling through a meat grinder.

He wanted to agree with her, but every protective instinct he had was spiraling tighter. The damn things didn't seem to be after him, only the women. But he'd learned from seeing Samuel Newton's condition that they didn't want any interference and would attack anyone who got between them and their target. Not that he had any idea how he could protect her if one of them did decide to rise from the pavement between them and the cab.

"Come on, Caleb. The car is waiting, and you know you

don't want Miranda to have to go out there."

"I don't want you to, either."

Juliet patted his chest and smiled. "That was sweet. I'll be fine." She pushed through the inner door into the vestibule. Her steps hitched once before she hit the door handle and took two long strides out into the sunshine.

Caleb double-timed it to hold the door open in case she needed to leap back in. One second passed like an eternity. Then another. Nothing happened.

"Come on, you two. I've had enough of this place," Juliet said, then slid into the cab.

"Damn her," Miranda muttered with a frown. "She's always got to grab the bull by the—"

Caleb stifled a laugh as she cut herself off. "I'll be right behind you on the bike." He ushered her outside and into the cab.

He shook Oliver's hand briefly and thanked him, then jogged across the parking lot to retrieve his motorcycle. He wove through traffic at a bit more than the speed limit to catch up to them, and pulled into Miranda's driveway just as they were exiting the cab.

The small, white, vinyl-sided house sat centered in a postage-stamp yard. Its best feature was the porch stretching across the front. A swing and several lawn chairs were arranged in a grouping at one end, where he'd sometimes been invited to share a glass of iced tea with Mandy of an evening. She'd been wary of more than food or drink.

Why did she continue to throw up barriers between them? She'd written him faithfully during his deployment, and then as soon as he returned home, she backed off so fast he'd been left confused and hurt.

Her letters had kept him going, probably kept him alive. They'd been filled with news from home, and insights about the townspeople who frequented the library since the college had opened its doors to them. In such a small community, everyone knew everyone else, but there was something elusive, something he couldn't figure out about her. Something she hadn't shared with him. He'd get her to open up soon or later, though. He was making progress.

He thanked Oliver once more before rushing up on the porch just as she was pulling out her key. "I want to check the house before you two go in. Just to be sure there are no surprises."

"There's no way to know until the two of us walk inside." Miranda reminded him. "I'm almost certain one was in the library last night."

"I saw one in the mirror at the club last night, but the light swung away before it could attack me, and it disappeared," Juliet added.

"Why was it able to come into the library and the club, but not The Dish?" Miranda asked.

No one bothered to answer.

"Before we go in, it might be a good thing to sit down and discuss why," Caleb suggested.

The twins exchanged a glance. Miranda settled on the porch swing and Juliet on one of the chairs.

He leaned back on the porch railing and studied them both. "The first rule of engagement is to learn as much as you can about the enemy before taking them on. We need to pool our knowledge so we can do that."

Both women nodded.

"I overheard what you were talking about last night." Some he'd understood, and other things he'd have to wait for Miranda to explain, if she ever opened up to him. "Why do you believe these things have something to do with Tanner Newton, Juliet?"

"One of the men responsible for killing him was captured yesterday and the other one killed. Detective Robinson said they hadn't figured out what had killed Porter yet. Not that he'd been stabbed or shot, but they literally didn't know what had killed him. Just like the doctors couldn't figure out why my throat looks burned or Miranda's arm looks like lighting zapped her. And the timing seems damn convenient for all this to go down as soon as Abbott was captured."

"You can identify this Abbott guy?"

"Yes. I identified him for the police right after Tanner's death."

"So do you think Abbott is responsible for these attacks?"

"He beat Tanner to death, and he knows I'm the one who identified him."

"Have you ever seen him at Steampunk Alley?"

"No, but the place is always packed, and the girls serve the drinks I fix. Or at least all but the people sitting at the bar. He could have been there without my ever knowing it."

Caleb turned to Miranda. "Do you know what he looks like?"

"Yes. I saw his picture in the paper after the killing. I haven't seen him at the library. It's a big place, though, so it would be easy for him to slip in unnoticed or come in on my days off."

He nodded. "It's just a theory, but if he's the cause of these attacks, he might have had to come into those places to open the way for these things to enter. We were at The Dish right after this started, and they couldn't get in there."

"It would be hard to do that in every store or restaurant a person frequents," Miranda said. "And there's no way he's ever been inside my house."

"Okay." He felt moderately better about letting them go inside. "But I still want to check the place out, to make sure nothing's out of place."

Miranda extended the keys to him.

Caleb slipped the key in the lock, twisted it, and disappeared inside.

✦ ✦ ✦

Taking advantage of their moment of privacy, Juliet asked, "If Abbott isn't the cause, has anyone new or different been in your house in the last few weeks?"

"No. I come home, go to bed, then get back up and go to work. It's been weeks since anyone has been here except me or Caleb."

They fell silent for a moment. It was almost painful to watch her sister and Caleb long for each other, love each other, and be so closed off by the past.

"It isn't fair to him, Miranda. He won't leave you as long as he believes there's a chance. You either have to let him in or shut him down and send him away."

Miranda clenched her hands in her lap.

"We've more than paid for the past. Paid with blood, sweat, tears, and any happiness we've ever hoped to have. It's time to let it rest and move on."

Her gaze jerked up to meet hers. "You're one to talk, Juliet."

"But I never really had a chance, Miranda. As much as I cared for Tanner, I didn't love him. You have a shot at the real thing. Take it."

"And if he finds out what I did, what I am?"

"No one knows but us. And I'd die before I'd tell anyone." The only way Caleb Faulkner would find anything out is if Miranda told him herself.

"Forget about the past, Miranda. Love him. Let him love you. You both deserve it." Juliet swallowed. "The ones you can trust are few and far between. Caleb is one of the good guys. He'd die for you."

"I know. That's what I'm afraid of."

Juliet started to say something more, but hearing Caleb coming back, hesitated.

Miranda's words hung between them until Caleb appeared and held open the door. "It looks clear."

CHAPTER 11

CHASE KNELT NEXT to the body and looked down into the man's glassy, dirt-brown eyes. The local coroner, Charles Brewster, squatted next to him. Brewster spoke his observations aloud. "There's no blunt force trauma, no stabbing, nothing. It looks like he went to sleep and just died. Estimated time of death is about three this morning."

Right after Chase brought him in and left for the hospital to interview the twins. Abbott had died, and no one had entered his cell or seen a thing. How was that possible?

"It could have been a drug overdose. I'll have to do an autopsy and send in a tox screen."

This man hadn't died of a drug overdose. He'd been searched before being put in a cell. And poison left some kind of clue, foam around the mouth, a bitten tongue, evidence of a seizure. The only evidence of anything was a small rim of blood around one nostril.

His autopsy results were going to come back the same as Willy Porter's. Chase would bet his paycheck.

Willy Porter's body had been discovered in an alley. He was stretched out peacefully on his back, as though he'd just lain down and died. No trauma other than the healing track marks on his arms and inflamed, eroded nasal passages from sniffing cocaine. At first the coroner had thought he died of an overdose, too. But the tox screen found no drugs in his system.

What would cause a hard-core addict to quit shooting up or snorting within a matter of weeks? Something that required him to stay alert. Like some kind of gray shadow creature?

"Can you put a rush on the autopsy? I need to know if he died of the same thing as Porter."

"Yeah, I can fax you the autopsy results in three or four hours."

"Thanks. In fact, call me when you get ready to do it, and I'll drive over and watch."

"If that's what you want."

The two of them stood back while the one of the patrol officers he'd called in took more photos of the scene, and two deputy jailers helped place the body in a body bag, zip it, and heft it onto the gurney.

Any death at the jail had to be investigated, and as the first responding officer, it would fall to him. He'd have to rule out staff neglect and clear them of any culpability first. Abbott's high-profile assault and murder of Tanner Newton guaranteed they needed every I dotted and every T crossed.

He wended his way back through the maze of hallways to the main security control center. They might be in Podunk, Kentucky, population in the city limits only fourteen thousand citizens and fifteen thousand college students, but the state had made sure they had enough security to properly serve and protect them all.

As his first order of business, he requested the security tapes from last night starting from the time Abbott was arrested until the present.

When Chase knocked on the edge of his doorframe, Chief

Jailer Herman Franks looked up. He ran a tight ship. In spite of the many prisoners cycling through the place, it was always clean, and there'd never been allegations of abuse against any of his deputies.

Franks went on the defensive before Chase ever made it into the room. "None of my deputies did anything to your suspect."

"I don't think they did, either. But I have to follow procedure, Herman. I need to talk to them. So I'd appreciate a list of everyone who was working last night and their phone numbers. I'll call them myself, and set up a time for them to come in for an interview."

Franks relaxed somewhat.

"This was a high-profile arrest, Herman. And you and I both know the sooner we clear your guys, the sooner life returns to normal."

"Okay."

"Did anyone visit or call the jail demanding to see Abbott?"

"No. We processed him and put him in a cell by himself. Scott and Bowhan took turns walking through, checking the prisoners every twenty minutes. There were ten other prisoners in the unit last night."

"I'll want to talk to the other prisoners. Maybe someone heard something."

"Okay."

"Did anyone besides your deputy jailers and the prisoners come into the unit?"

"No."

"Anything out of the ordinary happen?"

"Everything was quiet. Scott's wife dropped his dinner off about two-thirty. He'd left it on the counter at the house."

"Did she come into the unit?"

"No. She left it with Harvey Sutton at the front desk."

"Does she usually visit that late?"

"No. It was the first time she's ever been here. We don't let just anyone wander around here, Robinson. Some of the people who come through are just college kids who have made a mistake. We try to segregate the population so the party boys don't get mixed in with the drug addicts and hard cases."

"Okay. Scott's wife left the bag at the front desk around two-thirty and didn't come in. Anything else out of the ordinary?"

"No."

"All right. I'll be calling your guys to set up interviews. I'd appreciate it if you'd tell them not to drag their heels and try to avoid it."

"They'll cooperate or they'll be out of here."

"Good. Thanks." Chase offered his hand and Franks shook.

"Before I go upstairs, I want to interview the other prisoners."

"You're welcome to use my office."

Franks left to bring in the first prisoner, and Chase reached for his cell phone. With his partner still out on family leave, he'd need help or he'd be down here for hours. He called Garr. "They found Abbott dead in his cell this morning. I'm down at the jail and could use your help."

"We'll be there in twenty minutes."

He'd hoped for Garr alone. If Underwood fucked things

up, he'd see his ass back on patrol.

Chase had hit his rhythm with the second interview by the time Garr showed up. He handed off the list of questions he had formulated.

Two hours later they met in Franks' office to compare notes. "None of mine saw or heard a damn thing," Garr said as he slumped into the only chair.

"None of mine either," Underwood added.

"I'd like a copy of your notes for the file, and you'll need to write up a report on each interview."

Underwood grimaced. Chase wondered if he'd even taken notes.

"A prisoner died in the custody of our department. Unless you want the state guys coming in, we do this by the book."

"Okay," Underwood nodded and shifted his bulk from one foot to the other.

"Any news from the M.E.?" Garr asked.

"No, not yet. I've got a list of the men who were working last night. There were only five. I'd appreciate it if you two would call them and set up times for interviews before their shifts while I look through the video from last night."

"We can take care of this," Garr said.

"Okay." Chase rose, gave the list to Garr, and reached for his own notes and the CDs security had given him.

Chase took the elevator upstairs to homicide. With the other four detectives out on assignment, the room was quiet. He sat down at his desk and popped in the CD. It had recorded twelve hours of images, but all he needed was the time between when Abbott entered the cell until his body was discovered.

He watched the time stamp on the screen as Abbott, now dressed in an orange jumpsuit with his hair still slicked back from a shower, was escorted to his cell. He recognized Scott and Bowhan, whom he'd seen numerous times while walking prisoners down. The two deputies stood outside the cell while the deputy in the security room shut the door automatically. They turned and wandered back up the hall, each pausing here and there to check on other inmates.

As per protocol in the unit, one of the men walked the hall and checked the prisoners every twenty minutes. Bowhan took the first watch after sealing Abbott into his cell. He was carrying a paper lunch sack and a bottle of water, and he paused outside Abbott's cell and offered both items to the prisoner.

Abbott accepted them and Bowhan went on his way.

Twenty minutes later Scott had the duty. He sauntered by, paused to say something to Abbott, and continued down the aisle.

After watching the monotony of their routine, Chase was grateful for his job.

Chase removed his cell phone from his pocket and called Garr. "Make sure you ask Bowhan what was in the lunch bag he gave Abbott after he locked him in his cell. I'm sure it was food. But you need to identify what it was."

"Was there a possibility that Abbott died from poisoning?" Garr asked.

"There were no outward signs of poisoning, but we won't know until the tox screen comes back. We still need everything checked out."

"I'll make a point of asking them both about it separately."

"Good. Thanks." He hung up and went back to the video.

By the time he'd watched the video pass the five o'clock time stamp, he knew neither deputy had set foot in Abbott's cell after securing him inside.

He ejected the CD and popped in the other one. He'd asked for the video footage at the end of the hall so he could watch the security walk-throughs. This camera was positioned closer to Abbott's cell.

He started the CD in real time at 2:30. He could see how the light slanted into the cell, though the interior lights had been extinguished. At ten minutes after three, there was movement inside the cell. The cell door remained closed, but a gray figure rose against the bars, one arm and hand clearly visible.

Chase hit pause, freezing the image. A minute passed as he studied the frame. He took a screen shot of the image and enlarged it as much as he could. The arm and hand were strangely elongated, the outline of the fingers smudged as if the image were caught in the moment of action.

Abbott had been issued an orange jump suit and had been wearing it when Scott and Bowhan escorted him to his cell. No orange showed on the arm of the image. There was nothing gray in any of the cells. The sheets on the bunks were white and the blankets Kentucky blue.

Abbott had told him someone was after him, and he'd been terrified. But the story he'd told was too crazy to believe.

Just like the twins at the hospital last night.

And Tanner Newton's brother. The story the man had babbled to the nurse sounded nearly identical to Abbott's. Creatures rising from a pool of light to attack them. Creatures who had terrorized Porter and Abbott for the two months they'd been on the run.

It had to be Abbott inside the cell. To think it was anything else would be crazy. Wouldn't it? A quiver ran through the pit of his stomach. It had to be Abbott. Because if it wasn't—What the hell...?

He didn't even know how to finish the thought.

Chase wrote down the time stamp at the corner of the video. He'd have to take it down to the computer lab and get them to enhance the image.

He caught the elevator down two floors and quickly handed off the CD to a lab tech with a post-it note attached with the time frame where he wanted the video enlarged and explored.

On the way back up to his office other thoughts ran through his mind.

Who hated Juliet Templeton enough to want her dead? And why hadn't they followed through after Tanner was killed? He thought that through, running scenarios in his head.

Because their focus had been to separate Juliet and Tanner. When Tanner died, the focus had changed to killing the two men responsible for his death.

And now those two men were dead, the person who'd hired Abbott and Porter had all the time in the world to go after Juliet.

But two months had passed since the original attack, and though she'd been injured the night before, the chances of getting protection for her or her sister were slim.

He had to warn them both.

He tugged his phone out of his jacket pocket when it buzzed. But first he had to go to an autopsy.

CHAPTER 12

"**W**HERE DO WE go from here?" Juliet asked.

Miranda turned to study her sister. The blue scarf she'd loaned her hid the horrible reddish bruise around her throat. Dressed in a pair of jeans and a summer sweater from Miranda's closet, her face free of makeup, Juliet looked younger, less hardened.

"The library to do research. I thought it might be a good idea to see if we can learn anything about these creatures before it gets dark."

Juliet nodded.

"Caleb will be here with my car in a few minutes."

"Okay." Juliet reached for her oversized bag and dug inside to pull out a tube of lip-gloss and some blush. She used a mirror by the front door to smooth both on.

Miranda debated on whether or not to comment on her sister's new look. "I like you with less makeup."

Juliet raised a brow and looked at her through the mirror. "You're supposed to like me no matter what I look like."

"I always have."

"No you haven't," she answered with some of her normal edge, sounding like a six-pack a day smoker, which somehow made the attitude seem stronger. "But that's okay. I haven't always liked myself either."

"But you're better now?"

She nodded. "Sometimes."

Miranda struggled to suppress the tears and failed. "I'm glad." She turned aside to get her own purse.

"If I can set aside some of my issues, you can lay down some of yours, Miranda."

"With Caleb, you mean?"

"Yeah."

Miranda looked up from her useless search through her purse. "What if they find him?" She still couldn't bring herself to say her stepfather's name aloud.

"They won't. He's gone for good."

"How can you be sure?"

"Because three months ago I made certain of it."

Her heart skipped a beat before taking flight. Her breaths echoed loud in her ears. "What did you do, Juliet?"

"Clay Maddox will never be spoken of between us again in this lifetime, because he's no longer an issue for either of us."

"How could you—" Miranda cut herself off and studied her sister.

"You did the right thing nine years ago, Miranda. I did the right thing three months ago. Hell, I should have done it years ago, and I did try several times, but I lost my nerve. But now it's time for us both to be done with this particular burden."

Miranda searched her heart to feel how the suggestion resonated. "Are you sure?" Her gaze searched Juliet's soul.

"Short of being shot to the moon, he couldn't be any further out of reach."

The fear Miranda had lived with for so long lifted a little. "Why didn't you let me help you?" she asked.

"Because I needed to do it myself. To face him one more time and wreak my own revenge. And it was sweet." A triumphant smile lit Juliet's face.

Miranda's residual fear evaporated completely. She felt lighter, and her lungs could finally expand to their full capacity. "I wish you'd told me sooner."

"I got tangled up with the police investigation when Tanner died, and I thought I needed to keep my distance."

She'd protected Juliet nine years ago in the only way she could, and now Juliet had done the same for her. Miranda reached for her and they clung together. The distance between them no longer felt so wide.

She'd done the unthinkable, and one day she'd have to pay for it, but it was all worth it if Juliet could begin to heal. The guilt for not being able to protect her eased some.

When they heard a knock, they parted, and she went to open the door.

Caleb brought in with him the aroma of burgers and fries. He looked alert, though she knew he'd stayed up nearly all night on watch at the hospital.

He'd just gotten back from a war zone. What kind of effect was this having on him?

"Did you have any trouble?" Miranda asked.

"No. I thought we could use something to eat before we head to the library."

That brief *no* concerned her. There was something in his voice when he said it. But she certainly agreed with food. They adjourned to sit at her small kitchen table, where she took the drink orders for iced tea and got busy preparing them.

Caleb joined her at the refrigerator. "You can't do this

one-handed," he said, nodding toward the sling cradling her arm. He handed her the glasses to fill with ice, then reached into the refrigerator to get the pitcher of iced tea and pour it. He scooped the glasses up and carried them to the table while Julia got plates out of the cabinet.

They ate in companionable silence for a while. When Miranda sprinkled a few fries on her plate and put the rest on his, he shot her a grin. Every patient, kind thing he had done in the last six months unfolded in her mind's eye in a rush. He deserved much more than she had given him. For every moment he had loved her, he deserved everything in return.

The constant fear of having her secret discovered had eaten away at her life and Julia's like the gravity of a black hole. Every moment of joy had been sucked away. But no more. If they survived this, they were both going to put their lives back together as sisters, and as women. And witches.

Caleb stuffed the debris from their meal back into the bag while Julia put their plates in the dishwasher.

When he settled again in his chair he leaned forward and laced his fingers. Just the shift in his posture and expression alerted her.

"I checked the car over before I drove it here. I found something in the trunk, slipped between the liner and the wall."

A sinking feeling settled in the pit of Miranda's stomach. "What is it?"

"It's a rolled-up piece of paper with some writing on it. I didn't want to bring it into the house. Who besides me has access to your vehicle, Mandy?"

"No one. I don't loan my car out."

"But someone at the library might have access to your keys. Where do you keep your purse?"

"In my office, in my desk."

"Do you keep either locked?"

"No. But I'm in and out of the room all day, as are all the other people who work there."

"So anyone who works there could slip into your office, get your keys, fuck with your vehicle, then put the keys back. They might even have managed to get keys to your office and your house and make copies of them."

She and Juliet glanced at each other. Both rose at the same time and went into the living room. Miranda shook everything out of her purse onto the coffee table and looked through each object, but found nothing.

Miranda glanced up and froze when she saw the gun in Juliet's hand. Her heart skipped a beat. "What are you doing with that?"

"Protecting myself. Abbott and Porter were running around free until yesterday. I've been expecting them to come after me." She ejected the clip and cleared the chamber. She handed the gun off to Caleb.

Seeing her sister with a gun in her hand had shaken her. After everything Juliet been through, she didn't doubt she could pull the trigger. But could she live with herself after taking a life?

Caleb held the unloaded weapon like an extension of his hand as he checked it over. "Do you have a license to carry, Juliet?"

"Yes."

"You really need a holster. You don't want lint and shit

getting into the barrel or working its way around the trigger or firing pin.

Miranda brushed a hand across her forehead. What strange kind of world had she been teleported into? She'd never even touched a gun. There'd never been any in their house growing up.

The reason Juliet had kept her distance for so long became clear. Her sister's life had been threatened, and she'd played it down to keep from worrying her. And stayed away to protect her.

"Do you think bullets will affect the shadows?" Miranda asked.

Caleb frowned. "I doubt it."

"Why don't we put the gun away then?" She pulled a drawer open in the end table and he placed it inside.

Juliet pulled a tampon out of the blend of articles on the couch. "This isn't mine. It isn't the brand I use and I always carry mine in a small cosmetic case."

"Way too much info, Juliet," Caleb exclaimed, a slight flush coloring his cheeks.

She grinned, then laughed. "We're being attacked by shadow creatures and you're big bad Marine sensitivities are bothered by a tampon?" She ripped it open and pushed the device free of the small plastic applicator that held it. Instead of a tampon, a narrow piece of paper rolled up into a scroll dropped onto the floor.

She bent to pick it up and unrolled it. "Oh, shit! It's written in Latin. I recognize some of the words, but not all. Look in your things Miranda, there has to be something there."

Miranda looked through the contents on the coffee table

again. The normal flotsam of change purse, checkbook, and ink pens spilled out. She searched one of the zippered pockets and pulled out a tampon. She didn't use them. It wasn't hers.

Instead of ripping it open immediately as Juliet had done, she studied the wrapper. The end closest to the bottom of the applicator didn't have the same machine crimping as the other. It had been carefully trimmed and resealed.

As she ripped it open Caleb said, "It's a woman. A man wouldn't think of using...something like that."

The small scroll of paper resting in her palm curdled her stomach. For a long beat of time she and Juliet looked at each other.

Karma had just risen up to bite them on the ass.

"We both work with a lot of women," Juliet said. "But I can't think of any reason why one would come after me. I've been keeping a low profile for a while now. Even before Tanner was killed." She swallowed. "And I haven't poached anyone else's boyfriend, or slept with their husband. All I've done is work, mind my own business, and try to live my life." Her smile was forced. "What have you been up to, sis?"

Miranda laid the roll of paper in an ashtray and wiped her hand on her slacks. She controlled the urge to go scrub it with soap. "Nothing that could draw this kind of attention."

"Since we can't figure out who, then we have to figure out what they are and how we can get rid of them," Juliet said.

Miranda straightened her shoulders. They'd faced bad things before. She and Juliet could do this. She dealt in knowledge, and she knew just where they needed to go. "The library's our best bet."

✧　✧　✧

JULIET SLIPPED FREE of her seat at the computer and stretched. She'd been at it for two hours, and the only information her searches had kicked out was about shadow spirits.

The creatures they were dealing with weren't spirits. They interacted too aggressively with the living. Could they be demons?

Even the thought had chill bumps tiptoeing up and down her arms and her chest felt tight. They had done some amazing things in high school with Sherry and Aubrey, but nothing like this. She'd have never believed any of this shit was possible if she hadn't come face-to-face with one last night.

The translation she'd done of the words written on those small pieces of paper had sent her off in a different direction, though. She needed confirmation of what she'd discovered, and she could only find it in two places she hadn't visited in a very long time.

She wandered over to the second floor railing and studied the activity on the ground floor. Three women were working the desk, checking in, checking out, and shelving books. In light of what Caleb had said, Juliet studied each woman. One seemed familiar, but none looked like a psycho-bitch, but then appearances were deceiving. She was living proof of that.

Every few seconds the scanner beeped. How did Miranda stand it? The sound alone would drive her insane. But then her sister had always been more tolerant than she.

Juliet glanced in her direction. Miranda rose from her chair behind her desk and wandered out of her office to stand next to her at the railing. "Caleb texted me. He has an alarm system installed in my car. Anyone tries to mess with it again, the alarm will go off."

"Good." She glanced at Miranda. "He's afraid for you."

"I know. I couldn't have him hanging around like a body-guard all day, and he needed to work."

"What's that?" Juliet nodded toward the paper Miranda gripped.

She handed it to Juliet. "A thank-you note from a very pissed off student because I interrupted his conquest of another student in the upstairs bathroom. Or at least I think it is."

Juliet's brows rose at the word Bitch written across the paper in bright red ink. "It might not hurt to hand it over to the police. With all this other stuff going on, you never know." She handed the paper back to Miranda. "How's the employee search going?"

"So far, no one's standing out as suspicious, and their work histories are all coming back clean. There are three I suspect may be practicing the Craft. I've earmarked them for further study. I still have several more to look through." She cleared her throat. "We've got about six hours of daylight left. We need to stick with this and find some way to protect our-selves."

"Just the usual we already know. Salt, holy water, religious artifacts like crosses and Bibles, and prayer. That's all I've found. Or we could set wards to protect us, Caleb, and the house. Or we could wear protective jewelry."

Miranda's brows rose. "You learned all that in two hours?"

And she hadn't found anything she believed would really work, outside of fighting witchcraft with witchcraft. "Yeah. I think instead of doing more research, we need to get to a church and ask for some holy water and for a priest's help."

"We're not Catholic," Miranda said on a sigh.

Juliet glanced at her. "But priests and pastors are supposed to help people whether they're Catholic, Protestant, or whatever, aren't they?"

Miranda eyed her. "What makes you think one would even believe us?"

"He will if he's around after dark when those things start popping out of the sidewalk."

Miranda put a hand over her mouth and looked away, her shoulders shaking.

Ah shit, she'd made her cry. Juliet placed a hand on her shoulder in a demonstration of comfort. It took a moment to register it wasn't tears making her tremble, but stifled laughter. When Miranda finally looked up she was still smiling.

"What's so funny?" Juliet asked.

"You're so...I'm just glad to see you haven't changed the way you face off against things."

If only they'd both been able to manage that when they were younger. Juliet shrugged. "Necessity makes even the timid brave. I read that quote somewhere. After you've faced off against a belligerent drunk or two, you learn to be assertive."

She changed the subject. "I think we should divide our resources. You stay here and research, and I'll go down to the Catholic church and see if I can stir up some reinforcements for the cause. Then we'll both hit Aubrey's place on the way home. She may have some answers."

Miranda bit her bottom lip. "She was here last night. She warned me trouble was coming."

Juliet straightened from leaning on the railing. "You don't

think she…"

"No." Miranda shook her head. "Never. She's adamant about her beliefs, especially about harming none.'" She rubbed at her shoulder. "If we have to take matters into our own hands and protect ourselves the hard way, do you think things will come back to us? I mean it's been a long time."

"I think it's like sex. Once you know how, it doesn't just—disappear." In the end she had used magic to end things with Clay. So she knew her magic was still intact.

And she'd been going off by herself, up in the mountains, to practice by herself. The pressure inside her had built up to the point where she had to let it erupt. But it had been different by herself. As lonely as the rest of her life. "It probably wouldn't hurt if you did some meditation and a few…" She quirked a brow. "Exercises."

"It's been so long." Miranda's throat worked as she swallowed. "I've missed it, Juls."

"I know. It's like losing your sense of taste or smell. Everything is bland and less…"

"Yes. That's exactly how it is." Miranda gripped the chrome railing one handed. "I'm nervous about you going outside. What if those things decide to start crawling out from whatever lair they're hiding in? Last night was…"

She'd only dealt with one. Miranda had witnessed at least two creatures coming out of the lights. Or had it been the same one? They had to do something to stop them. "I'll be careful. Besides, what better place to hide from them than a church?"

Miranda shoved her hair back from her face with the one hand still in good working order. "You have a point. We'll have to keep that in mind for later. Just in case. Please be careful."

Juliet grabbed her purse hanging on the corner of her seat. "I translated the message on the slips of paper."

"What did it say?"

> *"In pools of man-made light,*
> *Shadows cast their fright,*
> *To wreak havoc and violence,*
> *And seal Juliet's silence,*
> *Death and destruction,*
> *Will end her corruption.*
> *Abide by my will, Let no man see,*
> *As I will, so mote it be."*

Miranda's eyes widened in surprise. "Have you heard of any witches besides Aubrey, Sherry, and us, living in Superstition?"

"Yeah, some. I've dealt with more than a few witches at the club. But I can only think of one who'd wish us dead.

Miranda frowned at the reference to their mother. "She wouldn't really wish us dead, Juliet. And besides, she doesn't have the power."

Noticing movement over Miranda's shoulder, she said, "One of the students just went into your office. You locked your purse up in your desk, didn't you?"

"Yes, but I still don't want her in there."

"What's her name? She looks a little familiar. Maybe she's come to the club. One of the women working the counter downstairs may have come in too."

"Her name's Vivian Ward. She's a very good worker."

"But?" Juliet urged.

"She's still proving herself, and is a little overeager."

"Did you look over her records?"

"She was one of the first. She's working on a degree in education and taking some classes in library science as a second major. I didn't find anything suspicious in her background."

Miranda was too trusting. Or was she? If she didn't trust Caleb enough to let him close, why would she let anyone else? Juliet nodded. "I'd get in there if I were you. I'm going to take off and do some errands to help us prepare for tonight."

Vivian exited the office and headed in their direction. The woman shot her a smile. "You two really are identical. If you weren't dressed differently, I'd never be able to tell you apart."

Not something they hadn't heard before.

"I was just wondering which of these books you'd like for me to use Saturday with the children. I'm still doing the history of fairy tales. Last week we did something more targeted to the boys, and this week I thought I'd do something for the girls."

The stack of books she held were all classic fairytales. Miranda tilted her head to read the titles. "*Rumpelstiltskin* might work, since it has a darker turn that will appeal to the boys."

"I suppose *Sleeping Beauty* would be too much like chick lit."

"Probably so." Vivian nodded, then smiled. "Especially since the prince has to kiss her to wake her. I can hear the eeews from all the boys myself. I'll write up the lesson plan and gather some other things to go with it."

"Thank you, Vivian."

Juliet waited for her to be out of earshot "She seems to know her stuff."

"She's very good. But she's one of those people who infringes on your personal space without realizing it."

Juliet had dealt with more than a few like that, but they were usually drunk.

Miranda dragged her thoughts back by saying, "Caleb's going to pick me up in about an hour, and we're going to search the house to make sure no one's planted any more of those spell papers. Call when you want to be picked up."

Juliet shot a thumb up. "Will do."

Juliet paused inside the library foyer. Leaving the hospital safely this morning had eased her anxiety somewhat, but as she pushed through the double doors, her heart raced and her breath clogged her throat.

Detective Robinson stood at the bottom of the concrete stairs. He took off his sunglasses and his strange blue gaze pinning her like a butterfly to a board. "I need to talk to you, Ms. Templeton."

CHAPTER 13

C HASE TOOK A seat in one of the hard backed wooden chairs in Miranda Templeton's office. He looked from one woman to the other. Had they not received different injuries, he'd have had a difficult time telling them apart. They were both beautiful, with warm, chestnut-streaked brown hair and high cheekbones. Since he'd done some research on them, he wondered at the different turns their lives had taken.

He broke the news quickly. "Gerald Abbott is dead."

The relief he'd expected to see in Juliet Templeton's face never appeared. But she was surprised.

She'd shut down before, when he mentioned her presence during Tanner's death and Samuel's attack. He'd seen similar responses in two different categories of the people he'd dealt with. Those who'd been abused, and the hardened criminals who'd gone through the system so many times they were neither intimidated by what lay ahead nor hopeful they were going to avoid punishment.

The more he looked into Juliet's background and past behaviors, the more he believed she was an abuse survivor.

"What happened?" Miranda asked.

"He was found dead in his cell this morning. We're investigating, and the coroner, Dr. Brewster, has performed an autopsy. We didn't want to wait for the state guys to do one."

The sisters exchanged glances.

"The reason I'm here, Ms. Templeton," he aimed his look at Juliet, "is because, according to what Gerald Abbott told me, he and Porter were paid to kill you. Tanner Newton was killed by accident."

Juliet flinched and pressed her fingers against her lips, the shock he'd expected to read earlier obvious.

Her throat worked as she swallowed. "Who hired them?"

"Abbott didn't know. He'd received payment through a go-between. That man too is dead."

"This is crazy!" Miranda exclaimed, her voice sharp with anxiety.

Chase scooted forward in the chair. "They were both drug addicts. Addicts will do anything for their next fix. Someone paid them to go after you. The person who hired them is still out there. I'd be remiss if I didn't caution you to be careful and stay alert."

Though Juliet's face remained composed, her hands clenched until the knuckles turned white. "We are." She ran her fingers through her hair, shoving it back.

Chase's attention snagged on the graceful line of her cheek and jaw. He tried to ignore the tug of attraction. She was a witness, a victim. He couldn't get involved with her. And with her history, it would be a bad idea anyway.

She bit her lip. "It seems that whoever is after me can't tell my sister and me apart."

He leaned forward in his seat. "Are you sure you don't know anyone who has reason, real or not, to want to harm you?"

"I've never dealt drugs, unless you count the drinks I serve at Steampunk Alley. I haven't taken drugs since I was eighteen, though some of your patrol officers continued to pull me over on a regular basis until I sold my car. I don't gamble, so I don't owe anyone money. And I haven't poached anyone's boyfriend. So no, there's no reason for anyone to come after me."

"When did you sell your car?" he asked. He'd put feelers out to some of the patrol officers and see what they said about her.

"In May."

"Have you noticed anyone hanging around at the club?"

"We have regulars who come in all the time."

"Anyone who's shown too much interest or gotten too aggressive?"

"Samuel Newton, but I think you can mark him off the list." She remained silent for a moment. "Justin Chalmers, one of the other bartenders, has been trying to get me to go out with him. He's been very persistent."

"Anyone else who's made you feel uncomfortable?"

"No one outside the occasional drunk customer who gets too mouthy when I cut them off. And those are too many to count."

Her job sounded a lot like his. He'd go by the bar and get a list of employees from the owner and talk to her coworkers.

Chase turned his attention to Miranda. "How many employees are there at the library, Ms. Templeton?"

"About twenty-five, counting the custodians who clean on the weekend and the two security guards. Plus we have five students on a student work program who come in during the week."

"Can you get me a list of employees?"

"Certainly."

"Anyone here who seems out of place?"

"We service the college and the town, Detective. No one's out of place when they come to the library."

"Anyone hanging around you or staying close to your work station when they shouldn't be?"

Miranda shook her head. "I don't hang out in my office very much. I'm in charge of scheduling and making sure all the other sections of the library are running smoothly. We have classes and community meetings coming in and out daily to use our conference rooms and AV equipment. Interlibrary loan materials to distribute, books to catalogue into the system, and a hundred other things to deal with."

"Anyone overeager to help?" he asked.

She was silent a moment. "We're here to be helpful. No one works here whom the college hasn't vetted. They've all been fingerprinted and a background check run." Her gaze shifted to Juliet. "We have to tell him."

Chase straightened in his chair. "Tell me what?"

Juliet shot Miranda a frown of displeasure. Her movements impatient, she dug in her bag and removed a plastic bag. When she rose he automatically got to his feet as well. She offered him the bag. "I found a small slip of paper hidden in a tampon in my purse. The paper had been rolled up in the applicator and put back into the manufacturer's wrappings. Miranda got one, too."

Impatience tightened the muscles at the back of his neck. "Why didn't you tell me right away?" Standing close to her for the first time, his gaze skimmed over the smoothness of her skin and the shell pink fullness of her lips.

Her eyes, a toffee brown, glittered with resentment. "We just found them this morning, Detective."

"We saved the tampons and wrappers," Miranda said, pulling out a bag from her desk.

"The notes are written in Latin, and I translated them, but you might want to get an expert to check it. I was on my way to the Catholic church to have the priest there look it over when you showed up."

Miranda added, "Caleb suggested it might be a woman. He didn't think a man would chose a feminine hygiene product to hide it in." She offered two bags to him. "He found one in the trunk of my car, too."

So Faulkner had been with them when they found them. He perused the slips of paper through the plastic. The words had been printed by hand in calligraphy. A reddish cast hung along the edge of each word, like the ink had bled.

He pulled the translation Juliet had done out of the bag and read it.

He thought he'd seen everything. He'd dealt with drug addicts, drunks, prostitutes, pimps, peeping toms, perverts and murderers. He'd arrested them all.

The translation of the words sent an uneasy chill up the back of his neck.

Miranda and Juliet waited for his reaction.

"It's a threat wrapped up in a voodoo spell."

"Not voodoo," Juliet corrected him. "It's written according to Wiccan custom. Wicca demands you harm none. And one more thing I believe this is something more. I believe the ink may be blood."

CHAPTER 14

C ALEB TIGHTENED THE screws on the new doorknob he'd installed on Miranda's front door. Once he did the deadbolt, the house would be more secure. Since he already had her car keys with her house keys on it, he'd gone ahead and installed the locks both front and back.

Would she be pleased with this, or upset he'd taken the initiative without asking? He never knew these days. She swung between pushing him away and looking at him as though she wanted... How was he to know what women's looks meant? He couldn't seem to stop loving her, and hoping she'd finally let him in...

He jerked out the rag he'd stuffed in his back pocket and wiped the sweat from his face and neck. The breeze was like a hot breath, and clung, sticky with humidity. The hypersensitive feeling of being watched slithered down the back of his neck for the third time in the last few minutes. The hair rose on his forearms. His heart rate skyrocketed.

He picked up the drill to use as a weapon and braced for an attack. How much good would the drill be against a supernatural shadow creature?

After a moment's pause, when nothing moved, he set the bit to cut away the dead bolt and leaned into the job. He had to believe whoever had planted those fucking slips of paper on

Miranda and Juliet hadn't had access to the house; otherwise everything he was doing wouldn't provide a damn bit of protection.

Ten minutes later he finished changing out the lock and bent to gather his tools.

He caught movement out of the corner of his eye and swung to meet it. In the shaded eave of the porch, a darker shape scurried along the vinyl siding to the ceiling. Was it only the light reflected from the windshield of a passing car or something more?

The longer he looked at the shape straight on, the more it seemed to fade. He looked just to the right of it, and it came into stark relief. It looked like a huge spider, suspended close to the door, ready to drop on the unwary.

It had been observing him for some time. He'd felt it. Was it there to watch, or would it attack him? He moved forward with the drill, and it scrambled along the ceiling to the edge of the eaves. Caleb lunged again, and it slipped around the back side of the gutter.

Come on, fucker!

Why wouldn't it take him on?

Because it hadn't come for him.

Shit. Locks or no locks, Miranda and Juliet couldn't come back here.

They were in deeper trouble now. The thing's legs crept around the edge of the eave and came back into view, its shape coming in and out of focus.

Something major had changed. This one could appear in daylight.

✧ ✧ ✧

MIRANDA STEPPED AROUND Vivian to reach her desk. The woman had no sense of personal space. She often stood too close when they spoke. "I've decided to leave a little early, Vivian."

"You probably shouldn't have come in at all today, Ms. Templeton. That bruise on your arm looks wicked painful."

Miranda settled into her desk chair and suppressed the need to rub her arm. It ached from the top of her shoulder to her elbow, like someone had drilled right through the bone. At the hospital she'd been surprised to find it wasn't broken.

She'd studied the bruise in the bathroom mirror this morning and gotten nauseous just looking at it. Something evil had stabbed her. And she had no idea what it was or where it had come from. Since Abbott and Porter had probably died of a similar attack, she'd been lucky. The shield she threw up had deflected the blow just enough to keep it from going through her body.

"It has started to ache a little more since this morning. I've made up a schedule for the rest of the day, and I was hoping you could pass it on to Ms. Carlyle when she comes in. I've already called security, and they'll be here to search the upstairs restrooms for stragglers in my absence. I've decided that from now on they need to be the ones to do that instead of one of us, for safety's sake."

Vivian reached for the schedule before Miranda had a chance to hand it to her.

That was another thing she found irritating. Vivian's over-eager behavior wasn't abating, and instead seemed to be tumbling into overbearing. "I appreciate you passing that on, Vivian. I have a few more things I need to take care of before

I'll be ready to leave."

The woman frowned, probably miffed at the dismissal in her voice, but said, "You're welcome, Ms. Templeton. I'll be sure she gets this."

Miranda stared after her. She'd looked through every employees file and found nothing but academic types who were as boring as she. Did any of them have hidden lives where they practiced the Craft?

Mary Janet and Susan, two of the work-study students, wandered by, stacks of books in their arms to return to the shelves. Did either of them have things in their background to hide? If they did, she hadn't been able to find it in their employee or student records. Vivian was a little more interesting, since she worked for a while as a secretary in her father's law firm before quitting to go back to school. Her father seemed to be footing the bill. If her behavior here was any indication, he might have sent her back to school to get her out of his office.

Her need to take charge might serve her well in her own classroom, though. High school students could be a handful.

Nora Donovan slipped through and settled at a table in the study area. She wondered if the girl was still seeing Robert Hoag.

Out of the corner of her eye she caught movement from the stairs, and her attention snagged on Caleb as he swung toward her office. Every time she saw him, her pulse raced and her heart tumbled. She rose to greet him with a smile.

"We have a problem," he said, his expression grim.

The adrenaline racing through her system at sight of him kicked up a notch and swerved in a different direction. "What is it?"

He edged her back into the office and closed the door. "I installed a new alarm in your car and I've changed the dead bolt and other locks on your doors at the house."

"Oh." He'd been in hyper-protective mode since last night. He couldn't continue this indefinitely. Already lines bracketed his mouth and his eyes were bloodshot. "That was a good idea. Thank you."

"While I was at the house something strange was on the porch."

Something in his eyes shoved her anxiety up another level.

"It looked like a dinner plate-sized spider, but I couldn't see it if I looked straight at it. It had some kind of strange shadow camouflage. It didn't try to attack me, but seemed more interested in just watching to see what I was doing. I know it sounds crazy…"

Miranda laid a hand on his arm. "I believe you."

His expression cleared. "I think you and Juliet should stay at my place. No one's been there. They wouldn't have had any reason to be."

Because she'd never been there. She as good as read the thought from his face. What did it say about her that she had never been to his home? That she had pushed him away at every chance. And what did it say about him that he'd continued for months to try to dig through the barriers she'd erected between them?

Six months, and all they'd done was lunch or dinner, movies, and pie and a few light kisses. She felt ashamed for having treated him so uncaringly when she—she loved him so, it bloomed into an ache inside her. Regret stuck in her throat, thick as peanut butter and twice as choking.

All day she'd dwelled on what Juliet had said about Clay. The fear of his discovery had been like a stone burrowed into the bottom of her heel and every time she stepped on it, the pain reminded her he was always there, waiting to destroy her life and Juliet's. If he was truly gone... He was gone. Juliet had sworn he was.

It had taken her so long to get past the legacy Clay left behind. Seeing what he had done to Juliet had scarred her, killed any desire to share herself with a man. Until Caleb came home. Was it even possible that she could have a life? A life with Caleb? But first they had to get past these creatures and whoever was responsible for sending them.

Miranda rested a hand on his arm. "I think it would be a good idea for us to stay with you, too. We'll need some clothes and toiletries." He bit her lip. "Detective Robinson came by, and we gave him the notes we found.

"It was a good call, Mandy. I know why none of us admitted the truth to the cops, but if all three of us go back in and lay it out for them..."

"They'll think we're all insane. If you hadn't seen them yourself, would you believe?"

"No. I wouldn't have. But then there a lot of things in this world that happen all the time that I can't believe."

He'd gone to war to get an education, and had learned more than how to rebuild engines. Those experiences had scarred him as deeply as Clay Maddox's abuse had Juliet and her. She moved to embrace him and he put his arms around her. After so many months, it felt natural to fit herself to his tall frame and just lean in. It felt right.

"Maybe they won't show up tonight. Maybe last night was a one-time deal."

He ran a hand down her back. "I hope so, but just in case, I still think you and Juliet should stay with me. I have plenty of room. There are five bedrooms."

Reluctantly she drew back to look up at him.

He glanced at his watch. "You said you saw one of the shadows in the library last night. It might be a good idea to get the hell out of here before dark."

The idea of some time alone with him before Juliet showed up was a temptation. How could she think of that when their lives were in danger from something none of them understood? But she had waited for such a long time to feel like this about someone. No matter what else was happening, she deserved to be able to acknowledge those feelings.

"I'm ready to go now, if you are. I can't really do very much with my arm out of commission." Her fingers briefly lingered on her upper arm. She'd see if Juliet felt up to trying some healing. She'd always been good at it before.

"How is it feeling?" he asked.

"Very sore." She unlocked her desk drawer and grabbed her purse. She took everything out and laid it on the large calendar that covered the surface of her desk. She searched each item, and when she found nothing, put everything back in her bag.

"Where's Juliet?" Caleb asked.

"She and Detective Robinson have gone to the Catholic church to ask the priest to check her translation."

"Why was Robinson here?"

"He came by to warn us. Abbott was found dead in his cell

this morning. They know he and his partner were hired to kill Juliet, but they don't know why or who hired him."

"Shit!" Caleb caught her good arm. "I don't think you realize what my seeing the spider on your porch means, Miranda. The thing on the porch was a shadow of sorts, but it was out during daylight."

The magnitude of what he'd discovered hit her. Safety in daylight, the one thing they thought they could count on, was no longer a guarantee.

"I need to call Juliet and warn her." She scrambled to jerk her phone free of her purse.

CHAPTER 15

CHASE AND JULIET sauntered down Sacred Heart's center aisle. The church hadn't changed since he was a boy. The darkly stained wooden pews gleamed with polished care. The scent of fresh cut flowers hung in the air. Large bouquets were set in the entrance foyer and at the front of the sanctuary.

When they reached the first pew, Chase went to one knee and made the sign of the cross.

Juliet paused beside him. "You go to this church?"

"Yes. My mom moved us here when I was twelve. I went to church here until I moved away to go to college. I started back when I moved back two years ago."

"You moved here from up north?"

"Yes."

"Michigan?" she asked.

"Yeah."

A small quirk of her lips and he could see amusement. "Everyone in Kentucky has at least one family member who lives in Michigan."

"Do you?'

"Cousins on my Dad's side."

"I'll start asking around and take a poll," Chase quipped and earned another of her small smiles. She didn't smile easily. That was a shame.

"You said Abbott died in his cell."

Her quick change of subject killed the easy mood between them.

"You might want to search his cell or the block where he was housed for a slip of paper with similar words on it."

He hid his keen interest by focusing his attention on Father Clarence's entrance from one side of the altar. "Why do you say that?"

When he looked up she shrugged. "Just a hunch, Detective."

"Do you believe in things like witchcraft?" he asked.

"I believe in evil, and sometimes that's all it takes to make things happen."

He couldn't argue with that.

"Father Clarence." He extended a hand in greeting.

The priest shook it. A shock of white hair hung over his forehead, yet his features appeared youthful despite his forty years of service to the church.

"Chase, how have you been?"

Chase smiled at the man's not-so-subtle reminder that it had been some weeks since he attended services. "Working weekends as well as nights, Father."

Father Clarence nodded. "I understand. You save souls your way and I do it mine."

"I do my best."

"Now what can I do for you?"

Chase motioned to Juliet. "This is Juliet Templeton. She and her sister were attacked last night. This morning they both discovered these hidden in their purses." Chase extended the plastic bags with the notes. "Juliet translated what was written on them, but I wanted to follow up with you and ask you to double-check her work."

Father Clarence studied the words through the plastic. "Come back to my office, and I'll translate them for you."

Chase momentarily wondered about allowing a victim to become part of the investigation. But Juliet was already a part of it.

They followed Father Clarence through the door to the sanctuary and down a wide hall to his large, cluttered office. Chase was amazed to note the room hadn't changed since he was a boy. The issues caused by his pale blue eyes and his sensitivity to light had been fodder for teasing by the other boys his age. He'd dealt with the issue in his usual straightforward manner and kicked their asses. His aggression had gotten him expelled twice from middle school before Father Clarence took him under his wing and taught him some coping techniques to redirect his anger. Techniques he still used on occasion.

The priest motioned to the chairs in front of his desk. "Have a seat. This will only take a few minutes." He sat down behind his desk and pulled a legal pad from the flotsam strewn across the surface.

Juliet's cell phone rang. She excused herself and stepped out into the hall to answer it.

When she returned, her expression remained guarded, but there was a tightness around her eyes that concerned him.

Father Clarence looked up after only a few moments. "Juliet you did a decent job translating this. It's definitely written as a magic spell. Are you Catholic?"

"No, Father."

The priest's brows went up like white caterpillars. "Do you claim any particular faith?"

"No. But I'm open to all possibilities."

"And you read Latin?"

"Some. I took Latin in high school. The rest I got from an online translator," she explained.

Chase studied her features. She was obviously as smart as her sister, yet she'd never attended college, and she clung to her bartending job like a barnacle. The patrol officers he's spoken to admitted to stopping her because of her past rather than anything she was into currently. She was beautiful, sassy, and usually dressed much more suggestively than she was right now. And cops would be cops.

Had she sold her car to keep from being harassed, or because she had money problems? He'd have to check.

Father Clarence remained silent for a moment. "I don't read this as a joke. I read it as a real threat."

"I did too," she said.

"You can't really believe someone could use witchcraft to harm someone," Chase said. "That it would really work."

"I don't rule out anything that can compromise a person's soul, Chase."

Surprised by the priest's attitude, he asked, "Do you know someone who practices this?"

"No. But I've seen things in other countries that would make the hair on the back of your neck stand on end."

Chase glanced at Juliet. "And you?"

"I was lifted off my feet and held in the air like a rag doll. It was either someone huge or something more."

He was slipping. He remembered her saying something

like that and had dismissed it.

"Does this look like a normal bruise to you?" She removed the scarf from around her throat.

The injury looked like a burn, just as it had the night before.

Father Clarence rose to his feet and moved around his desk. His concern as he studied Juliet's neck was palpable. "What did you see, Juliet?"

"Something gray. It was huge. And powerful. It screamed, sounding furious, enraged. It sounded like a baboon, only louder."

Chase butted in. "You didn't say anything about hearing a scream." What else had she left out?

"I was losing consciousness, I was being choked to death. Forgive me for not remembering everything at once."

Her smartass defensiveness pissed him off.

She returned to Father Clarence. "What would you suggest we do?"

"Are you and your sister close?"

"We have been. It's a kind of open relationship. We wander away from each other and always end up back together. We're sisters."

"I'd suggest you band together to fight it."

"How?"

"By loving each other and standing firm together."

"We're already there, padre. But you didn't feel the strength of this thing. It lifted me off my feet and held me in midair. Just throwing love at it will be like using a pea shooter to stop a locomotive."

Chase jerked in his seat.

"Giving up your fear will be even harder. Whoever has created this is depending on your fear to feed it."

Juliet's jaw went taut. Chase saw the same thing cross her face when he'd been interviewing her. She was shutting down, closing herself off.

Her voice, as hoarse as it was, held brittleness. "Is that all you have? No other weapons in your arsenal?"

Father Clarence laid a calming hand on her arm. "What do you think will work?"

"A water cannon filled with holy water. Shotgun shells filled with rock salt. Something more than holding hands with my sister and singing Kumbaya."

"You have to have faith in yourself and in God, Juliet."

She rose and detached herself. "It isn't God I have a problem with, Father. I don't expect anything from Him. I'll wait out in the sanctuary for you, Detective."

Chase studied Father Clarence as silence stretched like thick tar between them.

"She doesn't have much faith in humanity or otherwise, I think," Father Clarence said. "There is no clear-cut weapon to use to protect someone who is being attacked spiritually."

For the first time, Chase's own faith in the man wavered. "I have two men dead, Father. One was in police custody in a locked cell. His insides looked like they'd been sliced to ribbons. The other one's heart was pulverized in his chest without any external trauma. There's a real physical threat here. And you think something spiritual is what's happening?"

The priest's brow furrowed.

Chase got to his feet. "You look for the perpetrator in your domain, and I'll look for him in mine." He held out his hand for the evidence bags. Father Clarence twisted around and retrieved them with his translations and handed them to him.

Chase shook the priest's hand and left the office. When he returned to the sanctuary, he saw Juliet sitting at the back, slumped in one of the pews, her head down.

She opened her eyes as he approached her. "We'll be staying at Caleb's house. If you can drop me there I'd appreciate it."

"Did something happen at your sister's place?"

"Yeah. Caleb thought some...one was hanging around."

That pause between words set off alarms. What did he, Caleb Faulkner, think he'd seen, if not a person?

Jesus! What was he thinking? All this talk of spiritual attacks had given him the heebie-jeebies.

He'd looked into Faulkner's background, his military service. Though he and the twins had had some minor run-ins with the law as teenagers, none of them had been arrested, and now they were adults, they all seemed solid citizens.

What had they stumbled into?

Avoiding the kneeling bench, Chase walked over between the pews and sat down next to her. "What did you expect Father Clarence to do, Juliet?"

"Nothing." With her head down and the bruises on her neck a vivid red, she looked beaten. "I learned a long time ago not to depend on anyone but myself."

"And what about your sister?"

"I don't know why they're going after her, unless it's to hurt me. Miranda doesn't deserve this."

Chase quirked a brow. "And you do?"

"You said it yourself, Detective. I was there when a man

died. He's dead because of me."

Regret stung him. He should have taken things easier on her that first night. "It wasn't your fault. He's dead because someone hired two drug addicts to kill you and get you out of the way. Who would have wanted to do that, Juliet?"

She shook her head. "I don't know. None of my exes would have cared enough to have me killed. And Tanner never talked about any of his. We shared meals, did things together on our days off, and just talked." She swallowed and half raised a hand to her throat, then allowed it to flop back into her lap.

Had they been lovers? Of course they had. He jerked away from thoughts of her being like that with anyone.

She looked up. "He said his brother had a bad breakup last year. His girl put the move on Tanner."

"What was her name?"

"He never said. You'll have to ask Samuel." She stood. "It's getting late. We'd better go."

Chase rose to block her way. She smelled like green apples and some kind of citrus, and up close her skin looked so creamy smooth he fought the urge to touch her. "Why don't you tell me who you really think attacked you?"

She studied his face for a moment. "It wouldn't do any good. You wouldn't believe me." She hitched her purse over her shoulder and turned her head gingerly.

Father Clarence had been right. She didn't have much faith in anyone. "Try me."

She shook her head and flinched. "Sorry. I don't think so."

To hell with that. "If you withholding information that's germane to this investigation, Juliet, I'll throw your ass in jail."

Her brown gaze flashed. "That didn't keep Abbott safe,

did it?"

Chase ground his teeth in frustration. She was right. How had the man been killed inside the cell when no one had entered it? No one but a black shadow.

"Look around the jail. There will be a spell close to where he was staying."

Why was she harping on that? "Even if there is, what difference does it make? A magic spell isn't what killed him."

"What that spell invoked did."

"Your huge, angry, gray creature that screams?" Did she really expect him to believe that? There were some people dressed in masks and gray jumpsuits.

He saw the moment she closed down on him. It was like flipping a switch. She looked tired, and the set look about her mouth suggested pain. "It's getting late, Detective. I'd like to get to Caleb's house before dark."

"You're not going to work tonight?"

"No. I called in sick."

He nodded She still sounded hoarse, and she needed time for the trauma to her throat to heal. Without the scarf to hide it, the burn-bruise looked painful as hell. She flinched as she tilted her head back to look up at him. "My pain medication has worn off. I need some water to take some more."

Chase took a step back and motioned her out of the pew. He reached for his sunglasses. "Is there anything you can put on the bruise to help it heal?"

"No. It just has to go away on its own."

"We'll swing through a drive-through and get you a drink on the way to the house." He rested a hand against the small of her back as they walked the short distance to the front entrance.

She came to a sudden stop at the open door, forcing him to halt.

"What is it, Juliet?"

She scanned the parking lot. A tremor shook her. "Nothing." She took a tentative step out of the building.

More affected by her fear than he wanted to admit, Chase focused on getting to the car. He placed a protective hand against her waist, keeping her close.

Her body was spring taut. Her gaze zigzagged from one side of the lot to the other, reminding him of Abbott's panicked behavior while they'd struggled to extract him from his seedy motel room.

What had they seen that had frightened them so badly?

A piece of paper was wedged beneath one of the windshield wipers. A lazy breeze lifted it and it fluttered. Chase tightened his hold on Juliet. He scanned the parking lot. He reached for the paper and released her so he could unfold it.

The writer had used some of the same Latin phrases and the same strange reddish-brown ink. His name stood out at the top. When he reached the bottom a separate message had been scrawled.

Back away and you won't get hurt.

CHAPTER 16

J ULIET CAUGHT CHASE'S wrist.

He jerked his sunglasses off, and his pale blue eyes narrowed in anger and bored directly into hers. Her stomach went into freefall, and she found it difficult to draw a full breath. She shook free of the sudden buzz of attraction. Sitting beside her in the pew, she'd felt the heat of his body, smelled his clean, masculine sent. His body was muscular and fit, and the reddish-brown stubble dusting his jaw drew attention to the shape of his lips.

And now all that had been wiped away because of that scrap of paper he held clenched in his hand. "As long as that paper is in proximity to you, it will draw them to you."

"Them?"

She ignored the one word question. "It's like a freaking metaphysical GPS system for...whatever they are."

"It's evidence of a crime, Juliet. It's just a piece of paper with words written on it."

Her fingers tightened on his wrist. "You have to listen to me." With his healthy ego and the gun strapped to his hip, he'd walk right into something deadly if she couldn't convince him. "You're not dealing with human beings here. A human couldn't have burned and bruised my neck at the same time. Or bruised Miranda's arm in the way it was. A human couldn't have walked through walls and killed Abbott in his cell."

He searched her face. "You know how crazy that sounds?"

She'd known he wouldn't believe her. So why did it still hurt? She released him and took a step back. "I know it sounds crazy. But you didn't experience what I did. You weren't dangled like a toy."

"If they aren't human, what are they?"

He sounded more curious than anything.

She shook her head, then flinched at the movement. The pounding at the base of her skull amped up. "I don't know what they are, and I don't care. All I know is as long as you have those papers in your possession you have a target painted on your back. And as long as I'm with you, I do, too." She didn't want to see anyone else in danger because of her.

Chase's jaw suddenly went taut and his eyes narrowed again. Like ice-blue beams they, probed her features. "Stop trying to fuck with me and get in the car." He jerked the car door open.

Juliet debated about whether or not to get in. She was exposed and vulnerable standing in the parking lot. Walking down the street would leave her completely unprotected.

She slid in and reached for her seat belt. She followed his movements as he moved to the back of the car and got something out of the trunk. He slammed it closed, and when he slid in behind the steering wheel, the note was encased in plastic. He stuffed it into his jacket pocket and shoved the key into the ignition.

"We'll go by the station, and I'll log the notes into evidence."

"You can't. You have to destroy them."

He remained silent for a moment. His features hardened, his look stony. "When forensics works on these, are they going to lead back to you, Juliet?"

Her breath stalled. "What do you mean?"

"Did you put the note on my windshield?"

Shock held her motionless for a beat. He thought because she knew a little Latin and had been out of his sight for five minutes, she'd done it. "No, I didn't put it on your car."

"The note is a viable threat against a police officer, Juliet. You could get up to a year in prison."

"Screw you, Robinson. I didn't put that note on your car." She reached for her seat belt.

He grasped her arm.

"Take your hand off of me." Her voice had a raw quality that had nothing to do with her injury. She jerked against his grasp.

"That could be considered resisting arrest."

"Say the words. If you're arresting me, say the words. Otherwise you have no right to touch me."

His jaw worked with impatience. "Give me your purse," he demanded.

"Why?"

"I want to look in it."

Damn him. "You don't have a warrant."

"If you're innocent, that shouldn't matter. Let me look inside your purse."

She picked up the bag at her feet by the strap and swung it at him. Had he not caught it, it would have hit him in the face.

"Assaulting a police officer."

"Jesus Christ!" She gritted teeth in frustration and rage. She thought her head might explode. "You are such an asshole."

"I've been called worse. What the hell do you have in this thing? It has to weigh ten pounds. It could be considered a lethal weapon."

She fought the urge to roll her eyes for fear it would make her head hurt even worse. "My tip money's in the bottom." Pain and nausea rolled over her, and she propped her elbow on the armrest and rested her forehead in her hand. It hadn't been such a good idea to get so worked up while her head pounded like pickaxes were chipping away at her skull.

He went through every item in her bag, one at a time. When he opened her small planner, she mumbled, "That's private." He didn't turn the page, but studied the one that was open, then closed it. He returned everything to her bag and handed it back to her.

She looked up at him.

"You didn't write the note," he admitted.

"I know." There was an implied *duh* in there she was too sick to express some other way.

"You know more than you're saying about all this. If I find you're somehow involved in these two men's deaths—"

She'd had enough. Tears blurred her vision and she looked away. "That's rich," she scoffed. "I've been looking over my shoulder for weeks, waiting for them to show up at my door." Her chin shook and she put a hand against it to still the movement. "You're just like your buddy Brian Underwood. A bully with a badge looking for quick, easy answers instead of the truth. It's easier to harass me instead of getting out there and finding the real person responsible."

Chase's gaze narrowed again. "How do you know Underwood?"

"I went to high school with him. If you want to interrogate someone, start with him. But you better watch your back after you've done it."

He studied her, his gaze sharpening. He rifled through her bag and shoved her prescription pill bottle into her hand. "We'll hit Mickey D's for a Sprite to settle your stomach." He started the car, backed out and swung it around to pull out onto the street. "Try not to barf in my vehicle."

It took all her self-control not to punch him.

CALEB SHOVED THE key into the ignition and pulled out onto the street. Miranda had agreed to stay at his house. Without an argument. He was still processing that.

"I can swing by your house and pick up some clothes for you and Juliet." He smiled when her cheeks flushed. "What is it?"

"The idea of you going through my underwear drawer is a little embarrassing."

Caleb laughed. "I've seen you in less."

"When I was five."

"What about the bikini you wore to the city pool when you were sixteen?"

Her brows rose. "I didn't realize you noticed."

She had no idea. "I might have been the lifeguard, and I had to keep watch over everyone, but that didn't mean the image wasn't burned into my brain by teenage hormones. I can still remember how you looked."

Miranda smiled. "As I remember, you were rail thin, brown as a biscuit, and had a six-pack. And your hair was always sun-streaked, and shaggier than it is now."

"No one to read me the riot act and tell me to get a haircut." And no one to cook regular meals or buy food. His mother had spent her disability check on booze, not bread and milk. If his grandmother hadn't fed him, he'd have starved. A twinge of grief scraped at his emotions.

"You were all the girls could talk about."

"Even you?" he asked, enjoying this playful Miranda. She was more like she'd been in high school before her stepfather disappeared.

She smiled. "I wouldn't want to give you a big head."

"Please try." He wasn't thinking with the head on his shoulders right now.

She laughed. Her smile lingered, then fell away. "Things were complicated, even back then."

"Yeah, they were. But we made it through."

She laid a hand on his arm. "Thank you for changing the locks, and installing the car alarm."

He didn't want her gratitude. He wanted her. But if he said the words, she'd back off again. "I want you to be safe, Mandy."

"I know. And I love you for it. But Juliet and I will have to find our own way through this. Those spells were directed at us, Caleb. We have to figure out why, and who created them."

His heart still double-timed at the love you comment. "Maybe Robinson will come through with something."

"I hope so, but I don't think he will."

He glanced at her. "Why?"

"Because Detective Robinson is too cemented in what he believes is the *real* world. He won't be open to the possibility that there's more to it until it bites him on the ass."

Caleb grinned. Was this his Mandy talking like a badass? Well, a badass for her.

She touched his arm. "Can we stop somewhere along the way?"

He checked his watch. It wouldn't be dark until almost nine o'clock. "Where do you need to go?"

"To Aubrey McClellan's house."

He did a double take. "I didn't know you still hung with her."

"We haven't since high school. That was my fault, not hers. She's a regular at the library."

"Is she really what they say she is? I mean the real deal?"

Miranda remained silent for a moment then nodded. "Yes, she's the real deal. We used to be good friends, and we've remained cordial. I thought we could use a little guidance, and I'm hoping she'll be open to giving us some."

If it could protect her and Juliet from the creepy fuckers, he was open to anything. Flexible was his middle name. "Does she still live on Potter Street?" he asked.

"Yes."

A dry laugh broke from him.

Miranda's brows rose. "What is it?"

Caleb flipped on the blinker, turned onto King Avenue, and headed west. "Where else would a witch live but on Potter Street?"

CHAPTER 17

CHASE PULLED INTO the lot reserved for officer parking at the back of the police station and turned off the car. He studied Juliet's coloring. She'd turned sideways to rest her head against the back of the seat and closed her eyes. Her dark brown lashes fanned against her pale cheeks, thick and long, the tips a lighter color. She wasn't wearing any makeup, and she was still hands-down one of the most beautiful women he'd ever seen.

Her prickly personality had been curbed by the pain and nausea. "Is the pain easing off now?"

"Yes." She sounded drowsy.

Though he knew he shouldn't touch her, he smoothed back a wayward strand of hair hanging close to her eye with a fingertip. "You're supposed to take the meds every four hours. How long has it been since you took them?"

"They gave me something at the hospital at seven this morning. I was doing okay until now."

Her eyes opened a slit, and the tawny, brownish-amber of her irises peeked out at him, giving him a glimpse of what she looked like first thing in the morning. A fierce arrow of desired rushed straight to his groin and he hardened in a rush. Shit! He needed to get a handle on this attraction.

"That's seven hours, Juliet. The pain stresses your system

and keeps you from healing, so it's better to take the meds as prescribed until you're healed enough to do without them."

"I don't like being controlled, and taking meds is being under the control of something."

"Did you develop this attitude after your arrest in high school?"

She remained silent for a moment. "I was never arrested in high school. Who said I was?"

"It was just an impression I got."

"From the other cops here?"

He kept his features carefully blank.

"I'm not surprised." She turned her face away to look toward the station house. "I was a sophomore in high school. Miranda and I were invited to a party at Bobby Bush's house."

"Councilman Bush?"

"Yeah, his father was the councilman then. Bobby was a senior, and I had a crush on him. So, Miranda and I snuck out and went to the party. Neither one of us drank. Though there was plenty of beer there, we each got a bottled Coke from the cooler and held on to it for most of the night. And then Bobby came over to talk to me, and asked me to dance while Miranda danced with one of his friends.

"We came back to our drinks, and I drank a little of mine. A few minutes later I began to feel dizzy and nauseous. Bobby suggested I lie down upstairs."

"He'd roofied you?"

"Yeah. The only thing that kept him from carrying out the plan was Miranda. She saw him carrying me upstairs and broke away from the boy she was dancing with. Her dance partner told her we were just going to have a little fun."

"She got scared and snuck into the kitchen and dialed 911, then came upstairs. Bobby had taken my blouse off and was working on getting my jeans down when she came into the room. The cops showed up, and I was transported to the hospital. The lab work came back that I had Rohypnol in my system. They couldn't prove Bobby had given it to me, but I know it was an ambush. Because he hadn't gotten any further with the assault, and he was a minor, the police dropped everything."

She swallowed hard, and he could see it still hurt badly. "Councilman Bush went into politician protection mode, and I ended up with the reputation of being a druggie while his son danced away scot free." Her gaze grew distant. "I wonder how many other girls he drugged and succeeded in assaulting. After what happened to me, they'd have been too afraid to come forward."

She looked back at his face. "I'm not saying I haven't smoked a little weed or drunk a beer or two or three, but I've never popped pills, and I didn't deserve a rep at age fifteen for having a crush on a football player. It hounded me all the way through high school. The teachers treated me like I was some kind of troublemaker and were constantly on me. And the cops are still pulling me over for nothing. No one in Superstition lets anything go. Ever."

He didn't know whether to believe her or not. Dammit. "I have to go inside and sign the notes into evidence. I can't leave you in the car, it's against regulations."

She released the seat belt and grabbed her purse. "I'll call a cab."

He laid a hand on her arm. "I don't want you to do that.

I'd prefer to take you to Faulkner's house myself." It wasn't because he was beginning to feel protective of her. It wasn't. She was important to the case. His only witness to Tanner Newton's killing and to Samuel Newton's attack. She knew more than she'd said so far. And she was talking to him. Really talking to him. Eventually she'd get around to what had really happened on that street corner. He ran his fingers around the steering wheel, then gripped it. "I can't do anything about what happened to you back then, Juliet. The statute of limitations has run out."

"But if he's still doing it... You could check into that."

God there was such hope in her face. "Do you really believe he'd take that risk now?"

She shrugged again. "I work at a bar. I hear things."

God, he was slipping. A witness was trying to report a crime and he'd had his head somewhere else because of a physical attraction. "Will you write a statement about what happened last night for me?"

"I can do that."

"Did you write a statement for the police back then?"

"Yeah, I did."

"I'll pull it and read it."

"You won't find it."

"What makes you think that?"

"Councilman Bush had a lot of pull back then. If there was even a hint of suspicion cast on Bobby, he wouldn't be councilman today. The whole thing was tossed in the trash."

That she was probably right pissed him off. "We'll see."

He got out of the car and walked around to open her door. Juliet took some time to tie the scarf around her neck to cover the bruises.

Two patrol officers were leaving as they climbed the short flight of stairs to the door. One grabbed the handle and held it for them, and Juliet murmured a thank you. When he glanced over his shoulder he caught them both staring after her.

They took the elevator up to the third floor. He parked her in an interview room with a pen and paper to write her statement while he filled out paperwork to sign the notes into evidence. He made a copy of each one, sealed them each inside an evidence bag, initialed the tape, and handed it over to the officer manning the evidence room. He asked to see the evidence recovered from Gerald Abbott's cell. The officer buzzed him in and handed him a pair of rubber gloves. He brought him the box and placed it on a table reserved for that purpose.

Abbott's jail jumpsuit, shoes and underwear had remained with the coroner, as had the sheets and blankets from his bunk and the empty water bottle. Chase laid out the four pieces of evidence collected directly from the cell. A plastic baggy the sandwich came in recovered from the trash can, the crumpled potato chip bag ripped open to lay flat, the torn paper bag and a rectangular piece of paper. He picked up the plastic bag holding the piece of paper and recognized the writing and the reddish brown ink immediately. It had been lodged in the bottom of the bag the food came in.

What the fuck was going on around here?

He'd request a copy of the security video from the main desk downstairs and see who delivered the bag. It was supposed to be Scot's wife. He'd bet his next paycheck it wasn't.

Chase returned the evidence box and filled out a request

for all four of the notes to be analyzed. He took the stairs to the third floor to check on Juliet. If she was right about the ink being blood, they'd have a DNA sample from the killer. Or at least whomever they'd hired to write the damn spells. And that could possibly lead them to the killer and the associate.

He entered the detective squad room with its cluttered desks and ringing phones to see Brian Underwood standing outside the interview room.

"What's going on, Underwood?"

"You brought Juliet in for questioning again?"

"She's writing up a statement for me. Was there something you wanted to ask her?"

"No. I was just keeping an eye on her."

Chase leaned against the wall opposite the room. "She's not going to steal the table and chairs in there."

His bloated features folded into a scowl. "She's always been a troublemaker."

"Oh? So how long have you known her?"

"We went through the public school system together."

"You didn't say anything last night at the hospital."

"I let Garr question her when I realized who she was."

"I see." Chase studied Underwood's body language. There was tension in the way he stood, and his eyes kept shifting away. There was a history here Juliet hadn't shared, other than the bully with a badge comment.

He had seen a little of that in Underwood's demeanor himself.

"She's a witness to a murder and two assaults. She's not a suspect. You don't have to keep an eye on her."

"Two assaults?" His eyes widened.

"Samuel Newton's and her own."

"Oh." Underwood gave a brief nod and ambled off to his desk.

What the hell did he think he'd meant? He needed to pump Juliet for info about the connection between her and Underwood.

Was there anyone in high school she hadn't pissed off?

Sitting in Aubrey's modest one-story home, Miranda wondered at how things both changed and stayed the same. A new couch. A beautiful distressed sideboard in the dining room. A new large, round rug in the center of the living room floor. But the atmosphere of peace still flowed through the house like the refreshing coolness of the air conditioning. She and Juliet had spent hours here as teenagers. The small house had been a haven from things neither she nor Juliet wanted to face at home.

Aubrey's mother, a practicing Wiccan, had introduced them to meditation, taught them to call the quarters, and shown them how their inner strength could protect them. She had been a gentle, loving woman filled with spirit and joy, and had done more to boost her and Juliet's sense of self-worth than their mother ever had.

If they had discovered how to direct their true power earlier, would they have been able to stop Clay? As it was, they'd interfered with his plans when they learned to read the signs. They'd both had to keep their guard up, because he was wily and manipulative. They'd tried to bind him from harming Juliet and succeeded for a while. Until that last day, when he found his picture wrapped in black binding cord with the spell. She flinched away from that memory.

It seemed wrong to bring trouble to Aubrey's door without first warning her. But they were already here.

"How's your dad? Is he doing well?" Miranda asked.

"He's good. He and Sarah are doing great. He's learning to be happy again. For a time I worried that he wouldn't, but she's so determinedly positive he doesn't have a choice." She laughed as she said it.

"I'm glad he's found someone."

Miranda's grief at Sophie McClellan's death pierced her, like the sudden slice of a blade. Automatically she extended a hand, and Aubrey took it. The sudden rush of shared power between them eased the feeling.

Caleb shifted in his chair, a frown tugging at his brows.

"You've discovered what I sensed at the library," Aubrey said as their hands parted.

"Yes. It's not something I've ever seen before, or ever thought possible." She removed the copies of the notes and extended them to Aubrey.

Miranda watched her face as she studied them. "Copies wouldn't have the same power as the originals would they?" The last thing she wanted to do was put Aubrey in danger by bringing something evil and dangerous into her home. She didn't deserve to have to combat this.

Aubrey shook her head. Bright spots of color flared in her cheeks. Her green eyes looked livid. "No. But whoever wrote this has perverted the Craft by turning it into an intent to harm."

"Do you have a network of friends you could ask?" Caleb

asked. "Maybe someone would recognize the wording or even the handwriting."

"The handwriting is a traditional calligraphy font anyone can learn to do. But the structure of the spell might stand out."

"Juliet seemed to think the spells were written in blood," Miranda said.

Aubrey's face blanked and she went pale. "We have to figure out who did this, Miranda. There's a real danger here."

The urgency in her friend's tone intensified her own. With every minute that passed dusk crept closer. How dark would it have to be before the creatures appeared? And would they be able to find them without the spell scrolls?

"Believe me, I know. I have the injury to prove it." She brushed a hand down her arm. The bruise ached every time she moved it. She shifted restlessly. "The thing that came after me wasn't human, Aubrey. It was gray, had no eyes, yet it was able to sense where I was. It had a mouth, long arms, long hands. It wasn't of this world. It looked like the demons in a Hieronymus Bosch painting."

Caleb leaned forward in his chair. "Could someone take the concept of an imaginary creature and turn it into something real?"

"If they're walking the earth, they are real. And pose a real threat. The spell has the scent of dark magic, and with that, anything is possible. White magic uses blood sometimes as well, but the intent is always without malice."

"If I hadn't seen these things… I wouldn't believe…" He shook his head. "And why can I see them when other people are oblivious to them?"

"I think it's because you have such a strong tie to Miranda.

You always have."

When Caleb's gaze fastened on her, Miranda's throat thickened with emotion, and her eyes stung. She had to do something to protect him. If anything happened to him, she'd never forgive herself.

"How can we fight them?" Caleb asked.

"I'd rather wait for Juliet to arrive so we can talk this through together. She'll play an important part." Her attention swung to Miranda. "I know it's been years since you've practiced, but you and Juliet will have to bind together to fight them. You were always stronger than you thought, Miranda. And Juliet had the potential to be a master."

Miranda read the question in Aubrey's eyes and looked away. She hadn't harmed anyone with her magic, but she'd wanted to, and the strength of that intent had frightened her. But Aubrey deserved some explanation. "I had to take a step back, Aubrey. My control had become shaky."

"You used to practice witchcraft?" Caleb asked, eyes wide and voice louder than usual.

"Yes, from middle school through high school."

"You never told me." There was an accusation in the way he said the words.

"No one else knew either, Caleb. Only Aubrey's mother, the three of us and Sherry Connor. We had to keep it quiet. Can you imagine what would have happened if Brian Underwood or the other creeps on the football team found out? Or even worse, the school staff? Things were hard enough without having our beliefs brought into question."

Aubrey brushed her heavy red hair from her shoulder. "Any religion that travels outside the norm is looked upon as a threat. Had Miranda continued to practice the Craft, the college would never have hired her as head librarian. This is the Bible belt, and people aren't encouraged to think in terms of anything but God, country, and Kentucky basketball." She covered Miranda's hand with her own. "I understood when she and Juliet stopped."

That hadn't been the reason she and Juliet had given it up. But she couldn't divulge her sister's secrets, or her own. They had continued to be friends with Aubrey, but they had stopped calling the quarters or casting the circle. Their relationship had never been the same.

One of the last times she visited before going to college, Aubrey had told her they'd turned their back on who they were. And in a sense they had. But it hadn't been because of prejudice. It had been because of Clay Maddox.

Miranda's gaze wandered to Caleb while Aubrey studied the spells once again. His frown spoke of disappointment instead of anger. She had hidden a part of herself from him, but only out of necessity. But to learn this now, on top of everything else—especially her own skittishness—she could only guess how he was feeling.

She looked back at Aubrey, who nodded. "I'll make some coffee while we wait for Juliet. "I think some sandwiches would be good, too."

Miranda murmured a thank you. She had allowed her fear to keep her from reaching for what she wanted, but no more. Whatever else happened, she wanted Caleb to know who she was and how she truly felt.

Juliet was right. She had to either let him in or let him go.

Ending things and encouraging him to move on would be

the kindest thing to do.

The thought of never seeing him again, hearing his voice, looking into his eyes and finding that special expression he reserved for her... She couldn't do it.

She rose from her seat on the couch and paused beside his chair until he looked up. She moved closer and sat down on his thigh. Automatically he slipped an arm around her waist, and she longed to curl up against him and nestle her face under his chin. She ached for him to hold her.

"I love you, Caleb. I've always loved you. There's never been anyone else. But there are things about my life I've had to hide. I know it isn't fair to expect you to accept that."

Caleb thrust his fingers beneath her hair and brought her mouth to his, the pressure of his kiss firm and demanding. His tongue slipped between her lips to tangle with hers with probing heat, and her body flooded with heat. Her arm hurt like hell, but she ignored it as she melted against him.

He cupped her hip, holding her tight. The heated pressure of his erection pushing against her thigh triggered a needful ache between her legs. She reveled in it, in him, and looped a hand around the back of his neck. His hair curled around her fingers as if to return her tentative caress. He smelled of outdoors, laundry soap and him.

He was home. He was everything.

CHAPTER 18

JULIET STOOD AT the open station house door and scanned the street. A humid haze hung over the parking lot. The smell of hot sidewalks blended with the tang of fresh cut grass, and the light had turned soft despite the heat. It was on the cusp of dusk, and they needed to get a move on.

Two men sauntered down the sidewalk across the street. Something about the way one moved struck a chord of familiarity. His shoulders were narrow, his build lanky, his hair a medium brown. He turned the corner, and she caught a glimpse of his profile as a blue Chevy stopped and picked him up. It would come to her later where she'd seen him before.

Though the light had dulled, Chase slipped on his sunglasses and urged her forward. While they descended the stairs to the sidewalk, her eyes darted from one car to the other, searching for movement, for shadows, for danger. The touch of his hand against the small of her back should have been comforting, but it wasn't. He couldn't fight these things with a gun.

The setting sun struck a piece of glass beneath one of the vehicles and she jerked her head in that direction. A large spider the size of a tarantula scurried across their path.

"Jesus!" Chase exclaimed. "Did you see the size of that thing?"

Her mouth dry with fear, she quickened her steps. "Yeah, I saw it."

"It had to be someone's lost pet. Kentucky doesn't have indigenous spiders that big."

"No we don't."

She scanned the ground as they approached the car, dreading that it might crawl up her leg. She hated spiders, had always hated them. Their quick, sneaky movements. The way their web imprisoned their prey. Everything about them made her skin crawl. She nearly leapt into the car and held her breath, nearly gasping for air before he finally got behind the wheel.

She trembled with relief when he started the car. "Chase?"

He whipped off his sunglasses and looked up, his pale blue eyes intent.

If something happened to him, it would be her fault. She had tried to convince him of the danger. If only he'd been willing to destroy the notes. She should have asked him to at least allow her to put a binding spell on them. But then he'd know what she was, who she was.

"I need you to drop me on Potter Street instead of Caleb's. Miranda is waiting for me there."

He put the car in reverse and backed it out of the parking slot. "What's the number?"

"Three-three-three."

"Whose residence?" he asked.

"Aubrey McClellan's."

He slammed on the brakes, throwing her forward against her seatbelt. He gave her a long, hard look. "You said you didn't know anyone who practiced witchcraft."

"I said I didn't know any who would want to hurt me. Aubrey is Wiccan. She lives by the code of 'harm none.' She believes to use your magic to hurt someone would bring bad karma back to you times three."

His jaw tensed, and his hands looked like they were gripping the steering wheel hard enough to break it. "I don't give a shit what she believes. You *lied* to me. You said you didn't know anyone who practiced witchcraft. You're obstructing my investigation by withholding information."

"She's not involved in this, Chase. I've known her my whole life, and she's the kindest soul alive. If you're looking for a suspect, you're going to have to look somewhere else."

He put the car into gear and pulled out. "Ninety percent of the time it's someone close to a victim who's responsible for the crime against them."

"It wasn't her. She'd have no reason to harm me. There's never been any kind of bad blood between us. She wouldn't use magic to harm me even if there was. Whatever you send out, you get back threefold."

"Do you believe that too?"

"I do. Along with several million other people. But she lives it."

Though Juliet no longer practiced the Craft, she still lived by that as well. It was going to take magic to end this, but she couldn't do it in front of Chase. He'd lock her up for being a pyromaniac or something. And if there were other witnesses around—

He was furious. She could read it in his body language and the sharp tilt of his jaw. "I'm going in to interview her when we get there."

"Fine. But she's not a criminal, and if you go in treating her like one, you'll end up feeling like a fool and looking like one, too." At the sudden appearance of fine, spindly legs gripping the hood of the car, Juliet gasped. Adrenaline stormed through her system. "Chase?"

"That damn spider's hitched a ride."

"It isn't a spider. Hit your brakes and try to throw it off."

He argued. "It's just a—"

The creature leapt and hit the windshield with the force of a rock.

Chase took her suggestion too late, throwing her against her seat belt. The tires squealed and the front of the car swerved toward the curb and settled against it.

A web of lines burrowed through the glass, shooting out from the point of impact. "Dammit!" Chase swore, released his seat belt and reached for the door.

Juliet gripped his arm. His muscles bunched beneath his lightweight jacket. She couldn't protect him if he kept either ignoring the dangers or charging into situations before they were certain of what was happening. Though every nerve in her body screamed for her to get out of the car, she hesitated. The spider lay on the hood unmoving, but it might jump on one of them as soon as they got out. "Wait." When she was certain he was going to cooperate, she reached for her seatbelt and her bag at the same time.

Suddenly the larger body of the creature started breaking apart into smaller spiders. No, it had been carrying them. They charged the crack in the windshield. A gnawing sound filled the car, like rats eating through a wall. At the first pinprick of air coming into the car from the opening she yelled, "Get out now." She threw open the door and scrambled free of the car.

"Son of a bitch," Chase yelled and bailed out the other side. Tiny spiders swarmed the inside of the vehicle, their bodies reflecting light like cut glass. They turned in mass toward her, scrambling over the console and onto her seat. If she hit them with her magic, the whole car would go up. She slammed the door and heard the satisfying crunch as she caught some in the seal.

The large spider still lay, legs sprawled on the hood, unmoving. Was it dead or stunned? She wasn't sticking around to find out. "We've got to get out of here, Chase." Juliet turned and ran.

✧   ✧   ✧

CALEB CURVED AN arm around Miranda, holding her against his side. Bless Aubrey for giving them some privacy, but he could have used at least a week to make up for the number of times he'd wanted to kiss Miranda and hadn't. Had they been truly alone he might have pushed for more. But though his cock still pushed against his zipper, aching with need, it wasn't the time or the place. He'd just have to wait until all this crazy shit was over.

Whew. When Miranda lowered the walls, she didn't just roll them down, she blasted them to smithereens. She pressed against his side, her head against his shoulder, her hand resting over his hammering heart. He turned his head to press his lips to her forehead, because he could. She wasn't backpedaling away from him anymore.

He couldn't say there hadn't been other women in the years they'd been separated. But he'd never made a connection as deep as what he felt for the woman cuddled against his side. He'd felt passion for the others, sometimes affection, but never love. Never like this. She was it for him. She had been since they'd been in almost constant contact the last eight months he'd been in the Marines.

His chest and throat filled with emotion, and he murmured the words against her temple, "I love you, Miranda."

"It's about time you two got it together," Aubrey said as she wheeled a wooden cart into the room from the kitchen. She placed a plate with sandwiches in the center of the coffee table. Napkins and paper plates followed. "The whole town of Superstition has been making bets waiting for it."

"You're teasing, right?" Miranda's cheeks were pink.

Aubrey raised a brow. "I have it on good faith that the quilting circle at the Christian church has had a pot going since Christmas. And the whole crew at The Dish has one, too, that includes quite a few of the customers." She placed coasters on the coffee table and set tall glasses filled with ice tea in front of them.

Caleb laughed. He knew he had a stupid grin a mile wide when Miranda leaned back to look up at him, but he couldn't control it. Winning the lottery couldn't feel this good.

Even with all the weird stuff they were going through, they were finally together as a couple.

But Miranda wasn't smiling as she looked up at him. "There's something else I need to tell you."

He could see in her face that this wasn't going be as positive a confession. Shit.

"I guess it's better if I show you. You're going to find out when Juliet gets here anyway." She bowed her head and murmured. "Thank you Goddess, for allowing me to borrow from your bounty."

She bent her elbow and extended her hand, palm up and parallel to the ground. "*Exorior*," she whispered, almost gently. A sphere about the size of a softball appeared in her hand, its surface glowing with a rainbow-hued sheen.

Caleb's mouth dropped open and his eyes widened. Was this some kind of joke? He stared at the clear globe, fascinated by its structure. Its surface looked as thin and fragile as a soap bubble.

"*Impluo*." She spoke the word with authority.

Mist gathered inside, fogging up the entire shape like the inside of a shower. It slowly rose to the top, and the bottom half of the sphere cleared. The moisture condensed and began to take on indistinct forms that tumbled together into miniature clouds. A static flutter of light lit the bottom of them. A streak of lightning flashed down toward her palm.

Caleb stifled a gasp. In an instinctive urge to shield her, he raised a hand to hers. Miranda's remained steady, but he jerked his own back, his fingertips stinging from a shock. Beneath her skin raced a power stronger than static electricity, much stronger.

Her features had taken on the look of deep concentration, her eyes lightened from within to a tawny gold. A strange breeze ruffled her hair and his, and the wind was warm, almost balmy. He inhaled it deeply, and tasted moisture and ozone in the air around them.

Dear God, no wonder she had held him at arm's length. His throat was dry with fear. Yes, he was afraid, not of her, but of this power that seemed to have taken hold of her. She turned her head and looked directly at him. Her cheeks were flushed, her eyes aglow with not just power, but joy. The reserved, controlled woman had vanished, and Miranda had never looked more beautiful or more alive.

This was who she was, what she was.

His heart beat inside his ears so hard the sound of thunder was strangely muffled. The miniature clouds seemed to roll and shift, crashing together. It started to rain inside the bubble, the water gathering at the bottom.

"*Desino,*" The rain stopped and the water ran in streaks down the inside of the globe.

He heard rain dripping, and his gaze shifted to the window. The evening sun was going down and the light had dimmed, but there was no rain falling.

She tossed the globe up into the air, "*Ut Liberum.*"

The bubble popped, but no water hit the carpet beneath.

She had set the clouds and water free, and they had returned to wherever they had come from.

For long silent moments they continued to look into each other's eyes.

Caleb swallowed, his throat working against the dryness. Shock didn't even begin to describe what he was feeling. It was a lot to take in, this part of her he'd never known existed. "So you're the real deal too?"

"Yes." She swallowed. "My element is water, but we all have the power to harness a small portion of the others." She raised a hand to his cheek. "Can you still love me, Caleb?"

CHAPTER 19

C HASE HIT THE key fob to lock the car. If someone opened the door, would they be attacked? He leaped over the shallow curb, ran across the street, and jumped from asphalt to the other sidewalk. The skin-crawling image of the spiders scrambling inside the car hounded him. Juliet was running full out, her arms pumping unevenly, her heavy purse gripped in her hand, throwing her balance off. Who would have known she could make tracks like that? She turned the corner and out of sight.

Putting on a burst of speed, he whipped around the curve of the sidewalk after her. A boy of about twelve on a bike popped up from the shrubbery. He dodged to one side, avoiding a collision, but hitting the grassy strip between the curb and the sidewalk. He lost his footing and went down on one knee. Cursing the uselessness of leather-soled dress shoes, he caught himself with one hand, shoved himself back up, and got his feet going again.

Juliet had a half a block lead. Damn, she was either freaked out and running on adrenaline, or all those hours behind the bar had built some serious leg muscles.

Her ponytail swung back and forth with every stride. He concentrated on that as he poured on more speed and closed the gap to a quarter block. She zipped across the next side street. He followed, feet pounding, his breath rasping. He was a jogger, not a sprinter, and was really feeling it as he slowly inched up behind her.

From five feet behind her, he yelled, "Juliet—stop." As frightened as she'd been of the spiders, he didn't want to scare her any more. He wasn't pursuing a perpetrator, just a distraught woman. If he could match his pace to hers... He eked out a few more feet. "Juliet—please, just stop" He stretched to get a hand around her arm and put some drag behind it to slow her.

"We're clear of the car. Ease back."

She showed no resistance as she slowed, then stopped. She gasped for air and sweat beaded her forehead and upper lip. Her hair was wet, clinging to her face. His was soaked, too. Running in this heat and humidity was insane.

"You—need to—move your ass, Chase," she complained between gasps.

"We're clear. The spiders are two streets behind us." He wiped at his face with a coat sleeve and silently cursed about having to wear the damn jacket.

She dropped her purse on the sidewalk, bent at the waist, and gripped her knees, her chest heaving. "We need—to get off—the street." She pointed west. "Aubrey's house is two blocks down."

"I agree. But we're both going to drop from the heat if we don't slow down."

She finally straightened though her breathing remained ragged. "You're still not getting it, Chase. There's something happening here, and it doesn't involve your normal bad guy with a gun, or hyped-up junkie. Whoever they are tried that first, and when it didn't work they moved on to something harder to fight."

He had been resistant to the idea before, but he'd never seen anything like the huge dead spider lying on the hood of his car. He knew some spiders carried their young on their backs, but the swarm that had rushed into the car was unbelievable. And they had *eaten through the windshield*. What kind of spider did that? And what kind was covered in a glassy shell?

What the hell was going on here?

Exactly what she'd been trying to tell him.

And how the hell did she know about this stuff? Obviously there was more to Juliet Templeton than she had allowed him to see so far. Maybe much more.

"All right." He raised a hand in surrender. "I believe you."

Her face brightened, and she bent over again to take a few more deep breaths. "I think I just got lightheaded with disbelief."

She was afraid, he could read it in how she obeyed her flight instinct, but she wasn't cowed.

"Stop being a wise ass. Let's just walk it off and get where we're going. I need to contact headquarters and get someone to go get the car and process that damn spider." They'd left the scene of an accident, and he'd left his vehicle only partially parked against the curb.

And how the hell was he supposed to report this? He flipped his thumb over the face of his phone, and, finding the number he needed, phoned in the attack. He settled on an unknown assailant had thrown something against his windshield and busted it while he was transporting the witness home. He told the dispatcher where his car was parked, and that he was taking the witness to a safe location.

He hoped to hell it was.

"Just what was it you really saw that night?" he asked.

Juliet swallowed. "A demon."

His Catholic upbringing had introduced him to the concepts of purgatory, heaven, hell, and the possibility of other spiritual beings capable of possessing and tormenting you here on earth and beyond. All organized religion was based on the use of guilt and fear to keep you in line and to make sure you followed their construct of God and His rules without question. But to hear Juliet so calmly acknowledging the physical presence of an entity capable of true evil gave him a jolt.

"I haven't any other name for it. It was tall, hefty, grayish-black, with long arms and huge hands, and while it had no eyes, it could sense where I was, and it screamed in rage when it couldn't reach me."

He pounced on that information. "Why couldn't it reach you?"

"It's like a shadow. It has to have the light to appear."

"But it can't walk in sunlight."

"But the spiders can. Caleb saw one on Miranda's porch this afternoon, watching him change her locks."

He lapsed into silence for a moment, thinking. "And the spell has to be present to guide them to you? But we got rid of the notes at the station."

"Someone may have planted one in the car while we were inside and on Juliet's porch. I don't know if they can find us without the written note or not. When it gets dark and the streetlights come on, I guess we'll find out."

Shit!

The long street was lined with established oaks and maples, the neighborhood being one of the older ones just west of the center of town. The houses on either side were compact and well maintained, the yards as well. Chase scanned the street ahead, recognizing too many places where someone, or something, could lie in wait. Would his gun have any affect?

Juliet griped her purse by the strap like it was a weapon. She'd matched her strides to his, two to one, and realizing she was becoming winded again, he slowed, though the compulsion to rush and get inside burned strong.

They turned onto Potter Street. "Which house is it?" Chase asked. He stepped off the sidewalk to allow room for a young mother pushing a baby stroller. She smiled at them as she passed. He sought some way of telling her to get off the street but could think of nothing.

"The fourth one down on the right."

The light was getting hazy, and the streetlights would switch on at any moment. "Run," Chase urged.

She didn't need any encouragement. They sprinted the last hundred feet across neighbors' yards and hit the front porch just as the first light began to glow.

Juliet clung to the side of the house, as far from any ambient light as she could get. It was instinctive for him to position himself in front of her, blocking the light.

She grabbed his shirt and jerked him toward her. He braced an arm against the siding. His heartbeat kicked up as he tried to ignore the sensation of her breasts, soft and generous, pushing against him. Her head reached just beneath his chin. Even sticky with sweat, she smelled good. The incident with the spiders seemed days away instead of minutes. Would she smell like that after…? No, he wasn't going there.

"You need to get as close in against the side of the house as you can," she instructed. "Stay in the shadows. And hit the doorbell—"

He had a vision of her beneath him, demanding, issuing instructions while he thrust inside her. Blood rushed south to his groin, and he was rock-hard in an instant. Shit! He rolled along the outside wall, away from her, flattened himself against house, and pushed the doorbell.

The last light died and the streetlights brightened. Under each one, all the way down and on both sides of the street, stood a gray-black figure. They waited like sentinels, equal distances apart. Their long arms and hands hung, disproportionate and inhuman, at their sides.

A surge of fear rocked him, killing his erection, raising the hairs on the back of his neck and stealing his breath. Blood heated his face and his heartbeat soared. A chorus of roars and screams, rage-filled and hungry, rose and built to a crescendo. Juliet gripped his hand like a vise.

The door next to them swung open and a woman with red hair stood behind it and to one side. Chase didn't wait for her invitation, but barreled inside, pulling Juliet with him. Once inside, Juliet clung to him, trembling, and he held her. He was shaking more than a little himself.

He had believed what she said in concept after the spider attack. But now he believed in truth.

CHAPTER 20

MIRANDA CAME INTO the living room dressed in the long, deep blue-green shift with elbow-length sleeves Aubrey had loaned her after her bath.

While she waited for Juliet to finish her cleansing, she studied the pentagram painted on the floor. It was professionally rendered, and she wondered who Aubrey had hired to do it. No one local, she'd bet. The round rug that had covered it was rolled up and stashed along the wall out of the way. Caleb and Chase stood to one side in their borrowed sweats and T-shirts, their uneasiness clear in their stiff, almost jerky body language.

The detective's face showed equal parts of curiosity and wariness. But she couldn't read Caleb's.

It had been a shock for him. He had said he still loved her, but his understanding of who she was had been rocked. She had to give him some time to get used to the idea that his girlfriend was a witch. Or was she still his girlfriend?

How would she feel if he suddenly grew horns and a forked tail? Would she still love him?

Always.

Her love for him was a part of her. It had grown and evolved while they spent time together. What had started out as a childhood connection had turned to passion and something deeper after he returned from his two-tour stint in the Marines. After being apart for eight years, they had rediscovered each other through letters and phone calls, emails and Skype sessions. The connection had given her a safe haven, a link that transcended her normal reserve. She'd never dreamed he would come home to stay. But he had. Would they lose each other because of her inborn powers?

Maybe if she explained a small part of what was happening now, he'd come to understand.

She stood outside the circle "Aubrey and I consecrated each item inside the circle while you were showering. We do it in much the same way as your priest consecrates the things on the church altar, Detective. Each item has both a symbolic purpose and a practical one, and what's included depends on the focus of the ceremony."

"The focus tonight will be to ask for and forge some kind of protection against the creatures out in the street, and the strength to fight them," Aubrey said as she and Juliet entered into the room, both dressed much like Miranda.

Miranda breathed past the nervous fear triggered by the reminder. She recognized the same fear in everyone else in the room.

"Do you really think you can do that?" Chase asked.

"We're going to do our best," Aubrey replied.

Miranda used the consecrated broom to sweep the area; moving in a clockwise direction, she swept from the center of the circle to the edge. She glanced at the two men watching. "The broom was at one time a magical staff, a staff of power, used as a symbol of both protection and fertility. One end would be a phallic symbol, and a woman would ride it into the fields in a rite to increase their fertility and her own. The phallic symbol was later hidden with straw, and thus created the broom. It has the strength to brush away anything unneeded, to cleanse, and acts as an instrument of power to banish anything that doesn't belong in the circle."

Aubrey paused by the men. "I'll invite you into the circle as soon as it's purified." She took up a small clay bowl of water and followed in Juliet's path as she sprinkled it from her fingertips. "The water contains salt, elements of both water and earth, blended to purify."

Juliet took up the sage stick, lit it with a quick hand gesture, then blew it out. She strolled about the circle, waving the smoking sage stick to cleanse the space. "The sage releases any metaphysical elements in the circle and sends them on their way. We'll also be lighting incense to carry our prayers and sacrifices to the Gods."

Aubrey set the bowl on the altar in the center of the circle, reached for the small bell, rang it three times, and placed it back where it had been. She lit an incense stick, placed it in a small clay holder, then raised her arms. "Bless us, God and Goddess. We humbly invite you into our circle."

Juliet lit the red taper standing in a clay holder on the altar, while Miranda did the green. They each raised their tapers and lit a white one. "The red candle represents the God and the green the Goddess. When we light the white candle it symbolizes their unity," Miranda explained.

Aubrey motioned to the two men. "I'd like you to enter the circle before we close it. Take a position here, on the north side of the altar. Both of you seem very tied to the earth, so you'll feel most comfortable here." She handed Caleb a slip of paper. "You'll know when to read the words I've written for you on the paper. We appreciate your willingness to take part and stand in as our fourth."

Caleb's gaze rose to Miranda's, and she offered him an encouraging smile. She hoped his agreement to take part in their ritual would lead to a deeper understanding.

Aubrey moved to the altar and took the ritual dagger, an athame, in hand. "The circle must be cast from beginning to end. We'll be moving from the east where the sun rises, to west where it sets." She nodded to Caleb and Chase, and they fell in behind her and slowly walked the outer perimeter of the circle.

She pointed the athame at the salt-laced circle and, at each quarter, paused to draw a pentagram in the air. "With love and trust we build our circle with no beginning and no end. We construct its walls against the evil from which we seek to defend. We ask the gods for protection from harm for all those contained within this sacred space." Each of them stopped within their quarter. "And inside us may strength grow so we may be so armed. By the power of all and thee, so mote it be."

Miranda relished the surge of energy working its way up from the bottoms of her feet to the top of her head. She visualized bringing the circle up around them like an egg, protective, strong, enclosing them from all directions, as well as above and below.

An unexpected slide of warm, masculine power feathered through her, coming from where Caleb and Chase stood in the northern quarter. Was the feminine power filtering through the men to bridge the gap, or did one carry some latent ability he was unaware of? She pushed her concentration back into the task at hand, and drew upon the electricity spindling inside her to shore up the sphere. The sensation of pressure built inside the space, almost as if a door had closed, and she swallowed to clear her ears. For the first time since she'd sensed the presence upstairs in the library, she felt safe.

Everyone seemed to take a relieved breath in unison.

They gathered into a smaller circle, only few inches apart from each other, and sat cross-legged.

"To ensure there's no disruption of energy, and no interference from what lies outside the house, we thought it might be smart to plan everything inside this circle," Aubrey explained. "It will act as a barrier to anything metaphysical or otherwise that tries to eavesdrop on what we're doing."

Miranda interjected, "Chase, Caleb, is there anything you'd like to ask us about before we start to plan?"

"How long have you all known you had this power?" Chase asked.

That he asked, and knew what to ask, showed how far he'd come in a very short time.

"We were all three born with it," Juliet replied. "Our mother turned away from it because it frightened her. But our grandmother helped us all she could while she was alive. And we kept it secret until we met Aubrey and her mother.

Aubrey flipped back her long red hair. "We moved here from Wisconsin when I was twelve. As soon as I met Juliet and Miranda, we all knew we had a connection."

"Why keep it a secret?" Caleb asked, his gaze focused on Miranda.

"People don't trust things they don't understand, Caleb. And there are consequences for using magic. One summer it was hot enough to fry eggs on the sidewalk, like it's been the last few weeks. I was about seven then. And I decided we needed a way to cool down. "I willed the fire hydrant in front of our house to open. The pressure sent the cap twenty feet into the air, and when it came down it went through the windshield of my mother's car. She'd just pulled into the driveway, and it missed her by inches. She could have been killed."

"You have better control now," Juliet smirked.

"Yes, but if anyone besides our mother had figured out that I was responsible for it, we'd never have been permitted to play with any of the neighborhood children again."

"The quote 'with great power comes great responsibility' is true," Juliet mused. "If I had fried the spiders in your car today, Chase, the whole car might have gone up with them. We've all learned to be frugal about using our gifts, and careful when and how we use them. And there's a boomerang effect. Whatever you put out there comes back to you times three."

Chase's expression shifted to one of speculation. "Should your abilities be recognized, you could all be locked away as a threat."

Miranda's tension spiked. Was that a warning? "Or be forced to *become* a weapon," she added, shooting Chase a less-than-friendly look. "Either way, our lives would still be over."

His brows rose. "Are you strong enough to do that?"

She exchanged a glance with Juliet and Aubrey. "We'd all better hope so."

"We need to get to it," Juliet snapped, scowling at Chase, her face tight. "The night is long, and we need to have our defenses shored up in case those things outside decide to try to get in."

✧   ✧   ✧

WATCHING THE THREE women work together, Caleb realized they'd developed a sisterhood much like the brotherhood he'd experienced in the Marines. They had a common goal, not to destroy but to protect. Too many people lived on the residential street, and they'd all expressed their worries on behalf of the neighbors and the neighborhood.

While the women worked on a complex spell using crystals, Caleb shifted his attention to Chase, sitting next to him. He'd noticed Miranda and Juliet's response to his comment about being locked up. "I wouldn't try and fuck over these ladies if I were you."

Chase's pale eyes narrowed. "I was just stating what might happen if the rest of the world realizes witchcraft is real."

"That isn't how it came across. You might want to smooth it over with them before you find yourself on the wrong end of their broom."

Chase chuckled.

Caleb tilted his head toward the three. "Does it look like they're playing around?"

The large crystal Juliet held began to glow amber.

"No, it doesn't," Chase said. "I have four dead men tied to the same case, so I'm taking this pretty seriously myself." His frown deepened. "I can't do a damn thing to protect them. And I'm not about to interfere with their ability to protect themselves."

Caleb nodded. "Eight years in the Marines, and with all the skills I acquired, I can't do a damn thing either."

"I've read your file."

Caleb raised a brow.

"Why an auto mechanic? You could have gone into police work. Started your own security firm. You have a two-year college degree, and you're an expert marksman. You were coming up the ranks. I'm surprised you didn't stay in until retirement."

Caleb loosened the fists that had automatically clenched. "I'd had enough of taking orders, and giving them." *And when I do have to give them now, nobody dies. And nobody is shooting at me.* He rolled his head to relieve the knots in his neck. "When I'm under the hood of a car, with my earbuds in, I'm as far from that as I can get. I have two other guys working for me, providing for their families with what I pay them. Word's getting out about our work, and I'm making a success of it. I'm building something here. Providing a service to my community." *And I don't have to do any of it with a gun in my hand.*

He'd told Miranda all this and more. And she hadn't said a damn thing about any of her deepest secrets. The disappointment and pain pinged again. Although the detective's quick assessment had helped him understand why she held back for so long.

He'd fought against people who killed in the name of religion. Fought for people who had been oppressed by power-hungry assholes who used religion like a lash, a club. And she had given up hers and a huge piece of who she was to fit into a society that had at one time burned her kind at the stake.

Was this why she had held back for so long, or was it something more? She and Juliet had spoken about Clay Maddox last night. Their stepfather had left back when they were juniors in high school. After so long, what could he have to do with any of this, or them?

Miranda approached them. He read exhaustion in the way she stood, the curve of her shoulders.

"We're getting ready to open the circle, but we want to call the quarters first. We've delayed doing that part so we can recharge our power before we expose ourselves to what's out there."

Caleb rose to his feet and offered Chase a hand up. She handed Caleb a green pillar candle, the small bowl of salt, and a book of matches. "Place these at the corner of the square between the spokes of the pentacle and light it."

"Will do," he said, and turned aside to do as she asked.

She moved away to gather her own candle and a small clay bowl of water.

The candles lit, Aubrey raised the ceremonial athame, made the sign of the pentagram and pointed toward the East. "My element is air. I call upon the God and Goddess to boost my strength from up above, to twist and turn, lift, blow, and shove. To sweep aside the threatening evil, and carry away all its upheaval. By the power of all and me, so mote it be."

A stiff breeze whooshed through the room and spun around the circle clockwise, lifting their hair and causing the women's long skirts to billow. Caleb sensed Chase's restless movement beside him.

Aubrey turned and handed off the dagger to Juliet.

Juliet stood, feet braced, and thrust her arm toward the South powerfully before carving a symbol in the air. "My element is Fire. I call upon the God and Goddess to boost my strength, to light the way. To bind knowledge and justice, this course I'll stay, to smite this threat with a fiery lash, and burn its power to useless ash. By the power of all and me, so mote it be."

A current passed around the circle like static electricity. The lit candles placed around the circle sputtered and then the flames shot up a foot or more.

Juliet offered the athame to Miranda, who pointed it to the East, drew the pentacle, and said, "My element is water. I call upon the God and Goddess to boost my strength to fill and flow, to temper my quest with intuition and know, that good shall prevail, strong and right. This evil will end, starting tonight. By the power of all and me, so mote it be."

The waterfall sound of rushing water filled the room, and a mist billowed in the air, then dissipated.

Caleb accepted the ritual knife from Miranda and raised it to make the symbol and point to the North. He held the paper Aubrey had given him in his cupped palm and read the words. "My element is earth. I call upon the God and Goddess to boost my strength to cradle. In heart and hand I will hold those I love stable. Until 'tis time to bring my power to bear, against the evil who will dare, bring harm to those for whom I care. By the power of all and me, so mote it be."

A surprising feeling of warmth worked its way up through the bottoms of his feet to the top of his head. The hairs on his arms stood up. He glanced at Chase. The man was rubbing his arms, and his brows rose. Caleb waited for the feeling to ease back down before he passed the athame back to Aubrey.

She bent her head. "We offer our gratitude and our love for thy blessings and gifts, Lord and Lady." She raised the blade once more and again pointed to the East, "By thy breath." Turning, she pointed to the South, "By the power of thy loving spirit," West, "By the cradling waters of thy womb," North, "By the strength of thy body, we open this circle. So mote it be." She lowered the athame.

The sudden release of the barrier around them was like dropping a curtain, and Caleb was surprised not to feel another billowing of air as it hit the ground.

A bone-chilling chorus of screams rose and built from outside until it hammered against the windows, the walls. For a moment he expected the door to fly open or the windows to break, but all stood firm.

Miranda had shifted her stance and now relaxed and murmured, "Blessed be." The other two echoed the sentiment.

They'd have to take on the power sooner or later. But for now the barriers were holding.

CHAPTER 21

THE RELEASE FROM their hours of concentration left Juliet physically exhausted, yet her mind raced. Caleb and Miranda's conversation with Aubrey fell to a quiet murmur as the three went into the kitchen. Juliet glared in frustration at the shadow creatures. They paced back and forth in the pools of light, their movements strangely graceful and nearly identical. Were there really that many of them, or had the witch responsible mirrored the actions of just two or three to make it appear there were more?

If one witch was responsible for all this, and she'd sustained it all this time, she was bound to be getting tired. The three of them, working together, might be able to take them out right now.

Chase wandered over to stand next to her. He braced an arm on the wooden facing. "I don't like you being this close to the window." Beneath his light brown eyebrows, his pale eyes looked almost gray. "One of those things might reach through."

"Aubrey has set protective wards on all the doors and windows. We're safe—for the night at least."

"You have that much confidence in her ability?"

"Yes, I do."

"Just for my peace of mind, come have a seat with me on

the couch."

Juliet allowed him to guide her to the overstuffed sofa. When he sat close enough that his knee brushed her thigh, she looked up to study his face.

"I've been thinking."

"Uh-oh."

He shot her a wry look, then grinned.

Her stomach tumbled and she felt a twinge in her chest. She hadn't seen him smile before. It lent his masculine features a charm she wasn't expecting. His blond hair, cropped short, lay close to his head, as controlled as the rest of him. She wondered what it would be like for him to lose himself in passion. "What is it you've been thinking about?"

"It's more curiosity than a question. I was hoping you could satisfy me—ah, my curiosity." The tops of his ears reddened.

Was that a Freudian slip? Juliet bit her lip and looked away, the urge to giggle strong. "About what?"

He rubbed his palm along his jaw. He'd never shown any uncertainty before, so why now?

"If witches really exis—"

Juliet raised a brow. How much more proof did he need?

"What else is out there I don't know about?"

Would he believe her? And if he did, how much time would he spend wondering about his friends and coworkers? It might make him doubt them. It might also make him doubly wary of the people he arrested, which could save his life. But it could also affect the way he did his job.

Members of the preternatural community went out of their way to live under the radar. And they policed their own when someone decided to go rogue. It was better if they took care of business quietly instead of turning it over to the cops.

"This situation will probably be the only one of its kind you'll ever have to worry about."

She could see his relief, and guilt struck her. Was she putting him in danger by not telling him the truth? Maybe she should. In her experience, men could only deal with one thing at a time. After they got through this, she'd break the news to him.

Guilt drove her to her feet, and she went to look out the window again. The shadows were gone. The pools cast by the streetlights held nothing. Chase stood close behind her, his body heat reaching out to warm her. He was a detective. He carried a gun. He could protect himself against the Willy Porters and Gerald Abbotts of the world. The temptation to lean back against him was strong. "They're gone, Chase."

"I see that. What else is out there, Juliet?"

She turned to look over her shoulder at him, her arm brushing his chest. Instead of moving back, he splayed a hand against her back. She felt protected, and the look of demand in his eyes escalated her attraction into an ache of desire. Her gaze settled on the firm well-shaped curve of his bottom lip. She was tempted, very tempted, to align her body with his and reach for more. It would distract him from the question she was trying to avoid.

But he couldn't protect himself against what waited out there. And she couldn't be responsible for another man's death. She couldn't.

Pulling her thoughts back to his question she sighed. "Knowing won't make your job easier, Chase. And I can tell you love your job. Men identify with what they do so closely. They judge their worth by what they do. You don't want to allow all this crap to take root inside your head to ruin it for you."

"You wouldn't be trying so hard to avoid the question if it weren't something really bad. All the mythical creatures you see on TV?"

"Some."

"Shit!" He first looked surprised at her answer, then pissed. She could almost see the ideas working through his head.

"Most of the time things are taken care of on the down low. You won't be called in to deal with it. If Miranda wasn't such a Goody Two-Shoes, you'd never have known about the spells. I certainly wouldn't have given them to you."

"Who would you have given them to?"

"We're not associated with any coven. We'd have had to deal with it on our own. And you wouldn't be in danger right now simply because you got involved."

"I was already involved. The autopsy reports are on my desk to prove it. I'd never have stopped looking for the reason behind those men's injuries."

That pit bull attitude was what made him a good detective, but might also get him killed. But not if she could prevent it.

Her attention swung to the street again. Small glints of light sparkled on the lawn. She frowned. What the hell was that? Realization hit her, and she began to shake. Her stomach quivered. "Oh shit!"

"Spiders," Chase finished for her.

They turned as one and ran for the kitchen. "We have a

problem," Chase announced. Miranda, Caleb, and Aubrey jumped to their feet.

"The spiders that attacked the car are outside," Juliet finished for him.

"They can't get through my wards," Aubrey said, her tone soothing.

Chase turned an expression stony with concern on her. "We're talking about things that are able to eat through a windshield, Aubrey."

"My wards will hold."

"Do they cover the whole house, the roof, the attic vents? These suckers can leap like a fucking kangaroo and hit with the force of a baseball at ninety miles an hour. The big one cracked my windshield like an eggshell."

His language alone increased Juliet's concern.

Aubrey frowned, biting her lip. "If they come through a window, they'll burn to a crisp. If they touch the house, the same will happen. But I didn't think about the roof. Nobody told me they could jump."

"Fuck!" Caleb exploded.

Juliet tried to release her fear and ground herself. "I have an idea, but it will require that we all of us working together."

"What is it?" Miranda demanded.

"We were going to try to suck one of the shadow creatures into a crystal. We just need to work on a bigger scale. I can take care of the ones on the lawn, and you two need to gather up the ones on the roof."

"How do you know they're already on the roof?" Aubrey asked.

"Listen."

A muffled rustling sound much like a paper bag being crushed came from above.

"Those assholes are eating my roof," Aubrey's green eyes sparked, her red hair floating about her shoulders as anger fired her powers.

They all followed her into the living room. Aubrey reached for some of the crystals they had prepared, and she put some in her pockets. Miranda and Juliet did the same.

Caleb's features had hardened with concern. "How can we keep the shadows off of you while you three take out the spiders?"

"I'm going to kill the streetlights. You watch my back and warn me if they start to fire up again. I'll be using fire to dissolve the spiders. The shadows may try to manipulate the light from that to attack."

It had been so long since she'd felt empowered, and now the feeling of being in control of herself and her gifts rushed up to meet her like an old friend. She gripped the front door knob and jerked it open.

She threw out a hand. "*Terminus vicus lux luscis.*" Like dominoes falling, every streetlight blinked off, plunging the neighborhood streets into darkness.

"Showoff," Miranda muttered before shooting her a grin. As scared as they were, they were finally living as they should always have been.

Juliet motioned for Miranda to stay back and walked across the porch. She kicked a tarantula-sized arachnid off the stairs like a soccer ball, and heard it hit the street with a crunch. The weight of the thing surprised her.

She rushed to an open space on the lawn and pulled the

power up and through her body in a rush. The scuttling horde surged toward her as soon as she stopped in the center of the yard. She waved her hands back and forth as she would if she were brushing the grass.

A thousand small, skittering shapes hastened toward her, their bodies glittering like crystals. Her skin crawled, and the thought of them touching her provoked an itchy feeling in the back of her throat.

Her anger built to overpower her fear. "Within the grass, within their mass, with fire I will ignite, these things divined to inspire my fright." Each shiny body began to glow fiery red, like a hot coal, and they writhed and withered onto their legs, which curled like burned paper under them. Thousands of them glowed against the inky blackness of the grass, turning the yard scarlet with their heat and sending out the scent of burned sod.

In the dull red glow, tall gray shadows, hazy and indistinct, began to form.

Miranda ran to the edge of the porch and extended a hand, calling out, "*Impluo!*"

Large, wet drops of rain plopped onto the lawn, hitting the burning spiders. They hissed, and steam billowed upwards. Heat pulsed and built until the first one crackled, then popped with the ferocity of a gunshot, sending out shards of hard, molten glass. Like a chain reaction, the others followed in quick succession, sounding off like a string of firecrackers on the fourth of July.

As the light died, the shadows dissipated as quickly as they had appeared. Before the noise and rain ceased, Caleb and Chase ran off the porch, leaping over the smoldering patches to stand on the sidewalk and act as lookouts for any shadows.

Miranda and Aubrey followed to join Juliet on the rain-slick grass. They faced the house and looked up on the roof. Beneath the half-moon's light, the charcoal gray shingles glittered with tiny, skittering forms.

Aubrey bent her elbow, cupped her hand and spun it in a circle. *"Per suction quod verntus levo illa molestus."* The wind spiraled and swirled, circling in wild eddies along the ground, sucking the dead, broken carcasses up out of the grass. With the twisting speed of a dust devil, it took flight and climbed into the sky, bounced, then whirled along the roof, causing the damaged shingles to clatter as it scooped up the writhing mass of crystalline arachnids like a vacuum.

Miranda drew a deep breath and exhaled hard enough to blow up a balloon. A large, transparent bubble appeared and expanded until it stood six feet in diameter, suspended above the ground. "Wiggly arms and legs come hither, within my bubble you will slither," Miranda called out. The wind stilled, and Juliet was certain the sudden appearance of thousands of swarming spiders clumped together in a heaving mass with their burned and broken nest mates would haunt her with more than one horrible nightmare.

"Do you think you can break the bubble at the same time I send these things back to their creator?" she asked Miranda.

"Yes, I can do that."

"Maybe it will be enough to scare her into dropping this vendetta." Goddess, she hoped so. Juliet drew upon the earthy power beneath her. She stretched out a hand and touched her fingertips to the bubble. Immediately at least fifty spiders heaved against the sphere and tried to gnaw their way through to bite her. She couldn't entirely control the instinctive flinch, but held her hand steady. "From shadow to light, carry back this power, and end this final witching hour."

The sphere suddenly stretched out, elongated, as if it were being sucked through a keyhole by a ferocious vacuum. Then it began to shrink, getting smaller and smaller, as more and more of the spiders and their transparent prison were drawn away to another time and place.

"*Ut liberum*," Miranda commanded, just as the last remnant of the bubble disappeared into the either.

A waiting stillness hung in the air. And for several moments they remained frozen, silent.

"Remind me not to piss you ladies off," Caleb quipped. "Having thousands of those things dropped on my doorstep would be about as bad as experiencing the ninth circle of hell."

Aubrey laughed, breaking the white-knuckled tension of the group. "Juliet didn't drop them on her doorstep, Caleb. She sent them all back to her directly."

"Jesus," Chase murmured.

Juliet rolled her head to relieve the tension cramping her neck. It was both satisfying and depressing that she'd probably banished the one thing that could have led them to the person responsible. And that she'd been forced to break their cardinal rule of "an it harm none, do what ye will."

Her voice was tinged with a pinch of bitterness when she said, "Karma's a bitch."

CHAPTER 22

M IRANDA STOOD NEXT to the bed, Caleb's neatly folded clothes in her hands. Washing his clothes was such a small thing, yet intimate. His gray boxer briefs and white tube socks were tucked between layers of shirt and pants.

She had never allowed herself to dream of a husband and family. Had never thought she could want a man until Caleb. Not until Juliet had assured her Clay Maddox was gone for good. For a brief glorious few hours she'd believed it was possible. Until she showed Caleb what she was.

She'd ignored it, suppressed it, and the void inside her had grown to swallow her personality, her life. She had punished herself for the past by pretending to be someone other people could ignore. She'd hidden in plain sight. But she couldn't do it anymore.

"What are you thinking so hard about, Mandy?"

Caleb's voice, gravely from sleep, jerked her back to the present. He stretched and the fabric of his T-shirt pulled taut across his chest and shoulders, outlining the strong, masculine lines of his upper body. Her mouth dried with longing and her skin tingled. When Caleb folded one hand behind his head and patted the bed next to him, her heartbeat burst into an erratic rumba.

His small gesture inspired a tiny kernel of hope, although

she cautioned herself not to read too much into it. She placed his clothes on the dresser and closed the distance between them. Instead of sitting, she climbed on the bed next to him and curled on her side, facing him.

For a long moment he looked into her eyes. The dark beard stubble along his lower jaw tempted her to touch, but she curbed the impulse. He had made the first gesture, but she needed to take things slow.

"How's your arm?" he asked.

"Better." Juliet had done a gentle healing, and though the bruise had flourished with color, the bone-deep pain had eased a little.

He tucked a long strand of hair behind her ear with a fingertip, and the small caress resonated all the way down her neck. "What were you thinking about?"

"I was regretting how much time I've spent hiding in the shadows, afraid to be what I am."

"I understand the need to hide what you can do, but why did you think you had hide the rest?"

The question aimed right for the heart of the whole situation and hit its mark. Fear and guilt welled up, threatening to paralyze her. Her voice came out a whisper. "I didn't think I had a choice."

Caleb's throat moved as he swallowed. "It had something to do with your stepfather, didn't it?"

Oh, Goddess, he was going to guess what it was. How could he not, with her every emotion clamoring beneath the surface of her skin? She tried to swallow, but her heart had lodged in her throat, making it impossible.

He urged her against him.

She shivered as a numbing cold took hold of her, and she burrowed into him, seeking the closeness she had denied herself…and him.

"I love you, Mandy. Nothing will ever change that."

It would. Whatever he thought had happened, nothing could compare with the reality of it. Now that he had connected her behavior to Clay Maddox, it would get stuck in the back of his mind until he began to ask questions. And the Gods help her, she'd answer them.

His fingers found the back of her neck and he rubbed the taut muscles there until she began to calm. "There were things that happened in Afghanistan I will never be able to talk about to anyone. It's fine if you can't talk about things, either. I understand."

Tears burned her eyes as relief flooded her. For however long it lasted, she'd take it.

✧ ✧ ✧

CHASE BRACED A forearm against the window frame and studied the front yard. Scorch marks peppered the grass, reminders of the battle that had raged the night before.

With the normalcy of drinking coffee and the murmur of quiet conversation coming from the kitchen, what had happened last night seemed distant and dreamlike.

He took one more swallow of coffee. It was time to get back to the real world and catch who was responsible. There were three men dead, and it had to be connected to the attacks against Miranda and Juliet. He couldn't use any of the things he'd seen last night as proof, however; he had to build a case using real world facts.

First he needed to interview Samuel Newton. He'd called earlier and checked with the doctor to make sure Samuel was well enough to be questioned.

"I've pressed your clothes, Chase," Juliet said from behind him.

Surprised, he turned to see her dressed in the clothes she'd worn the day before and holding hangers with his trousers and shirt neatly hung on them. His attention shifted to his underwear, T-shirt and socks in her other hand, and he was struck momentarily speechless. "Thanks." Uncomfortable heat climbed into his face and he went closer to exchange his cup for his clothes. No one had washed his laundry since he left home for college. He always kept a change in the trunk, but battling the spiders to get them had been out of the question at the time.

"I'd like to go with you to the hospital to visit Samuel."

He raised a brow. He should have known there'd be a hitch. "In order for this to remain within official guidelines, I can't have you with me when I interview him, Juliet."

"I can go in and thank him for saving my life. If he hadn't knocked me free... Maybe I can reassure him how open-minded you are, so he'll tell you exactly what happened. Otherwise he might not be candid with you."

"If I allow you to talk to him, it contaminates his testimony. Any contact the two of you have, and the timing of it, will be the first thing a defense attorney will home in on."

"I understand, but he may not be completely truthful if he doesn't feel you're open to—the unusual."

"After last night, I believe I'll be open enough." He offered her a wry half smile.

"He may have convinced himself he was hallucinating by now." She shrugged. "Isn't that what most people do when they can't explain something away rationally?"

"Yeah, sometimes."

"I'll go in and see him later to thank him." She cupped his mug in her hands.

Could he trust her on her own? When she started to turn back to the kitchen he said, "What plans do you have for today?"

"I'm going to make the phone calls we talked about and hang with Miranda at the library."

"You're not going to work tonight, are you?"

Though her voice had improved, it still had a bit of a rasp. Just enough to be sexy as hell. Dammit. The handprint on her was less fiery, and was moving on to purple, green and blue, making more of a statement. "No. I'd like to have this situation resolved before I'm trapped behind the bar surrounded by customers. It would probably be wise to limit public participation if this psycho-bitch attacks again."

"You're very certain it's a woman."

"I don't usually anger men enough to want to kill me, and Miranda never makes anybody mad. Well she did once, but that was years ago."

"Who was it she ticked off?"

"Your buddy, Brian Underwood."

Whoa. He'd suspected something because of Underwood's behavior at the hospital and the precinct. "He isn't my buddy. He just happens to work in my department. What did he do?"

"My mom and stepfather forced us to sign non-disclosure agreements when his father laid a big check on them. We're not allowed to talk about it."

Fuck. A wave of heat hit his face as his anger spiked. "He hurt her?"

"No." She remained silent for a beat. "He couldn't tell us apart back then. He probably still can't."

Double fuck. He'd hurt Juliet instead. Jesus.

"He hasn't changed. So watch your back."

That was the second time she'd warned him. Underwood had already pulled the bully routine on him to see how far he could push. But he wouldn't again. He'd trip the lazy son of a bitch up at the first opportunity. He had to take several slow, deep breaths to cool his temper. "Any old boyfriends who might hold a grudge?"

"No, and certainly none who practiced the Craft. I don't think Miranda has dated enough to stir up any trouble. You can ask her, though."

"Why do you think it's a woman?"

"It has to be someone tied to either the library, or the Newtons, or both. About ninety percent of the employees at the library are female. Then there's the tampon thing. Men seem to have a big ick factor associated with feminine hygiene products." A brief smile quivered across her mouth and was gone. "I agree with Caleb, a man wouldn't have thought of hiding anything in one. If she sent Porter and Abbott after me, but Tanner was killed instead, she'd go after Miranda just to hurt me as payback. My sister's the most important person in my life."

It all made sense, but who the hell was it?

A frown flickered across her features. "But I could be wrong. I saw someone outside the police station yesterday I recognized just before the spider ran past in front of us. It was more from the way he moved than anything. It's taken me a while to figure out who it was, because he usually wears Goth makeup at work and darkens his hair with gel. It was Justin Chalmers, the bartender who works with me."

"So you think he might be involved?"

"I don't know. I wouldn't have thought so. But he's been pushing pretty hard for a date."

"Why didn't you go out with him?"

She stared down into the empty mug she held. "He's not really my type. Pretty boy and used to getting what he wants." She looked away. "I decided after Tanner's death that there were some personal things I needed to work on before I would be ready to date anyone else." She swallowed and glanced up. "I've been seeing a psychologist at the college."

"Good for you," he said, and meant it. He'd seen how wounded Juliet was the first time he met her, but she was strong as well. "I've had a round or two with one myself."

"Was it one of those department required things after something on the job?"

"Yeah. And at the time I didn't want to admit I needed it. But I did."

"Did it help?"

There was such hope on her face, he had to swallow before he answered. "Yeah, it did."

She shifted from one foot to the other. "Good." She turned away.

"I'll be ready to go to the hospital in ten minutes. You can ride over with me, and I'll drop you at the library afterwards."

She half raised a hand to her throat when she turned her

head, surprise suffusing her lovely face. She studied him for a moment. "Thank you. I'll be ready."

While he stood in the shower, Chase mentally listed all the reasons he needed to keep the hell away from Juliet Templeton. He was just going through a wounded bird phase with her. She was emotionally scarred. But with her strange natural abilities, she was a warrior. He admired the one and wanted to protect the other. He was still heaping on self-recrimination when he came out of the bathroom dressed and ready to go.

She rose from the couch. The house was silent. "Is everyone already gone?"

"Yes. Aubrey had to get to work at the Social Security office. And Miranda and Caleb went to the mall to get some things. Neither of us feels comfortable going home just yet, and one outfit apiece isn't very practical."

He swore silently. "I forgot about my car being out of commission."

"It's okay. Caleb called us a cab. The driver can take us to the garage, and we'll pick up my new ride."

"New ride?"

"I sold my old car and bought a new one. Well, it isn't new, but it's new to me."

"Are we meeting again tonight, or are we splitting up?"

"We're meeting at Caleb's. If we move around, they might not be able to track us."

He was beginning to realize what Abbott and Porter had gone through. No wonder they had looked and acted psychotic. "It might be better if we split up."

Juliet bit her lip, her regret palpable. "I wish we'd never involved Aubrey. She wasn't even on their radar until we led them here."

"We're going to figure out who's doing this today, and I'm going to bring them in."

"There's nothing to tie them to Tanner's death or the others. Nothing concrete."

She was right. He had to keep moving forward with the cases, and maybe something would slide into place. "We'll find something. There's always something to find." He hoped he was right.

CHAPTER 23

B Y TEN AM heat radiated off the parking lot and the air was saturated with an oily scent. The unusual mid-July heat had stirred up the humidity and threatened to parboil them all. Caleb leaned into the trunk to search for scrolled notes or spiders.

"It's clear. I put wards on the car before we went into the mall," Miranda said over his shoulder.

"I'll feel better knowing for sure." He unscrewed the wheel well where the spare was kept, took the hatch off and looked inside. Everything appeared okay. He fastened everything down again and reached for her packages. He had the trunk loaded and looked over his shoulder to see if there was anything else. He caught Miranda eyeing his pants. "What is it?"

Her smile was slow, and her amber gaze sparkled with amusement. "I'm just checking out your behind."

Caleb grinned, then laughed. "How is it?"

"I like it fine, but I have a preference for your forearms and thighs."

Mandy Templeton was checking out his butt. No, she was checking out more than his butt. Wow. It was corny as hell, but that was the only word his brain could come up with at the moment, because all the blood had drained from his head and was heading south.

Before she could back off again, he slid a hand beneath her hair to cup the back of her head and angled his mouth over hers. He had waited for six months for her. Agonized over why she wouldn't let him in. Ached to hold her, kiss her, and more, every single day of those six months. When her arms went around him and she nestled in tight, he groaned in pleasure. Her lips parted and his tongue found hers. He lost himself in the eager tangle of their lips and tongues.

A horn blared close by, startling them both. Caleb reluctantly raised his head but kept an arm around her, pressing her close. The guy responsible was two rows over and had nearly hit a car pulling out.

Miranda's smiling, flushed face tilted up at him. "We may have been a distraction."

He planted a brief, intense kiss on her lips. "I was a tad distracted myself." Which had been great, but dangerous. If the bad guys had chosen that moment to unleash the spiders on them, they wouldn't have reacted in time. He slammed the trunk shut in frustration, guided her toward the passenger side of the car, and opened the door for her.

After he settled behind the wheel, Miranda touched his arm. "Can we go by your house? I'd like to change before going to work."

"Are you sure work is a good idea?" He started the car and backed out of the parking space.

"I'll be surrounded by people. I don't think she wants an audience for these attacks. They've only happen when we're with only one person. Well, until last night."

"It was dark, the middle of the night, and the street was empty." He pulled to a stop at the main entrance of the mall, and waited for the light to change.

"Maybe after she made the mistake of getting Tanner killed, she's being cautious, making the spell as person-specific as possible."

He turned left onto Cayce Drive. "Wonder why I'm not on her hit list?"

"We don't know that you aren't at this point."

As soon as he noticed her distress, Caleb reached for her hand. "There isn't a force on earth that can make me leave you, Mandy." He loved her, witchy stuff and all.

"If something ever happened…"

"We'll get through this and move on to better things. You have my six and I have yours."

Anxiety edged her smile.

"Last night, while we were in the circle…when I said my part, I felt this stream of energy pour through me from the three of you. It was the same when we were out in the yard and you were doing your mop-up operation. Did Aubrey do something to make that happen?"

Miranda gripped his hand tighter. "No. She wouldn't use you as a conduit without asking your permission."

"So, it's possible to do that?"

"We focus power through objects when we cleanse the circle and bless the materials we use before a ceremony. And I've heard of some witches being able to pull power through animals. But to use a human would be—*unthinkable.*"

The idea of them siphoning power through him didn't sound too bad, as long as it was just them and no one else. It hadn't hurt. "Then what was happening?"

She shook her head. "When we get to the house, I'd like to

try something with you."

He bit his lip to keep from smiling. "Anything you want, darlin'."

Miranda's lips parted, and then she smiled. "I didn't mean that. But…" Her voice softened, "We can talk about it."

Caleb grinned. "Talk about it?"

"Well, yes. You have to be certain."

Another *Wow* overtook him, and it was damn hard to catch his breath. His cock pressed hard against the unyielding metal zipper of his jeans. "Not a problem."

"Even after the witch thing?"

He grew serious for a moment. "I'm okay with the witch thing. And your reasons for keeping it from me."

"I thought I'd left it all behind. I was trying to just be…like everyone else."

"Not possible. You'll never be like anyone else." He pulled to a stop at a red light and turned to look directly at her, so she'd know he meant what he said. "I love you, Mandy."

Her eyes went glassy with tears for a moment before she smiled. "I think you're just saying that so you can get into my panties."

Caleb grinned. "Not just."

She laughed.

He raised their laced hands and rubbed his cheek against the back of her hand.

Having her so relaxed with him was a powerful turn-on. He'd begun to think it wasn't going to happen. He released the tight rein he'd held on his feelings for so long. Things were going to be great between them.

✧　✧　✧

MIRANDA LIFTED TWO of the bags from the trunk and preceded Caleb around the back of the house to the back door. He juggled several bags in one hand and tugged his keys free of his front jeans pocket. Unlocking the door, he shoved it open and stood back for her to enter. He laid the bags on the huge island between the kitchen and dining room.

She looked around the room, obviously surprised by the modern layout. "This is really lovely, Caleb."

"I had it remodeled for my grandmother. She's the one who fed and took care of me most of the time, and she loved to cook. I also promised her I'd modernize the upstairs bathroom as soon as I got home."

Miranda remembered she had passed away before he had the chance. Miranda rubbed a hand up and down his back in sympathy.

His blue eyes looked intense as he turned. "Wait here. I want to check the house out before we get too far inside."

She propped the two bags against the others. "I don't feel any lingering energy signature."

"You can do that?"

"Yes, if anyone has used magic in the house. I don't feel any."

"Good." His shoulders relaxed. "Would you like to check it out anyway?"

"Yes." She held out her hand and Caleb's enfolded it.

There were gleaming hardwood floors throughout. They wandered through the dining room and turned left into a spacious living room. The walls were painted a light green, and crown molding graced the length and breadth of both rooms. A wide fireplace covered in travertine tile rose from hearth to ceiling and took up the center of the east wall. A flat-screened television was mounted above the mantle. On either side were built-in bookcases rising even with the mantle. Large windows along the east wall allowed light to stream into the room. A bulky couch, love seat, and a couple of chairs were arranged around a walnut coffee table.

"I've been doing some updates at night."

Regret lanced through her. She could have been helping him instead of pushing him away. Offering him solace from his grief, instead of stalling.

"It's beautiful."

They walked down a hall to look inside the first room on the left, a bedroom. The next was a full bath. Everything was neat as a pin and freshly painted. The small office was the last room on the first floor. Paperwork stacked across the desk gave the impression he was doing some bookkeeping. She looked around with interest. Being with him in his home helped her visualize him as a family man. It gave her a tiny flutter of desire in her stomach to think of him in that way.

"I haven't gotten around to updating the upstairs yet. I've painted a few of the rooms and the hall." The oak stairs were bare of carpet, but had been refinished. Their footsteps echoed loudly as they climbed. A full bath in need of an update was at the top of the stairs, then three more bedrooms, and a master suite which included a small bathroom with a shower stall, vanity, and toilet. His bedroom had been painted, and had a distinctly masculine feel to it, with the blue walls and a brown and navy comforter.

"I never noticed you were such a stickler for neatness," she said.

"I guess I'm still in military mode. I can do beer-swilling slob if you prefer."

She laughed. "No, thank you. I'm a little OCD myself."

"Maybe all that repressed energy?" he suggested.

And the need to control everything in her environment to empower herself. "You could be right. I haven't had the urge to clean the sinks since all this started."

He smiled. "What was it you wanted to try with me?"

There was nothing suggestive in his tone, but her cheeks warmed. The bedroom was as good a place to experiment as any. Her face got hotter at the thought. She tried to ignore his grin.

She held out her hands palm up. "Place your palms over mine." The steadiness of his gaze, so vibrant blue, sent a quick, pleasurable frisson of desire racing through her. Chill bumps broke out on her skin, and a warm, moist ache settled between her legs. She needed to concentrate on what they were doing, not on how his every look and touch triggered a desire to jump his bones.

She actually wanted to jump a guy's bones. Not just any guy's, but Caleb's. She thought about all the emotions that went along with reaching for those feelings, and didn't find a moment of distrust among them.

"When I draw energy from the elements, I visualize inhaling it into my body from all around me. I can draw from the air, the plants and animals, the earth, every natural thing. But it cycles through me like I'm a switch on a circuit. I'm only borrowing from them for a while before returning it."

"Sounds pretty—intimate," Caleb said.

"It is. It's a sort of energy partnership."

He nodded his understanding.

"I'm going to borrow a tiny bit of energy from you, and I want you to tell me how it feels."

"Okay."

She took several deep breaths and drew upon the physical connection between their palms. Tender warmth blended with sexual energy to wash through her. She bit back a groan as it ramped up her own physical responses.

She swallowed, uncertain she could even speak.

"We're on the same circuit. You weren't just pulling it away, it was flowing back through me at the same time." His eyes searched her face. "Miranda..." His throat worked as he swallowed.

Her legs felt spongy and weak. She had to get this need he'd triggered under control. She braced her feet apart so her stance was stronger. "Do you want to see if you can borrow it from me?"

"No. I don't know what I'm doing or how to control it. I'd rather try to give you the energy."

"Okay."

He closed his eyes, and the look of concentration on his face made her smile. He looked so determined. And dear.

Her hands tingled with heat, and a slow wash of power flowed up her arms and through her. It nestled deep inside, like a touch, and she bit her lip. The feeling of pleasure building behind it threatened to overwhelm her, and she tugged her hands away. She took two staggering steps back and half sat-half tumbled down on the corner of the bed.

Caleb rushed to her and put an arm around her. "I didn't hurt you, did I?"

"No. Never." Oh God, the feeling wasn't going away, and she wanted to rock her hips until she satisfied the delicious ache he'd triggered. She gripped his shirt with one hand and turned her face against his shoulder.

"What is it?"

How was she supposed to tell him? They were just beginning to ease into a new kind of intimacy. "It's—" Her breaths came in short pants and her heart was drumming inside her ears. "Caleb, it's pure sexual energy. And it's—I want you to touch me so much."

He lifted her face to him and kissed her. The adamant pressure of his lips fed the amazing need that tightened and tightened inside her.

"It's the same for me, Mandy," he murmured against her cheek, her jaw, as his mouth brushed against her skin. "You've set me on fire for you."

She reached for the bottom of his T-shirt and ran a questing hand beneath to touch his skin. Caleb yanked it up and off, and threw it aside. The muscular slope of his shoulders and chest looked so wide and powerful. She had to be closer to him, and feel his skin against hers. She swung a leg over his lap and straddled him.

Caleb cupped her bottom with one hand as he slid back onto the bed, taking her with him. He reached for her sweater and tugged it up. So focused on the driving need to feel him inside her, Miranda shed the sweater without a second thought. He reached for her bra, and she allowed it to slide forward so he could toss it aside. She shivered at the delicious brush of her nipples against the hair blanketing his upper chest. She wanted to nestle into him like a second layer of skin and wrap herself around him.

He cupped one breast and kneaded it gently. She had dreamed of having his hands all over her, craved them. She pressed into his palm in response, and relished the sensation that trailed from her breast downward when he squeezed her nipple.

She cupped his jaw and tilted his head so she could kiss him. Her tongue tangled with his in a slow dance that had her blood racing, and she groaned at the onslaught of a sweet rush. He ran a hand up her back to cradle her against him and turned so she could stretch out beside him.

His gaze swept down her naked torso, and his eyes had never burned so hot a blue. He trailed his fingertips down between her breasts and over the dip between her ribcage to her waist and the top of her slacks. "You're trembling."

"I want this so much." Her voice shook. "Want you."

"You're the only thing I thought about for months overseas, and all I've wanted since I got home." He unhooked her waistband and slid down the zipper, his movements unhurried, apparently savoring every moment as much as she. When he slipped a hand inside the fabric and around her hip she lifted up so he could tug them down and away.

She didn't feel embarrassed or uneasy being naked, vulnerable with him, only cherished, wanted. When he ran a hand along her bare hip, she turned against him, seeking the warmth of his skin against hers. She traced his collarbone with her lips, then the heavy pulse beating at his throat.

Caleb drew a ragged breath. His hands moved slowly, insistently, caressing her. He pushed her back and slid down to caress her breast with his lips and tongue. When he took her nipple into his mouth and sucked, she gasped at the titillating pleasure coursing deep inside.

She raked her fingers through his hair, discovering the texture of the faintly coarse waves and curls that twined around her fingers. The brush of his stubble against her breasts heightened her desire, but not as much as the realization that she was experiencing this with Caleb, sharing it with him.

Fear had held her back for so long, she was amazed by the tiniest sensation. She couldn't touch him enough, share a deep enough kiss. Every heartbeat felt like the first. She loved freely for the first time. When he shook free of his jeans and rose above her, she welcomed him. The brief feeling of pressure and discomfort lasted only a moment, then he was inside her, filling the hungry, sensual void, and her heart. The sweet intimacy of being a part of him was almost overwhelming, and she fought back the tears.

He froze for a moment, a question in his gaze as he looked down at her.

"Don't stop," she pleaded.

She caught the rhythm of Caleb's slow, steady movements, and the desire building to give to him as he was giving to her rose up and carried her forward. She reached for the surprising, encompassing pleasure he gave her with joy. It built to a tantalizing crest, until she was almost afraid she might fly apart. She curved her arms up his back and held on as it took her.

Caleb looked down into her face, still aglow from their lovemaking, and smiled. They had been perfect together. Her tawny eyes opened and she smiled. She trailed her fingers down his spine to his ass and cupped his buttocks. He pushed into her again in response, and she made a sound that made him harden in a rush all over again. He bent his head and kissed her. Her response was so loving, his throat clogged with emotion.

He'd been wrong in his assumptions about her stepfather? But if Clay Maddox hadn't molested her, what had happened to make her close herself off from everything?

Though he wanted to make love with her all over again, Caleb withdrew and lay beside her.

Miranda curled against his side and bent a knee across his thighs.

He brushed her temple with his lips. "I didn't hurt you, did I?"

"No. It was more wonderful than I ever expected." She ran a hand over his chest. When the silence stretched between them, she stilled. "Just give me a few more moments. I know what you're wondering, and I'll explain everything."

He tried to keep his voice even, but a sense of betrayal was tightening the back of his neck. "How many more secrets are there, Miranda?"

"Only this last one."

He was used to waiting. He'd waited half his life for his mother to get her act together, and she never had. He'd waited for his father to come back after abandoning them both, and that hadn't happened either. He had waited for Miranda, but did the woman he had thought she was even exist?

"This isn't just my secret, Caleb. It's Juliet's as well." He felt tension take over her body. "My mother married Clay Maddox when Miranda and I were twelve. We moved into his house, and for a time Mom was happy and so were we.

"Then when we turned thirteen, Clay decided we needed separate bedrooms. We didn't want to be separated, but he insisted, and because he was so adamant, my mother insisted we go along with it. He waited about six weeks for us to settle into being separated..."

Every muscle in her body seemed to clench, and she pulled away. She reached for his shirt on the floor and put it on. "I didn't realize what was happening when she started to pull away from me. We'd always been so close. Then I was going to the bathroom one night and saw him coming out of her room. He was zipping his pants."

Caleb reached for his pants. She didn't need to see a naked man while she relived what she was telling him. He slipped them on and moved around the bed to sit next to her.

"Clay molested Juliet, but he used the threat of what he might do to me to control her. He used to lie in wait for me when I least expected it, and whisper to me what he was going to do to her if I didn't keep my mouth shut."

Jesus! Caleb raked his fingers through his hair.

She looked up at him, her eyes haunted. "You can't say anything. She never wanted anyone to know."

God, he felt sick. He had promised himself he wouldn't push her to tell him things like this, and it was the first thing he'd done. He had to clear his throat before he could speak. "I won't say anything."

"She was the one who had to endure it, but it nearly destroyed us both. I'd go into her room after he left and hold her while she cried. Then she just stopped feeling anything. And I didn't want to feel anything either. It was safer that way."

"Until now," Caleb said softly.

She tugged at the T-shirt, stretching it to cover her thighs. He grasped her hand to still the movement and tipped her face up to him with the other. He ran his thumb along her jaw. He'd destroyed the wonderful glow she had when she lay under him, their bodies still joined. Regret clawed into his chest.

Miranda pulled his hand away but continued to hold it. "For years we've both been haunted by Clay Maddox and everything he did. Juliet and I are both trying to leave it all behind. I couldn't let a man touch me. I didn't want anyone to. I'd seen what it did to Juliet all those years ago, and it killed any desire I might have had for anything physical."

She swallowed, and then gave him a radiant smile. "Until we started talking while you were deployed. I got to know you again, trust you. Love you. And then you came home and you were here, eager to touch me, hold me, kiss me. All the normal things a man wants to do with a woman. I didn't think I could have those things. But I wanted them with you, Caleb."

While he'd been thinking about giving up on her, she'd been working through all this, building up her nerve to try. He slipped an arm around her and gathered her close. His voice sounded like a rusty hinge around the lump in his throat. "We have it all in front of us now, Mandy. Whatever we want to build between us." When her tension dissolved and she melted into him again, he relaxed with relief. He wouldn't push again. Whatever she chose to share would be on her terms from now on.

CHAPTER 24

SILENCE STRETCHED BETWEEN Chase and Samuel Newton.

The cafeteria service personnel had picked up Samuel's breakfast tray shortly after Chase arrived. Only a cold cup of coffee remained on the tray positioned across his lap. Propped up into a seated position in his hospital bed, Newton's posture was stiff from trying to avoid moving.

Chase felt some sympathy for the guy, but dammit, the man was stonewalling him.

"Are you sure you don't remember what happened, Mr. Newton?"

"I remember being on the street with Ms. Templeton, and then the next thing I'm here, receiving intravenous pain meds and pissing blood through a catheter.

"I've interviewed Ms. Templeton several times since the two of you were attacked. She describes your attacker as being tall, thin, with long arms and hands and dark gray in color. As crazy as that description sounds, I have five other people who've seen similar attackers and agree with that description."

Newton eyed him. "I didn't get a good look, but yeah, it was gray."

"It took some balls to confront it like you did."

Newton remained silent.

"I believe that this attack on you and Ms. Templeton is connected to your brother's assault, sir. Before Abbott died, he told me he and Porter were hired to kill Juliet Templeton. Your brother was killed trying to protect her."

"So he died a hero, but it won't bring him back." The pain of his loss blended with his physical pain to cut deep furrows on either side of his mouth.

"Abbott admitted to being paid to get rid of Juliet Templeton. The money was given to him through a go-between. Did Tanner have a possessive girlfriend who'd look upon Juliet as a rival?"

At the dramatic change in Newton's expression, Chase shifted in his seat.

Newton raised a hand to cup his forehead as he fought off some strong emotion. "I dated this girl in Lexington. Tanner and I used to live there until my father went into semi-retirement and asked us to come back and take over the firm. Her name was Suzette Chalmers. Tanner came over one night before we went out, and the moment she met him she became obsessed. At first she continued to date me, but only to ask questions about my family and Tanner. When I broke it off, she went after him directly. She got into his apartment somehow and cooked dinner. She was waiting for him when he got home. He tried to be nice and told her he was flattered, but that he already had a girlfriend."

"The woman he was dating... Her tires were slashed, and she received threatening phone calls and letters. We could never prove it was Suzette sending them. Then something weird happened to Bethany. She got sick for like two weeks. Every time Tanner would get anywhere near her, she'd get worse. Like she was allergic to him or something. Finally she broke it off."

"Directly afterward was when we moved back to Superstition, and about three months later he met Juliet Templeton. I know I had a preconceived idea about her because she's a bartender, but he seemed really crazy about her, and the other night... She seemed to really care about Tanner."

Chase concentrated on the pad in his hand. It felt strange hearing about how another guy felt about Juliet, how she'd felt about him. And yes, there was some jealousy involved, but it was hard to be jealous of a guy who'd saved Juliet's life.

"Tanner seemed to be putting all the craziness from Lexington behind him. Then he mentioned seeing Suzette here in Superstition. He thought it was her. It was just a glimpse, but it freaked him out. When two weeks or so went by and nothing happened, he said he must have been mistaken and relaxed again."

"Will you give me a description of her?"

"She was about five foot six, slender, had light brown hair streaked with blonde and greenish-brown eyes. She was well built and very athletic."

"How long between the time he saw her until his death, Mr. Newton?"

"Maybe three weeks."

"Do you know if she has any family in the area, or friends?"

"No. I know her family was pretty well-to-do. And she had a younger brother."

"What was his name?"

"Justin."

✧ ✧ ✧

JULIET AVOIDED LOOKING at Samuel Newton's arm. After just a glance she'd felt nausea creeping up her throat. It was blue, the whole arm to the wrist. How could anything injure someone like that?

"I'm sorry you were hurt."

Samuel leaned back against the pillows on the hospital bed, his body stiff. "It wasn't your fault."

"It was indirectly. If you hadn't intervened, I'd have been killed."

"I'm glad you're okay."

She wasn't surprised at Samuel's wooden replies. He was exhausted after the interview with Chase.

A distant look clouded his eyes. "I'm still not sure what I saw."

Juliet stood and grasped his hand. She drew some of his pain to herself so it would ease him. She breathed through the first wave until she could control it. "It doesn't matter. The men responsible for Tanner's death are dead. Neither of us has to worry about them again."

"But the person who hired them is still out there."

Something about him reminded her so much of Tanner in that moment that her eyes clouded with tears, and she had to look away to maintain her composure. "Detective Robinson will get them. You've given him a lead. I could tell from the way he looked when he left your room. He's very determined to find who's responsible and see justice done."

"Good." He seemed to relax a little more. "The other detective was close to retirement and didn't seem all that interested."

"Detective Howard passed it on to the right man. Detective Robinson is the right one." She gave his hand a squeeze. "You need to rest. The more rest you get, the faster you'll heal." Juliet closed her eyes for a moment and drew upon the natural power around her. Some of it came from the other people in the building. She was careful to block that off. Most filtered into her from the natural life force of air, water, earth, and from the fire she found in the natural sunlight spilling into the room next to his bed. She siphoned some from the electricity slithering through the room. "Why don't you close your eyes and rest?" She touched his cheek briefly and his lashes fluttered. She waited a moment until he settled into slumber.

She first set protective wards around the room, then turned her attention to Samuel. Careful not to touch his skin, she held her hand just above his shoulder and directed the healing into the bruised tissue. She didn't have to raise the fabric of his hospital gown to tell how much of his body the injuries covered. The hungry tug upon the force spilling from her directed it. She was the conduit, Mother Nature the doctor.

His body relaxed more as his tissues mended, the pain from the bruises eased. The door opened behind her just as she reached Samuel's knee. She stepped back from the bed, her hand dropping away.

Chase's attention slid from her to Samuel. He came all the way into the room. "What are you doing?" he whispered.

"Nothing. He fell asleep talking to me. We should leave." She collected her purse from the chair next to the bed and strode toward him.

Chase didn't move back as she expect, but stood intractable and determined, blocking the door. He laid a hand on her shoulder.

"I can feel the power in the room, Juliet. It's like static electricity."

Damn. She should have known. He'd experienced it before, so of course he'd recognize it. She reached out and made a twisting movement, gathering the residual power to her. It washed over her and nestled into her body, the sensation comforting.

Chase's mouth took on a stubborn look as he gripped her upper arm, his fingers curled around the limb firmly, but not tight enough to hurt. He guided her down the hall to the elevator. She was reminded of how he'd done the same thing the first night they met, when he clasped her arm as if he expected her to attempt an escape.

He spoke to the police officer standing at the desk with a cup of coffee. "We're leaving. Sparks will be here at five to relieve you."

"Thank you, sir." The man handed the empty cup to one of the nurses to throw away and wandered back down the hall.

"I don't know how much protection he'll be against witchcraft, but it's better than nothing."

"I've placed protection wards on the room. As long as Samuel remains inside he'll be fine. They have no reason to go after him. He was just at the wrong place at the wrong time."

"Like his brother?"

Juliet stiffened at the unexpected slap.

He removed his hand, and she shifted away from him in the elevator. She was relieved when two more people got on the elevator and stood between them.

Why did she feel this tug of attraction toward him when he could so effortlessly punch at her with his suspicions and hurt her? Why was she a target for this every time something happened?

The elevator door opened and she rifled through her bag one-handed until she found the car keys. Once outside in the parking lot she tossed them at Chase with no warning and he snagged them out of the air with quick reflexes, but shot her a scowl. She got into the passenger side of the car and he caught the door before she could close it.

"We should check out the car before we leave the parking lot."

"I placed wards around it. If anyone had touched it they'd either be lying on the parking lot writhing in pain from the shock, or the alarm would have gone off."

He stared at the palm holding the door open and jerked it back. She slammed the door shut and fastened her seat belt. Let him be afraid of what she could do. He deserved it. She was tired of trying to pass for something she wasn't. She'd let him into her life much further than she had any other man, and he was still sniping at her and blaming her for what someone else had done.

She folded her arms against her when he got into the car. She snagged her bag and pulled it onto her lap for something to do with her hands so he wouldn't know she was feeling defensive.

She hadn't done anything wrong. It wasn't her fault someone had hired Abbott and Porter to kill her.

She was finally starting to believe it. But the pain of Tanner's loss was still just as sharp.

Chase got in the car but didn't attempt to put on his seat belt or start it. "What were you doing with Samuel Newton?" he asked, his demeanor less angry.

"I was easing his pain."

His head came up and he looked at her. "Healing him?"

"Yes."

"Your voice is better just since this morning," he observed.

"A side benefit of channeling so much energy."

He reached for the scarf around her neck. She forced herself to remain passive as he untied it. His fingertips glided over her skin with feathery lightness. Would his touch be so gentle while making love? Her pulse leapt against it.

"The bruising has faded. It's not completely gone, but it's fading," he observed. He laid the scarf in her lap. "You did more than CPR on Tanner, didn't you?"

Sharp pain rose up to slice at her, regret and grief blending to make her throat ache. "I tried to save him, but the EMTs arrived before I finished." Tears ran down her face. "Once they were working on him—they wouldn't let me touch him." She pressed the scarf to her face as tears flowed. "He died on the way to the hospital."

"Did you do the same to Samuel when you were attacked?"

"Yes. He had internal injuries, a concussion. When he started to wake up, I had to stop. So I dialed 911 and EMS came to get us."

"Jesus," Chase hissed. He braced his elbow on the steering wheel and cradled his forehead in his hand. "I'm sorry, Juliet. I opened the door and felt all that power circling the room." He shook his head.

"It can be as gentle as a whisper or as fierce as a bomb, but there's a price to pay each time it's used. If you use it for good, the price is lower. If you use it for evil, it's cumulative and can turn on you. I've heard it can drive you mad. Nature has its own checks and balances. If it didn't, you'd be getting a call every few minutes about a fire, a flood, or what have you."

"I don't find that very comforting, honey. The possibility of things like that happening behind my back—disturbs me."

Honey? Honey? He could take his *honey a*nd stuff it. "You weren't getting those calls, were you?"

"No. Not until Porter and Abbott were killed."

"The imbalance she's created will boomerang back to her threefold. We all pay eventually."

"Like the spiders you dumped on her last night?"

She shrugged. "We just helped the process along a little."

He raised a brow.

"We are allowed to defend ourselves. What did you want us to do? Sit there and wait to be chewed up? We sent a message: leave us alone or reap the whirlwind." She looked out the side window, back toward the hospital. "You can drop me at the library and keep the car. I'll catch a ride with Juliet and Caleb later."

He started the vehicle and backed out of the parking lot. "I wasn't saying you weren't supposed to defend yourself."

When he looked in her direction she stared at him hard.

"My badge and gun are useless against this. How do you expect me to feel, when I've been entrusted with enforcing the law and protecting the citizens of Superstition, and suddenly find there's a whole subculture here I can't even begin to identify, let alone protect? None of my training will stand up to what you three women can do."

"It doesn't need to. There are members of your force who have the ability to deal with things like this. All you have to do is ask for help."

"I'm not handing over my case to anyone."

"I didn't say you had to. You might want to find out who they are and ask them to work with you."

"And how do you suggest I do that?"

"When I make the phone calls, I'll put out feelers about people in the department who might be able to help."

His fingers tightened around the steering wheel, his masculine features set in a scowl of frustration. With his jaw shadowed by stubble, he looked dangerous.

She had shed her craving for bad boys a while back when she gave up pot, cigarettes, and a few other things she didn't want to think about. She'd been trapped in a senseless quest to either feel normal emotions like other people or dull the pain from the past.

But now, for the very first time, she was tempted by real attraction. And it scared her to death. He was unapologetically all man. No beta tendencies with him. And that was probably why they were butting heads every time they spent more than ten minutes together. They both needed to be in control. Him because he was used to it, and her because she was afraid to allow anyone to have power over her ever again.

"Tanner's death wasn't my fault. I did everything I could to save him. Don't ever try to use it to hurt me again, Chase."

He heaved a sigh and brushed a hand over his jaw. "I won't. But from here on in you're straight up with me about everything, Juliet. Even the witchy stuff."

She studied him for a long time. Would he be able to control his instinct to push? She doubted it. But she could trust him to try to discover the truth. She extended her hand. "Deal."

CHAPTER 25

A S SHE LOOKED out over the library's main floor from the second floor landing, Miranda evaluated her morning with as much objectivity as she could. She and Caleb had actually flirted and been playful, and she'd felt like a normal woman with the man she loved. They'd made love. As if they'd been made for each other. He'd been inside her, and she hadn't felt sick or afraid. For one brief, glorious moment she'd been happy—truly, fantastically happy.

And then Clay Maddox had once again stolen it from them. No. She was responsible. She should have guessed how Caleb might misconstrue her reaction when he mentioned her stepfather the night before. Of course he needed to push to understand what had held her back for so long. She only prayed he'd accept what she told him and not keep digging.

Miranda turned back to her office. Juliet lounged on the small sofa against one wall reading some information she'd printed off the computer earlier. Now she held a pencil gripped in her hand and was busily scribbling something on one of the sheets. There was an inherent grace in her pose, with her legs tucked up on the cushions and her hair draped over one shoulder. Her sister was more vibrant and passionate. She recognized in herself the need to be more introspective. They were mirror images of each other physically, and complete opposites emotionally.

Juliet struggled so to put her life back together, and come so far just in the last year.

"Because I work here, and you're my immediate family, the college has a policy that I can donate the free classes I earn each semester to a family member if I don't use them myself. You'd have to pay for your own books, but the tuition would be free."

Juliet raised her brows. "You're not interested in working toward your doctorate?"

"There isn't a doctoral program here. I'd have to go to summer school or commute to UK on the weekends. An independent study might be an option or online classes. Right now I'm not ready to take on anything more."

"I'll think about it."

Encouraged, yet trying to keep her excitement under control, Miranda asked, "What would your focus of study be?"

"If I said social work, you'd go all warm and fuzzy on me, but I'm more interested in business."

She couldn't really picture Juliet behind a computer working as a CPA, but running a business might be an option. "Sounds good. If you decide to try it, I can help you get up-to-date for the entrance exam."

Juliet smiled. "Thanks, sis."

Miranda sat down in a chair across from her. "I've been thinking about how we could—"

Juliet cleared her throat, her gaze cutting to someone behind Miranda. She turned to look behind her. Susan stood, waif-thin and pale, in the doorway. In contrast, her hair hung a vibrant black down her shoulders and stood out like ink against her skin. "Ms. Ward called and said she was having some issues with her car but she'd be here ASAP."

"Thank you, Susan. Do you need me to come out and help at the front desk?"

"No, thanks. Mary Janet and I can handle things until she comes in."

"Buzz me here in my office if that changes and you need me."

"Yes, ma'am." The girl's gaze focused on the drawing in Juliet's hand. "That looks a lot like a Sasha Carlton character."

"Sasha Carlton?" Juliet repeated. "You know what this is?"

"It looks like one of her shadow demons from the graphic novel, *Twist in Time.*"

Excitement brought Miranda to her feet. "Do we have a copy of it here in the library, Susan?"

"Several. I can get one off the shelves for you if they're not all checked out. They're very popular among the art students."

"I'd like to see a copy if one is in."

"Sure." Susan darted away in the direction of the south corner of the floor where the art texts were stored.

Juliet came to join her at the door. "I've never heard of anyone being able to create an imaginary creature to kill someone."

"I haven't either. But if they've patterned it after this book, they may have inadvertently built in the same weaknesses as the one in the book."

"And what if they don't have a weakness?"

"Authors always build in strengths and weaknesses to their characters. It gives the characters something to overcome to increase the conflict. The shadows can't appear without the artificial light. I want to know what the spiders' weaknesses might be."

Susan was back with a large, rectangular coffee table sized book. She handed it to Miranda. "Thank you, Susan. We've been looking for information about this for a few days."

"Glad I could help." The girl's wan face lit up with a smile.

"Are you into the characters?" Juliet asked.

"Yeah. I've read all her books. The graphic novels were patterned after them, but are separate stories."

Juliet smiled. "Why don't you come in and tell us about them? I was planning something of my own, but I don't want to infringe on another author or illustrator's idea."

Susan glanced in Miranda's direction. "They might need me downstairs."

"I'll get one of the other work-study students to cover the desk for you while you help us out, Susan. We're both eager to hear your perspective on this." Miranda left the office in search of one of the other students to sub for Susan for a while. For the first time she felt like they might have an opportunity to level the playing field.

Forty-five minutes later, Miranda sent Susan on her way. The young woman had provided a wealth of information about the author, the books, and the graphic novel's characters.

"She needs to eat more," Juliet said softly.

"She and I have had several conversations on that subject. I think she has a boyfriend with whom she shares an apartment. He must get the bulk of things."

Juliet's brows crimped. "Not a good situation."

"No." Miranda sighed her discontent. "I've approached

her several times and offered to help."

"You can offer, but it's up to her to make the change, Miranda." Juliet stared through the open office door after Susan. "Her name is Susan, but she's definitely not our Suzette. She doesn't look like someone who would hook up with Samuel Newton. And she's not a witch. Whoever is doing this is a witch, very powerful, and is fixated on the creatures in these books."

"I've given Chase all the background info on the student employees, contracted employees and fellow faculty. Maybe he'll find something I couldn't. In the meantime, I'm going to look up all the students and faculty who have checked out the graphic novels."

"That will be hundreds. From what she told us they're extremely popular."

"I know, but it might give us a list to compare to others."

"Chase has the info on the employees at the bar. He's looking hard at one of the bartenders who works with me. I'm certain I saw him outside the police station before the spider attack on the car. Samuel's psycho girlfriend had a brother named Justin."

"That sounds promising. If he's on the checkout list, we have a tie-in with this idea. Why don't you call Chase and update him on what we've discovered?"

Juliet laid aside the papers she'd taken notes on and reached for her cell phone.

✦   ✦   ✦

THERE HAD TO be some record of Clay Maddox once he'd left Superstition. He couldn't have just disappeared. Unless he'd left the country or was living under an alias. After what he'd done to Juliet and Mandy, he very well might have done both.

Caleb had been searching the web off and on for hours, and had looked through a number of Clay Maddox profiles. There were over a thousand, but none he'd looked at so far was the man he remembered. Since he had neither Clay's social security number nor birth date, his research was slow going.

And what the hell did he expect to do once he found the perverted fucker? Hunt him down and call him out? The painful repercussions of such a move would harm Miranda and Juliet. Juliet possibly the most. But dammit, there had to be something they could do about the son-of-a-bitch. What he'd done for ten long years had ruined their lives. He deserved to pay for it. And what if he'd moved on to someone else?

Caleb's concentration on the computer screen was broken by the jingle of the door opening and closing. He looked up to see one of the students from the library. He recognized her at once. "Hi. Vivian isn't it?"

"Yes, it is." She smiled. "And you're Caleb, Ms. Templeton's friend."

Caleb waited for her to continue.

She shifted close to the counter. "I'm having a problem with my car, and I was hoping you could help me."

Caleb shut down the computer search, grateful for something else to focus on. He got down from the stool he was perched on behind the counter. "Sure. What's the vehicle been doing?"

"I think it's leaking oil. I came out to go to work, and when I moved it there was dark fluid on the ground."

"We can put it up on the rack and see what's happening. It

might be a leaking seal."

She frowned, gripping her purse so hard her knuckles turned white. "Can't you look at it right now? I really need to get to work, but I was afraid if I waited it might damage the engine."

He leaned back to take a look through the heavy plate glass windows separating the office from the mechanic bays. "All the bays are full right now, and I wouldn't be able to track the leak from just looking at the engine. From underneath we'll be able to see where it's coming from. If you'll leave the keys, I'll pull it in as soon as I have a free bay."

"Well, if I have to leave it, can you give me a ride to the library?"

"Sure, I can arrange that. We can call you when we've figured out what it is and let you know what repairs if any are warranted."

Her frown cleared and changed into a smile. "That would be great."

He pulled out the form and filled it out with the problem cited by the customer, make, model, and color, and scooted it over the counter for her to sign.

He studied her long-sleeved blouse. Long sleeves in ninety-degree heat seemed odd, but she worked in an air conditioned library at night.

He slid the paper into a plastic sleeve and dropped the keys in with it. He hung the plastic bag on a hook reserved for work orders. He leaned in the door leading into the garage and yelled at Edgar, one of his mechanics. "I'm dropping a customer off at work. Next one up will be that blue Malibu parked out front."

Edgar threw up a hand. "Ten-four, boss." He disappeared back under the hood of the car he was working on.

Caleb turned and froze. Vivian stood across the counter, a Beretta pistol, too large for her hand, pointed at him. His heart rate soared and a quick rush of adrenaline flooded his body. "We don't keep much cash around, most of our business is done through check or credit card."

"I'm not interested in your money, Caleb. I want something much more important."

He judged his chances of survival if he rushed her. From this distance, even with the counter between them, there was no way she'd miss if she pulled the trigger.

"You know what I'm capable of. Unless you want your mechanics to die in an avalanche of spiders, you'll do what I say."

He met her gaze head on and recognized the unflinching resolve of a zealot. He'd seen enough of them in Afghanistan and Iraq.

"Come out from behind the counter. You're going to give me a ride, just like we planned."

He walked around the desk, his eyes never leaving her. She moved immediately to grip his arm and rest the barrel of the gun against his ribs. "Which vehicle?"

He'd parked Miranda's car just outside the door, and the keys were in his pocket, but his truck would be more difficult for her to get into and might create an opportunity for him to disarm her.

"My work truck is right over there." He nodded in the direction of the vehicle.

Vivian strode toward it with a no-nonsense gait, though he

tried to drag his feet. "You were a Marine, Caleb. Don't dishonor your brothers in arms by acting like you don't know how to march to a tune." Her gaze narrowed. "I can make you dance like a puppet if you force me to."

The thought of her power pouring through him made his skin crawl.

"Passenger side," she directed.

He opened the door and she waved him in. He'd barely rested his butt on the seat when she hopped in beside him, almost landing in his lap. The console dividing the seats held him captive as the pistol dug into his midsection. If she pulled the trigger he was a dead man.

"I can understand what Miranda sees in you. With your strong jaw and blue, blue eyes, you probably had to beat the girls off in every port. You have to have some smarts, too, to run your own business and survive two tours of duty overseas. If you use your brain instead of your brawn, you might just survive this." Her hazel eyes were as cold as her smile.

She lowered the gun and leaned back just enough for him to climb across the console and get behind the wheel.

"Just how long have you known Miranda and Juliet?"

"Since grade school." He started the truck.

"Turn right," she directed. "So you and both the Templetons are pretty close, aren't you?"

He wasn't interested in talking about his private life with her. It might help her find more leverage to use against the twins.

"I can tell from the way you and Miranda look at each other that there's more than friendship between you. And you're so protective of her. Of them both."

He glanced her way, but didn't speak.

"That's all right if you don't want to talk to me about them. I promise you, you will soon enough."

"Where are we going?" he asked.

"Somewhere you've been many times in the last six months. Having Juliet hanging around recently must have put a crimp in things. Or have you done them both? I've heard Juliet isn't as circumspect as her sister." She smiled, but it looked more like she was grinding her teeth. "Had you been at my door just begging for sex, I'd have taken you in."

He kept his eyes on the road and his expression controlled. No matter what happened, he wasn't telling this bitch a damn thing.

CHAPTER 26

C HASE SLAMMED THE car door with more force than necessary and jerked his seatbelt in place. Dammit! Justin Chalmers had quit his bartending job at Steampunk Alley two days ago, and according to his landlady had left his one bedroom apartment in a hurry an hour ago with a large suitcase. He was in the wind and dangerous as hell.

He and his sister Suzette were a lethal combination. Their own parents had barely survived them. During an earlier phone interview, their father hadn't said it straight out, but the records alone showed that the two had developed issues at an early age, and they'd left a swath of injured people in their wake, as well as at least one dead, Tanner Newton. Samuel Newton didn't know how lucky he was to have escaped.

And where the hell was Suzette Chalmers? He'd been through every employee record with the help of Garr and Underwood, and couldn't identify her. She had to be among the files he'd gotten from the library. There were no other connections between Miranda, Juliet, and Tanner Newton.

The files Miranda provided had photographs attached. He should take them to the hospital so Newton could identify the sister. He flipped open his phone and hit Garr's number. "Any other info on the women's files I gave you to go through?"

"I've finished the files on the bar employees and done

some telephone interviews to follow up on work history. None of the employers I've spoken to had an issue with any of the females. I've looked at social security numbers hard. Aside from a few unpaid parking tickets there are no red flags."

"Are you following up on Underwood's files?"

"No, but I'm about to right now. He hasn't gotten as far into them as I think he should have."

Chase wasn't surprised. "The files from the library have photos attached. Can you set them out like a photo array and make a copy of them for me? I'm going to take them to the hospital and see if Samuel Newton can identify the woman. His description of her could have been anyone. He said she had blonde streaked hair and hazel eyes. But the way women change their hair color—look closely at the social security numbers."

"Will do. I'll have the photo array ready by the time you get here."

"I'm on my way." He snapped the phone shut and reached for his seat belt. Ten minutes later he pulled into the precinct parking lot, jumped out of the car, and hotfooted it up the stairs and into the building. After seeing the crush waiting for the elevator, he decided to take the stairs.

Inside the office, Garr was waiting for him.

"This report on the photographic analysis just came in, and is weird as shit." He offered the folder to Chase.

He flipped open the paperwork and looked at the blown up, enhanced image of the shadow inside Gerald Abbott's cell. The hulking shape appeared to have substance, its long arms and hands hung at its side, but what drew Chase's attention were the tiny spiders gathering outside the cell in a swarm. He hadn't been able to see them on the video.

"And this is the report from the autopsy on Abbott." Garr handed him the next folder.

Chase didn't have to see the report to know what had killed the man. His insides had looked like soup with chunks of internal organs swimming in it. He got nauseous just thinking about it.

"Any ideas?" he asked.

Chase perused the document, then propped his hip on his own empty desk with a shake of his head. "I need to think this through." He turned away so Garr couldn't read his expression. "Underwood, have you run those social security numbers yet?"

Brian's face was sullen as he looked over his shoulder. "I've gotten about half of them done."

"Anything unusual?"

"I have something," Garr announced. He shot Brian a look that could have singed the hair off his head. "Vivian Suzette Chalmers-Ward. She drives a 2012 blue Chevy Malibu. She's registered at the college as Vivian Ward under her married name. Her husband died under mysterious circumstances, but she had an ironclad alibi provided by her brother, Justin Chalmers. She wiggled out from under the investigative team's thumb because of it." Garr handed Chase the copy of the information he'd compiled.

Vivian. He'd met her at the library when he went in to interview Miranda and Juliet yesterday afternoon. God, had it really been less than twenty-four hours? "I'll put out a BOLO on her, her brother, and the car."

"Why not an APB?" Underwood asked.

"We don't have the evidence to arrest them yet. I'd lay odds she was the one who paid Abbott and Porter to kill Juliet Templeton. Weed Keller was shot right after Tanner Newton's death. I can see her or her brother either one doing the deed themselves. If they still have the weapon and we can gain access to it, we'll have them for Weed's murder. I can't see any way of tying them to Porter or Abbott's deaths. Abbott made a statement, but he didn't know who paid them."

"She's been right under Miranda's nose at the library." Underwood lumbered to his feet, excitement kindling his eyes. "Probably gathering information about her and Juliet. Waiting to finish the job."

Was Underwood excited about the discovery, or was it the possibility the two people who knew about his assault on Juliet might end up dead?

Shit! Miranda and Juliet were at the library right now. Vivian and her brother could walk right in and take them out, and no one could stop them.

"We have to issue a BOLO with orders for the Chalmers not to be picked up, but to let us know if they're spotted. I don't want them getting rid of the gun if they haven't already. We have to tread lightly." His cell phone rang and he reached for it. It was Juliet.

"I have to take this. Garr, can you put out that BOLO? Instruct units to patrol the area around the library. Miranda and Juliet are there."

"I'm on it." He reached for the phone.

"Where are you?" he barked into the phone.

Juliet hesitated. "At the library where you left me."

"No. I mean where in the library?"

"Miranda's office, why?"

"Has Vivian Ward shown up for work yet?"

"No. She called in with car trouble and hasn't come in yet. Why?"

"She's Suzette, and she's dangerous as hell. Justin Chalmers is her brother, and they're working together. If they show up—" Shit, it would be carnage for the normal people in the library.

"She must be the one who picked him up in a blue Chevy near the police station. I couldn't see her in the driver's seat. It was too far away."

Chase's blood pressure spiked. The woman was going to kill him and get herself killed by holding back information. "Why didn't you tell me?"

"I didn't realize the make of the car would be important."

Jesus, he was going to stroke out. "Did you make those phone calls for me?"

"Yes, I have a couple of names for you."

He reached for a pad off of one of the nearby desks. "Give them to me. We may need them for backup." With the first name he turned to look over his shoulder and met Garr's gaze in surprise. No way. He wrote the other one down quickly.

"There's something else you need to know. The creatures they're using are from a graphic novel by an author named Sasha Carlton. One the students here recognized it from a doodle I was doing. We have one of the books here, and Miranda's running a search to see who's checked each copy out."

"I can't use a copy of a book to arrest them for murder."

"You can't, but I know of a council who can if we have

enough witnesses to their actions. And we already do, if we can prove it's them. They're dangerous, Chase. They both need to be put away."

"A council, huh?" Why wasn't he surprised?

At his lingering pause she said, "I told you we police ourselves." She cleared her throat, and he realized her voice was almost normal now. "They're using black magic. Probably have since they were old enough to master the Craft. It has a way of building up and turning on you."

"You keep telling me that, but it hasn't done them in yet."

"No, but their thinking won't be logical. Their behavior won't be, either. The way Vivian pushed Miranda, standing too close, being overbearing, her brother behaved the same way with me. They've lost their checks and balances. At this point they probably believe they're omnipotent, which makes them more dangerous than you can imagine."

She and Miranda had obviously been talking about everything they'd discovered. He could see where she was going with this a mile off. "I'm not taking a back seat on my case."

"Then you'll need some protection. Be sure to bring at least one of the guys I mentioned."

"All right. I will."

"If you could bring the spells you put into the evidence room it might be helpful. Miranda and I want to try a binding to block the power of the spell or at least lessen it."

"Okay." Not being able to call in regular backup seriously fucked everything up. "I'll be there in a few minutes. Faulkner is closer than I am. Call him for backup until I get there."

"He wouldn't be able to do any more than you will. Less, because he won't be armed."

"Miranda may need him. There was something going on with him the other night in the circle. The power poured off him."

Her response was slow. "That's…interesting. I'll ask Miranda about it."

He flipped off the phone with a flick of his thumb. Then he approached Hollis Garr. "I think we need to talk."

✧   ✧   ✧

HE WAS IN hell. He'd only thought the middle of the desert surrounded by bombed out buildings, refuges, the enemy, and wounded soldiers was hell. This was hell. The pain went on and on. His skin was on fire. So was the inside of his skull. He writhed in the kitchen chair where they had him tied and gritted his teeth to keep from screaming.

Vivian came into his line of sight, and the flow of energy cut off. "Tell me and all of this can stop."

No it wouldn't. She and her psychotic brother were going to kill him, whether he told them anything or not. He stalled by collecting himself through the lull, using techniques he'd learned in the Marines and used in combat, and prepared for the next round. What she wanted he couldn't give her. It would be like laying Miranda open to every moment of guilt and pain she'd experienced at Clay Maddox's hands, and he wouldn't do it. He wouldn't betray her.

Vivian grabbed him by the hair and jerked his head back. "Tell me, or so help me, I'll set you on fire and watch you burn."

He had to figure out how to let the power flow through him and back into her like he'd done with Miranda. If he could do that, it might burn her as badly as it did him and she'd stop.

His head hurt so much he barely felt when she tugged on his hair again. "Tell me, damn you."

"Fuck you." Was that slurred sound his voice? Hell, he sounded pretty good considering half his brain was fried.

With a wave of her hand she hit him again with that horrible, burning tidal wave of pain. This time he tried not to fight it, instead imagining it flowing over him, around him. The steady burn that threatened to burst his heart fell off a little, then entirely. The energy suddenly zipped through him and away.

A high-pitched squeal of pain was followed by a curse. "Damn you." Vivian rushed in front of him again and she swung her open palm like she was playing tennis and slapped him across the face, slamming his head sideways with the force of the blow. His cheek and jaw were lit by a different fire, then became numb. She grabbed his hair, and stuck her face close to his, her features twisted with rage, her skin red with it. Or was it the power she'd been frying him with? "How did you do that?"

"Go to hell." His words were less slurred this time, his vision clearer, although his cheek might be swelling already.

How long would it be before Edgar noticed he had been gone too long and started calling around? Would he know enough to call the library and ask Miranda where he was?

Damn, why did he always hold things so close to the vest? He was in love with Miranda Templeton, and the only people who knew were her sister and one friend. Why hadn't he crowed about it, so when he went missing they'd be out hunting for him?

Vivian picked up the Beretta she'd used to get him here and shoved it under his jaw. The sight at the end of the barrel dug into his skin. "You can't redirect a bullet, can you?"

He met the woman's gaze and tried not to think about what it would be like for the piece of metal to travel through his skull and take the top of his head off. "I love them both, and I'm not going to give you anything that will hurt them."

For the first time, Caleb was able to open his eyes wide enough to notice movement to the right when a man jumped down from his seat on the countertop next to the sink. "Leave him alone, Suz. You know enough to torment them both without having him say the words. You've dug up enough dirt to scorch them out of existence. Go ahead and kill him and be done with it?"

"No, not yet. I want to wait until they're both here, so Juliet can see what it's like to be responsible for her sister's pain."

Both the twins knew what it was to face pain and guilt. Everyone who lived knew something about it. Would these two have any concept of it, though? They were like simple children playing a vicious game.

"When the time is right, I'll send the shadows to harvest their emotions." Vivian said.

"Why? Because you can't feel anything yourself?" Caleb asked.

"Bastard. I feel plenty. I loved, Tanner. We were supposed to be together forever. I knew it the moment I met him. He looked at me and I just knew. But everyone got in the way. That bitch he was dating, his brother. Then Juliet Templeton got in the way. He was just too attractive to women. They all wanted him."

"And then you killed him."

"I didn't kill him. Juliet Templeton did."

He knew better than to antagonize her, but if he could plant a seed of doubt in her mind... "No, the men you hired to kill Juliet killed him. Accept it. His death is on you."

Vivian suddenly grew completely calm and her eyes went flat, predatory. "And so will yours be."

CHAPTER 27

MIRANDA PUSHED THE button on her cell phone one more time. She'd called Caleb three times. He hadn't picked up. Oh, he was probably just busy. He had his hands in an engine and couldn't reach his phone. The reassurances didn't calm her.

Something was wrong. She felt it. She dragged out the phone book from beneath a metal file holder and looked up the garage number. On the sixth ring a male voice answered, "Faulkner's Garage, Edgar speaking."

Anxiety sent a shiver of nervous tension through her, leaving her hands and feet cold. Juliet stood tense at her side. "Hello Edgar, this is Miranda Templeton, I've been calling Mr. Faulkner for the last twenty minutes, and I know he must be busy, but I really need to speak to him."

"He isn't here, Ms. Templeton. He left an hour ago to drop a customer off at work and hasn't come back."

Miranda's heart drummed against her throat and she began to shake. "What did this customer look like, Edgar?"

"I don't know. I had my head buried in an engine, but her car is still here."

Her. It was a woman. The realization offered her no comfort. "I know you're probably not supposed to give out information, and I understand that, but it's very important...

What kind of car is it?"

"A blue Chevy Malibu."

Miranda pressed her fingertips to her lips even as she murmured, "Please no, please no." She forced air into her lungs. "Is the name on the work ticket Vivian Ward?"

"I'll have to check." The sound of plastic rattling was followed by, "Yes, that's the name."

Fear swamped her and she couldn't breathe.

"Is something wrong, Ms. Templeton?"

"There may be. I'll send someone down there to talk to you."

The receiver clattered against the base as she hung up, her legs weak she lowered herself into the desk chair. "Please call Chase, Juls. Vivian has Caleb." Though her voice remained calm, it shook. She swallowed back a scream of denial. Was he already dead?

Please. Vivian couldn't take him from her. He was everything. Love, trust, everything, and she wouldn't survive losing him. She wouldn't want to.

Juliet rested a hand on her shoulder as she dialed the number. "You need to send someone down to Caleb's garage. Vivian's car is there. We believe she's taken Caleb."

Tears streamed down Miranda's face. An hour. Why hadn't Chase worked faster? If they'd known who Suzette Chalmers was earlier, Caleb would have been prepared.

What was that woman doing to him? Was she hurting him? Miranda couldn't bear even to think it.

The sound of hurried footsteps out in the commons area preceded Chase and the older detective they'd met after their attack. When they walked in, Chase's grim expression scared her even more. Garr closed the door and stood in front of it on guard.

"I've sent a unit to the garage with Underwood. They'll conduct a thorough search of the car and interview the men working there before taking it in. In the meantime, is there any way you can track Caleb's whereabouts? To get the phone company to access the GPS on his phone will take hours."

Juliet shook her head. "I don't know."

"Miranda, is there anything you can think of?"

She had to pull herself together. Caleb needed her. She dried her face with her hands and dried them on her slacks. "Edgar said he was giving her a ride to work. Caleb only has two vehicles, his motorcycle and his truck. It's a Ford. You can put that out so officers can be out looking."

Hollis Garr nodded. "I'm on it."

"Anything else you can do?"

"I don't know." She fought back a fresh wave of tears. "We need to call Aubrey and ask her. She may have some ideas." She reached for her cell phone, then hesitated. If they dragged Aubrey back into this situation, it might put her in danger. But she didn't know what else to do. She moved to hit Aubrey's number on the screen and the phone rang. It was Caleb's number.

Relief nearly crushed her. "Caleb?"

"No, but I'm certain you know my voice," Vivian said from the other end of the line.

"Don't hurt him, Vivian. He has nothing to do with what you feel is between us."

Chase and Garr froze.

"Too late. You weren't here for me to take my frustration

out on. Do you know how irritating your perfect princess routine is, Miranda?"

A fuzzy, disconnected feeling swept over her, and she fought it off. If she'd hurt Caleb... "Do you know how irritating your pushy broad routine is, Vivian? Let me speak to Caleb."

"In good time. Is your sister around? I'd like to speak to her."

Miranda motioned to Juliet. "I'm putting you on speaker phone."

"Go ahead. I'm sure Juliet's pet police officer is there listening." Her voice filled the room. "You know it isn't to our advantage to conduct business in front of the general public. It only gets the regular humans stirred up. In fact, the two of you broke the rules when you brought in Detective Robinson. I'm not interested in confusing the situation any more than it already is. So we'll play it straight."

"After last night's little Mexican standoff, I thought a duel might work out better for all of us. You and Miranda against me and my brother. Winner gets to claim Caleb Faulkner and do with him as they see fit. I already have something in mind I'm sure he'll enjoy much more than he did being with you, Miranda."

Miranda slumped against the desk as some of her anxiety eased. Caleb was still alive. *Thank you, Goddess.*

Juliet's eyes already burning with rage, and power settled on her face, Miranda nodded. "You're on, Vivian. Where do we meet, and when?"

"Where everybody meets in this two-bit Podunk town. The library. After closing, of course. I'll leave it up to you two to get rid of the security guards—unless you want them to get hurt. Be sure to leave Detective Robinson and his sidekick at home. I know all about Detective Garr's extra activities. He doesn't want to be a part of this unless he's ready to die."

"Put Caleb on, Vivian," Miranda said when it seemed she might hang up.

"Mandy?" Her heart leapt in relief and joy at the sound his voice. He sounded tired.

"I love you, Caleb. We'll be together soon."

"First thing, we'll go out for a burger and fries like yesterday."

"Whatever you want. Are you okay?"

"See you tonight at the library," Vivian's voice came across the phone, then nothing.

"What did he mean about the burger and fries yesterday?" Chase asked.

"He brought burgers to the house yesterday for lunch." Juliet answered.

Miranda gasped and glanced at her, a small ray of hope blooming. "They're at my house. Caleb changed the locks, and he still has the keys."

✧   ✧   ✧

JULIET STARED AT the random destruction wreaked throughout her sister's home. A deep, powerful rage built to add to the concern for Caleb clutching at her stomach.

Miranda was hanging on by her fingernails. She'd finally found a man she trusted and was building something special with him, and his kidnapping had devastated her. Her home being trashed added to her stress. She wandered around the kitchen like a lost soul, picking up broken dishes and placing them in a plastic bucket.

Chase looked like he could bite a bullet in two like a pistachio and spit the casing out for the shell. "We can write up a report, Miranda."

"And what? Fine them for vandalism?" Her laugh held a bitter hardness. "Forget it. These are just things. If they hurt Caleb, though, they'd better find a center-of-the-earth-deep hole to hide in." She threw the pieces of a small pottery bowl in the bucket.

"I'll empty that in your trash out back, Miranda," Hollis Garr said. "It's all right if I call you Miranda, isn't it?"

"Sure."

"They didn't find my gun, which is a good thing," Juliet said.

"Gun?" Chase's brows rose.

"It's a Sig, and yes, I have a permit to carry." She shot him as deep a frown as he was giving her, and grabbed Miranda's arm before she bent to pick up another sliver of glass from the floor. "Come back into the bedroom with me for a minute."

She pulled Miranda down the hall and into the bedroom. Vivian and Justine hadn't had time to trash this room or the guest room, only the kitchen and the living room. The soft peach comforter still covered the bed, smooth and perfectly aligned. Everything seemed in place.

The best way to distract her sister was to jump into planning how they meant to break Vivian and Justin. And they would have to be broken, their magic destroyed, in order for justice to be done. "You can't allow your anger to rule you when we go into the library tonight, Miranda."

"I know." The panic she'd suppressed bubbled up like lava. "He sounded okay didn't he? A little worn but he sounded normal."

To cover her own shaky composure, Juliet wrapped her arms around her sister and held on tight. "He sounded tough. And he knew what he was doing when he mentioned the burgers."

"You don't think they punished him for it, do you?"

Yeah, she did, but nothing on earth would get her to say so. "He's going to get through this, and the two of you will be fine."

When Miranda's arms tightened and she buried her face against her shoulder she was reminded of how often she'd done the same years ago. Her sister felt guilty for not being able to protect her. But in truth, Juliet felt just as guilty for dumping that burden on her. "When I went with Chase to see Father Clarence, he said we would need to band together to face this. I didn't think he knew what he was talking about, but I believe he was right."

Miranda pulled back to reach for a tissue from a box on the nightstand.

Juliet looked around the room. "How do you sleep in here? I'd be afraid I'd wrinkle the sheets."

Miranda laughed, though her eyes and nose were red. "And I'd be afraid I was sharing the bed with a litter of mice in yours. Do you ever make it?"

Juliet grinned. "Not if I can help it." She sat down on the area rug next to the bed in a lotus position and Miranda joined her.

Then Juliet's face turned serious. In order to survive, they had to set aside the sackfuls of negative emotions they'd both lugged around for so long. "No more guilt for anything that happened, Miranda. You read the same passages about the shadows as I did. They'll be waiting to extract any negative emotion from us any way they can, and that's what increases their power."

"I know."

She leaned forward and grasped Miranda's hands. "No more. We've paid for everything, and then some. Justice has been served."

"I agree."

Juliet studied her. "You're saying it, but do you really believe it?"

Miranda's face was earnest. "Yes, I do. But you have to promise me something. Whatever happens tonight, you won't feel guilty. Vivian and her brother won't hold back, and they won't have any compunction about harming or killing us. We may have to use lethal force. If it comes to that, we leave it behind after it's over."

An it harm none, do what ye will was more than a belief. It was etched into their souls. To go beyond it would be a terrible thing to live with. Miranda knew that better than she. "I agree."

"I think a little meditation is exactly what I need. Then we'll do the bonding spell and return to the library to prepare."

Juliet nodded, then straightened into her lotus position and closed her eyes. They would do binding spells to limit the power of the creatures, but there was no guarantee they would work. Vivian would write more and renew their power. And then there were the spiders and several other nasty surprises mentioned in the book. But for now they would let it all go and prepare themselves for battle.

CHAPTER 28

C HASE HAD NEVER felt more useless. He was supposed to be the one to capture and put away the bad guys. The Chalmers had committed a crime and left behind proof guaranteed to put them in prison, and he couldn't arrest them. They probably wouldn't be around to serve a day in jail, and there wasn't a prison built that could hold them. They were responsible for five deaths. They deserved life behind bars.

The alternative Juliet and Miranda had come up with was just and damn clever—if they could pull it off.

From his position on the second floor, he watched Miranda work behind the checkout desk as though it were any other night. He'd been amazed at her composure when she and Juliet had emerged from her bedroom. Even if she had glanced at the clock a hundred times in the last hour, she was still holding it together.

Juliet and Hollis Garr exited the second floor elevator and sauntered over to stand with him at the railing. "How did it go?"

"They're taking a long, restful nap in the lounge downstairs," Hollis said.

"How can you be sure they'll stay asleep?"

Juliet glanced up from under her brows. "Even if they don't, they're locked in and won't get out until Hollis releases them." Her mouth tightened and a line appeared between her eyebrows as she eyed the clock.

Chase rested a hand against the small of her back to comfort her and felt the revolver tucked into the waistband of her jeans. Dammit, there was just something hot about a woman who could both shoot a gun and zap someone with magic. When this was over, he was going to find out what it was like to spend some time with her without having psychotic killers trying to take her out before he could.

He grimaced at his own cop humor. It didn't keep the tightness of concern from cramping his stomach. This had to be Juliet and Miranda's show, and he didn't like it one bit. His every protective instinct was screaming there had to be something he could do.

The midnight chime sounded and students wandered by, heading for the stairs. Needing something to do, he backed away from the railing. "I'll go up on the third floor and check to make sure everyone is out."

"Be watchful. There's a chance she left some surprises behind we didn't find," Hollis cautioned.

"I'll go with you. I need to keep moving." She shot Hollis a look and he nodded.

He'd noticed how the two of them had fallen into partner stance as soon as they reached the library.

Juliet fell into step with him as they climbed the stairs to the third floor.

"You okay?" he asked.

"Yes. I'm more concerned for Miranda than myself. If they've hurt Caleb, or worse, she won't be able to hold it together, and the emotion spell we've done might not be able to buffer everything."

He realized what a responsibility both women carried to harbor so much power and yet force themselves to use it sparingly or not at all. If they turned it on the Chalmers in rage, the entire plan would come apart at the seams.

They reached the landing on the third floor. When she started to go one way and he the other, he turned and walked beside her. He wasn't leaving her alone for a moment. These might be their last moments together. "How do you feel?"

She drew in a breath. "As ready as I'll ever be. We've been practicing all afternoon. And we've been on the phone with Aubrey off and on all day. We didn't want to drag her back into this. Miranda's a little rusty, but she'll be okay."

"You didn't really go all these years without using your abilities."

"For the most part, yes. But there were times the pressure would build up inside me and I'd have to go out into the mountains, away from everyone, and let off some steam. More than a little. I'm a fire witch. I'm kind of like a solar panel, gathering energy all the time." She pushed open the men's bathroom door and went inside while he stood on the threshold. "Clear."

"And Miranda?" He shoved open the ladies' room door and saw at a glance it was empty. "Clear."

"I think she really held herself to a higher standard and completely denied herself. Being a water witch, she was able to distance herself from her element a little better than I could."

He had been focused on the dynamic between the two women the entire time he was with them. There was more to the story than they were admitting. "You mean punish herself."

She remained silent for a moment. "We both did."

They fell into a tense silence as they patrolled the rest of the floor.

"I've done a little digging. I discovered what a sleazebag your stepfather was. He'd pissed a lot of business associates off and cheated them out of money before he disappeared." They walked down the stairs to the second floor.

"Yes."

"There were other criminal allegations before he married your mother. Allegations of a different nature that were dropped from lack of evidence when the woman and daughter left the state and refused to testify."

Juliet stopped at the foot of the stairs and braced her feet apart to face him. "They weren't just allegations at our house. And our mother turned a blind eye."

Jesus. Having what he'd suspected verified hit him with the force of a roundhouse punch. He wanted to take her in his arms and offer her comfort, but to do so now might undermine her resolve in the coming minutes.

He probed her eyes, her face. A man didn't just disappear without any trace unless something permanent had happened to him. The pieces of the puzzle fell into place. It would have been Miranda, protecting Juliet. The signs where there.

He was an officer of the law, and it wasn't his place to sit in judgment, only to apprehend. But in this case he couldn't divorce his feelings. And no evidence existed. He'd bet it had gone up in flames long ago. And without a body, he wasn't interested in trying to build a case. Or air their childhood traumas for the world. They'd more than paid for anything that had happened.

Besides, they were putting their life on the line to take two murderers off the street. Juliet was right. Mother Nature had a way of balancing things out.

"Sometimes criminals like your stepfather get exactly what they deserve. I figure one of his business associates took care of him."

Her throat worked as she swallowed, but she remained stiff with tension.

He reached for her and cupped her face in his hands. "You told me you were working on some things before you wanted to date again. And I know my timing sucks, but how long do you think those things might take?"

Her fingers looped around his wrists and she searched his face.

"No pressure. But I care about you, Juliet. If you never want to see me again after all this is over, I'll go with that, but—"

"I want to."

Those three words released his tension and hers, and they both took a deep breath. "How long?" He was being pushy, but dammit, he wanted this. Wanted her. And he wanted her to know he had her back.

"I don't know. I have a lot of baggage."

"I'm strong. I can help you carry it."

Her eyes grew glassy with tears.

If she cried, he'd lose it. He covered her lips with his, and he was careful to keep the pressure soft, undemanding, just a comforting connection between them. Her hands slid from his wrists. She leaned into him and slipped her arms up his back to hold him.

This might be the only time they had together. He wanted more. He wanted her to want more. And then his wish was granted. Her lips parted, and his tongue reached for hers. The kiss flared, torrid with desperation. He tasted her passion, felt her need to be close. His hands dropped from her cheeks and he reached for her, molding her against him. She smelled like citrus and her. Her breasts nestled in against his ribs.

A cracking sound from downstairs intruded, and he raised his head. Every muscle clenched in sudden alertness.

Miranda's sharp, alarmed, "Caleb!" tore them apart.

"If this goes south, don't hesitate to use your gun, Chase. They're too dangerous for human and witch alike. Stay hidden until it's over. She'll use you against me if she can." Juliet ran for the stairs.

✧   ✧   ✧

JULIET'S HEART CAUGHT at the sight of Caleb suspended in midair twenty feet from the ground. The entire room was nothing but hard surfaces, so if he dropped, it would kill him.

Miranda's face glowed white with fear as she looked up at him. He appeared to be unconscious. His limbs hung limp and his chin rested against his chest. Dried blood darkened the front of his T-shirt, and bruises marred his forehead and jaw. One eye appeared to be swollen shut.

Vivian sauntered further into the commons area while Justin turned and closed the two large, wooden front doors. He twisted the lock and announced, "All snuggled in, secure and safe."

Without his Goth makeup and gelled hair, the resemblance between him and Vivian was as striking as were the pair's gleeful faces while they soaked in Miranda's fear. She came out from behind the desk, knocking a book from the counter to the floor. She ignored it.

Juliet's heart drummed against her ribs so hard it hurt. She slowed her pace and sauntered down the stairs in an unhurried gait, refusing to look up at Caleb's body again. She shoved away the idea that he might already be dead and what it might do to Miranda and her. If he was...the two witches before them would pay with their lives.

She stopped at the bottom of the stairs and rested a hand on the wooden banister. She looked from Justin to the Vivian. "Why don't you quit fucking around and get to it?"

Justin's smile died, a small hint of uncertainty around his eyes. After a brief pause Vivian threw her head back and laughed. "If that's what you want." With a flick of her hand, Caleb's body plummeted like dead weight toward the check-in desk.

Miranda shouted out a command and a large bubble encompassed him, catching him inches from the ground. She rushed toward him, only to have her way blocked by a slithering mass of black snakes. They hissed and rose to strike at her, and she staggered back.

Justin yelled as he was jerked toward the skylight by an invisible bungee cord, coming to a stop upside down, hanging by one foot only a few inches below the skylight. His eyes looked round with shock. "God dammit, put me down. Suz, get me down."

Juliet squelched her momentary satisfaction. He was the follower, the weak link between them, but just as deadly. He'd hung around her trying to worm his way into a date. Had she agreed to go out with him, he and his sister would have killed her without a second thought.

"You know your physics theories, Vivian?" Juliet asked. "For every action there will be an opposite and equal reaction. There are descriptions used in other contexts. An eye for an eye. Karma's a bitch. That kind of thing."

Juliet gestured the symbol for snake. A tiny serpent crept out from behind Vivian's ear and dropped to her shoulder. The woman yelped, jerked it free of her hair and tossed it to the ground. It curled around to face her and lifted up, ready to strike.

Justin continued to scream above them. They both ignored him.

"What kind of action do you believe should result from your killing Tanner?"

Vivian's features turned sullen and angry. "I didn't kill Tanner. You did. If you'd left him alone he'd still be here with me."

"How was I supposed to know to leave him alone, Vivian? I'm a witch, not psychic. You never called. You never wrote. I wonder why? Could it be because you'd already done those things before and you were afraid he'd know you were stalking him again?"

Vivian whispered something under her breath, and a pool of black appeared at Juliet's feet. A bulbous head rose from the center, followed by narrow shoulders and a wide, concave chest. His long arms hung to his knees and his legs spread thin and bowed.

Looking into that blank, blackish-gray face was like looking into the pit of pain and guilt she had suffered since she was thirteen. But he had no eyes, no heart to see what was inside her. She had known those feelings long enough. But the memory gripped her of how those on the street had screamed—hungry, furious. At the quick pinch of fear she stepped back. Would the emotional buffering Miranda and she had created hold? Even if it did, she still needed to control her emotions.

She glanced toward Miranda to find her sister facing a similar creature, and standing protectively between it and Caleb. Concern choked her, and she turned away. If she watched too long, she'd be so frightened for Miranda it might set the thing off. She had to get her own emotions under control. She reached for the moment of peace during meditation and her feelings leveled out.

The creatures swayed from side to side, waiting for either a signal from Vivian or for Juliet's emotions to rise.

"You hired the men who killed Tanner. They beat him, beat him until he couldn't stand or defend himself. Then stomped him. Kicked him. He was one of the most decent human beings I've ever known, and they killed him. You created the situation that caused his death. And for what?"

"I never meant for him to die." For the first time Juliet saw remorse, but it quickly passed, to be overpowered by her Vivian's rage. "I just wanted rid of you. He was with you everywhere. He walked you home every night. He ate dinner at your apartment. Spent the night there. *With you.*" Her voice rose with her rage. "If you had left him alone, he'd still be here. We were meant to be together."

"If you'd loved him enough to walk away, he'd still be

alive. That's what love is Vivian. Sacrifice."

She glanced at Miranda for a brief moment. "I'm going to show you what you did, Vivian. What you took from us all." Juliet's hand shook as she gestured to the empty area before her. Her throat tightened with grief, and she quickly shut down her pain. She closed her eyes, pulled the memories from her, and set them free, producing more than just a movie screen. The room was filled with a three-dimensional image of what had taken place on the street that night. Juliet turned her face away to keep from watching. Every moment was imprinted on her psyche.

A quick moment of Tanner laughing, watching television with his feet propped on the coffee table, reaching out a hand to grasp hers, was followed by the attack. The meaty thuds and grunts were animalistic as Abbott, hyped up on cocaine, punched, kicked and stomped Tanner into unconsciousness while Porter held her by the hair and twisted her arm behind her back until he dislocated her shoulder. She screamed in pain. Her anger and fear had screamed with it. His high-pitched squeals when she set him on fire echoed through the room. Abbott ran to him and beat the flames with his hands, so hyped on drugs he didn't feel the pain. The two ran back to their car and peeled away.

Tanner's labored breathing filled the room, his broken ribs and punctured lungs making it sound soupy as blood rushed in to drown him.

"This is what you took from us, Vivian. What you did. What you caused."

Vivian's face was pasty white when she approached the image and stood over Tanner.

Justin's voice rose, high-pitched and desperate, as he twisted and turned to try to escape Juliet's tether above them. "Vivian, don't listen to her. It wasn't you, it was them, and we killed them. They're dead now." His face twisted and he balled his fist.

A glowing orb of power shot down at Miranda, and she threw up an arm and a shield against it, its impact spreading out, dissipated by her defense. She yelped in pain as some of the residual energy showered blue down on her, and she leapt away. With an angry glare at Justin above her, she thrust a hand out and the energy pooled in her palm.

Juliet released her spell, and he hurtled toward the floor just as Caleb had done. He caught himself feet from the hard tile, but stumbled as he found his footing. Miranda hit him in the back of the head with his own ball-shaped energy. He tumbled forward into a slithering stream of snakes.

He yelped and surged to his feet.

Vivian shouted, *"Umbra exsisto hic."* Black pools filled the tiled floor, so dense only inches of space remained between them. Shadow creatures struggled up out of the depths from the center of each one.

Miranda kicked the book at her feet out of the way and it slid forward, the pages opening in a flutter. She faced off with the creature before her.

The fifty or more shadows around them screamed in unison. Juliet flinched and covered her ears.

"Look at him, Vivian." Juliet yelled when their screams subsided. "What would you say to Tanner now? I'm sorry? What good would it do? He's dead. You'll never have him. And he'll never be able to love you. He'll never be able to love anyone."

"Shut up," Justin shouted, his features twisted with fear and rage. The shadows around him skimmed closer, hemming him in. "She's doing to you what you were supposed to do to her, Suzette. She's the one who should feel guilty, she's the one who caused his death."

Vivian moved closer to Tanner's image. "He would have loved me if you hadn't taken him." Her eyes began to glow with emotion. For a moment Juliet thought she saw tears glaze the woman's eyes. She jerked around to face the creatures standing sentinel behind her. "Kill them! Kill them both!"

Everything went still, silent. The shadows wove back and forth, sightless, seeking emotion. Juliet turned to look at Miranda and raised a fist in a signal to hold on. She braced herself for their attack. Would anything she tried work to fight them off? They turned en masse toward Miranda, and her heart skipped a beat. "No!" The word escaped her in a whisper. She stumbled backwards, up two stairs, and realized they weren't going for Miranda, but Justin.

He screamed as two of the creatures locked onto his arms. His panic drew others blindly, hungrily.

Vivian's shout was just as panicked. "No! No! Not him— them!" She pointed toward Juliet and Miranda, but the creatures were blind to all but emotion. "Not him!" She shoved her way through the sea of black, and for a moment she was almost obscured. They couldn't attack her, she was their creator, but Justin was just another unprotected source of emotion they could drain to feed their hunger.

Juliet slipped along the wall behind the creatures, and, reaching Miranda, gripped her hand. "We have to do it now.

While they have him."

They clasped hands and gathered as much energy as they could. A full moon beamed down through the panes overhead.

While she spoke in Latin, Miranda spoke the words in English.

"From characters inside a book you began.

To characters you will end.

Into the book you must all descend."

A heavy whistling sound filled the room as air began to drag and pull at their clothing. The pages of the book Miranda had kicked whipped back and forth. The first shadow reached it and was sucked into its pages, then the next. The snakes Vivian had called forth streamed through the air, their hisses lost in the cry of the wind, their tails a lash that could maim or blind.

With each creature's disappearance the speed with which the next was sucked in increased. The two who held Justin hostage were dragged forward, their bodies elongating as they sought to continue feeding off his emotions and kill him. One wrenched its hand free of the vacuum's pull and plunged it into his chest.

Justine's scream was an inhuman warble wracked with torment. Vivian leaped forward and tore the thing's grip from him and attempted to cover his body with her own.

The wind ripped at Juliet's clothing, flinging her ponytail over her shoulder and into her eyes making them sting. Miranda shook head to clear her own vision. "We have to end it."

"For your own good, for others' safety,

You will be locked away for all eternity."

One of the shadows lost its grip and was pulled away, but the other clung like a tick, dragging Justin with it. Creature and man's feet disappeared into pages while Justin's anguished scream filled the cavernous space.

Vivian, realizing the danger, tried to pry his fingers loose from her arm and roll away. Her teeth clenched in a grimace as his fingernails dug into her arm, leaving bloody trails. He threw an arm around her neck.

"Don't let me go, Suzette," he cried. Desperate and beyond panic, he clung to her. His torso disappeared until only his head and arm remained free. Vivian braced her hands on the floor and heaved back to either pull him free or break his grip. A long, grayish-black arm extended from the pages then, its huge hand tangling in Vivian's hair, pulling her off balance until she fell headfirst into the book, her feet kicking like someone plunged into deep water, struggling to surface.

Caleb's protective bubble slid forward, heading for Vivian's scissoring legs.

The vortex they'd created was intensifying and was about to suck him in! Juliet tore her hands free. "Get him." Her tennis shoes squeaked as she twisted toward the book. Miranda released the bubble and nearly collided with her as she rushed forward.

Vivian's shriek echoed as she was sucked all the way down into the pages. Juliet dove head-first, using her body to block Caleb's momentum, and his greater weight struck her from behind, shoving her forward. Her arm sank elbow-deep into the pages and she gasped as something gripped her wrist and pulled hard.

Fingers grabbed the waistband of her jeans and wrenched

her back. A large foot encased in a black dress shoe kicked the book closed and stomped on it. The immediate silence lay poised like the moment following a laugh. She looked up at Hollis Garr. He stood on the cover of the book with all his weight.

"Thanks."

He grinned so hugely his wrinkles had wrinkles. "My pleasure." He carefully scooped up the book and deposited it into the lead-lined box he'd shown up with earlier. There was a satisfying click as he locked it. "The council will be keeping this."

Juliet turned, and found herself folded close in Chase's arms. "I've heard of losing yourself in a good book, but you damn near took it too far, Juliet." Still panting from the near miss, she threw her arms around him and rested against his broad chest. His heart beat hard beneath her ear. His arms tightened around her.

"Juliet." Miranda's voice broke on a sob.

No. This couldn't end in tragedy. They'd come too far in three days to have it end badly. She sat up to look past Chase's arm to Miranda. She cradled Caleb's head tenderly in her lap, tears streaming down her face.

"No." After everything they'd been through, if Caleb were to die...Juliet pushed free of Chase's embrace. The hard tile floor bit into her knees as she crawled to her sister. She swept her gaze over Caleb's battered features.

"He won't wake up," Miranda breathed.

He lay still, the rise and fall of his chest shallow but regular.

Exhaustion weighted Juliet's limbs. The huge expenditure

of power had drained their resources. If he was badly injured, they might not be able to heal him.

Her hand shook as she extended her palm over him and drew a meager healing power to her. She slowly swept it over Caleb in search of an injury. The bruises on his face drained some of it away and she paused there a moment, then moved down over her chest, stomach and his lower limbs to his knees.

"It isn't an injury that's keeping him asleep. And I don't sense any drugs."

"It's a spell?" Miranda's hand flew to her throat. "Since Vivian created it, we may not be able to break it."

"You just sucked two psychotic witches into a book they were obsessed with…" Chase paused, then grimaced.

"What is it?" Juliet asked.

"It sounds corny as hell, but maybe Vivian put Caleb to sleep like Sleeping Beauty."

A picture of Vivian holding a book about that fairy tale flashed through her mind. Juliet could picture the sadistic pleasure the woman would have gotten when she kissed Caleb awake only to tell him she'd killed the woman he loved.

Miranda had nothing to lose. "Kiss him," she urged.

The hope and love she read in Miranda's face as she gazed lovingly at her man brought a quick rush of tears. Miranda eased his head off her lap and curled her legs beneath her. Holding her hair back away from his face she bent and pressed her lips to his.

A moment then two passed, and she kissed him again. "Caleb, please wake up."

Caleb's breath hitched, and one of his hands twitched.

Juliet's hope latched on and clung, waiting for a reason to

rejoice. Chase took a step closer and rested his hand on her shoulder. She reached for it and gripped his fingers tight.

Caleb's lids rose and he blinked, perhaps to clear his vision. His smile was something special. "Hey, Mandy." He sat up enough to pull her close, and two clung together. Without releasing her he looked around the room. "Wow, look at that mess."

Juliet took in the destruction. Papers were strewn around like a ticker tape parade had driven through, hundreds of books littered the floor, and the two of them looked a little disheveled.

Caleb smoothed Miranda's hair from his face. "What did I miss?"

EPILOGUE

MIRANDA STUDIED HER kitchen with deep satisfaction. Boxes with her name on them lined one side of the room, and on the other, near the small kitchen table, stood boxes with Juliet's name on them.

And at the moment her sister seemed to be taking a break to read one of the many newspapers she'd gathered to wrap her stuff. Joining her, she bumped Juliet's hip with her own. "Hey, you're supposed to be helping me pack."

"I am, I'm just reading this article in the paper about Bobby Bush."

Miranda looked over her shoulder at the picture on the front page of the Superstition Times. Bobby's normally perfect hair was ruffled, and his tie hung askew. His hands were cuffed behind him so he couldn't hide his face from the cameras. The story hadn't only been in the Times; it had hit every paper in the state. Beside him, gripping his arm, his features grim, Chase Robinson was leading him to a patrol car.

"He's finally gotten what he deserved years ago. Sleazebag." She met Juliet's gaze and smiled. "Karma's a bitch, isn't it?" The two of them laughed.

"I may be imagining it, but it seems Detective Robinson's name has been in the paper more and more recently."

Juliet smiled. "Yeah, it is. Did you read where Brian Underwood left the police force? Rumor has it he was going to be demoted back to patrol officer but quit instead."

"I heard the same rumor." She raised a brow. And her gaze flicked back to the picture of Chase. "He's settling injustices for you, Juliet."

"I know." Her voice softened.

"Has he called?"

"A few times to check in on me."

"And?"

"We had an agreement. We'd hold off seeing each other for a few months until I got deeper into my therapy."

The stirrings of hope fluttered in Miranda's belly, and she turned aside to hide quick tears. She wrapped another coffee cup in newspaper. "That was a responsible thing to do, and a brave one." Her throat hurt with the attempt to conceal her emotions. She'd waited so long to find happiness herself, and she wanted desperately for Juliet to find it too.

She stuffed the cup in the box and turned back to Juliet. "We could use an extra pair of hands and some strong shoulders to help us load and unload," she suggested.

Juliet bit her lip. "I went a lot of years and slept with some questionable men looking for something they couldn't give me. I couldn't feel things. They couldn't even give me pleasure at first. Then I finally discovered a couple who could and thought maybe it was a way to feel better. But I didn't. I couldn't feel anything in here." She pointed to her heart. "I tried so hard with Tanner." Grief shadowed her face, but she contained it. "I'm afraid to try again. And I'm afraid not to."

"You've grieved for him for months, Juls. I think you did love Tanner, but were afraid to acknowledge it. And I was the same way with Caleb. But I took a chance, and it worked out beautifully. Chase may be that one man who'll break through everything and help you find what you need."

"Well, he has given me something I couldn't get for myself."

"What's that?"

"Closure. The cops aren't stopping me anymore to ogle my bartending leathers." She held up the newspaper. "Bobby Bush has gotten exactly what he deserved. And Brian Underwood has been outed for the fat, lazy, sadistic bully he is."

"After all that, I think Chase deserves at least a chance. If he didn't really care about you, he wouldn't have put himself out there to make things right."

"No he wouldn't have, would he?" She looked one last time at the photograph, then reached for another coffee cup off the island. She rolled the paper around it and Miranda turned away in disappointment.

The rattling of the paper stopped and she glanced up. Juliet pulled the paper free, set it aside and reached for a different piece.

Miranda smiled and emptied the last few cabinets of dishes onto the counter to be packed.

Caleb came to the door carrying a large box. His blond hair was mussed and the muscles of his upper arms bulged with the weight. "Hey, hon, you forgot to write what room you want this in. Want to write it on there real quick? I'm about to make a trip to the house and unload."

Miranda smiled. "I'll go with you." She turned to look over her shoulder. "We'll be back in a little while."

Juliet nodded and kept working.

✧   ✧   ✧

NOW HER SISTER was gone, Juliet pulled the article back to her and smoothed it out. She studied Chase's photograph. He'd waited for her more patiently than she ever thought he would. Miranda was right. He was setting things right for her.

She'd relived Chase's kiss a hundred times. No, she was lying to herself, it was at least a thousand.

Why not call him? They could take things slow. An instant excitement assailed her and she smiled. She set aside the paper and reached across the counter for her cell phone.

He picked up on the second ring. His resonant, masculine hello set off a nervous quiver, making it difficult for her to catch her breath.

"I don't suppose you have some free time on a Sunday afternoon to help a lady move, do you?"

"Move where?"

Instead of taking umbrage at his sharp tone, she smiled. "I'm not going far. Well, actually, Miranda and I are both in the middle of a move." She wasn't doing this very well, but she felt tongue-tied and anxious. "She's moving in with Caleb and I'm moving into her house. I'm there now."

"I'm on my way. I'll be there in ten minutes."

He was just as brusque and decisive as he'd been when they first met.

She rushed to the bathroom to wash up and check her appearance. Yikes! She didn't have on a scrap of makeup, and her hair was tied back in a messy ponytail. Maybe she should have thought this through a little more. She washed the newsprint from her face and hands and brushed her hair.

The doorbell rang, and she scrambled to tuck the wisps of

hair that hung on either side of her face behind her ears.

Nerves battled with her eagerness as she opened the door. Chase's eyes were still icy blue, but full of a warmth that triggered a flutter in the pit of her stomach. Dressed in jeans and a sweater, his tall frame looked muscular and fit. His shoulders seemed somehow broader as they stretched against his sweater. The late afternoon October sun turned his blond hair to silver.

Her mouth dried with a swift sweep of physical longing. She cleared her throat in an attempt to speak.

"No one's ever fought my battles for me the way you have."

"I wasn't around when you needed someone to do it, but I'm here now."

She felt his words touch the tender, hungry part of her heart and had to fight back tears. "I don't need you to carry my baggage for me. I just need you to give me a hand to cling to now and then while I do it."

Chase nodded. "I can do that, Juliet."

She extended a hand to him, and when he clasped it she drew him into the house and shut the door. They grabbed each other as if it had been a year instead of four months, clumsy in their eagerness.

His voice was husky as he tilted her face up to him. "I've been waiting weeks for your call."

"I'm so glad you did."

Then he kissed her. There was hope in this kiss, with this man. She'd been waiting a lifetime for this moment. With an open heart, she embraced it.

ABOUT THE AUTHOR

New York Times and USA Today bestselling author Teresa Reasor was born in Southeastern Kentucky, but grew up a Marine Corps brat. The love of reading instilled in her in Kindergarten at Parris Island, South Carolina made books her friends during the many transfers her father's military career entailed. The transition from reading to writing came easily to her and she penned her first book in second grade. But it wasn't until 2007 that her first published work was released.

After twenty-one years as an Art Teacher and ten years as a part time College Instructor, she's now retired and living her dream as a full time Writer.

Her body of work includes both full-length novels and shorter pieces in many different genres, Military Romantic Suspense, Paranormal Romance, Fantasy Romance, Historical Romance, Contemporary Romance, and Children's Books.

Books by Teresa J. Reasor

BREAKING FREE (BOOK 1 of the SEAL TEAM HEARTBREAKERS)
BREAKING THROUGH (BOOK 2 of the SEAL TEAM HEARTBREAKERS)
BREAKING AWAY (BOOK 3 of the SEAL TEAM HEARTBREAKERS)
BUILDING TIES (BOOK 4 of the SEAL TEAM HEARTBREAKERS)
TIMELESS
WHISPER IN MY EAR
DEEP WITHIN THE SHADOWS
HIGHLAND MOONLIGHT
CAPTIVE HEARTS

SHORT STORIES
AN AUTOMATED DEATH
TO CAPTURE A HIGHLANDER'S HEART: THE BEGINNING
CAUGHT IN THE ACT

NOVELLAS
BREAKING TIES: A SEAL TEAM HEARTBREAKERS NOVELLA
TO CAPTURE A HIGHLANDER'S HEART: THE COURTSHIP

CHILDREN'S BOOKS
WILLY C. SPARKS: THE DRAGON WHO LOST HIS FIRE.

FOR NEW RELEASES

Visit me at my:
Website: www.teresareasor.com
Blog: mymusesmusings.blogspot.com
Facebook: .facebook.com/teresa.reasor
Facebook Author Page: facebook.com/SEAL.Crazy
Twitter: @teresareasor
Substance-B: substance-b.com/TeresaReasor.html
Goodreads:
goodreads.com/author/show/2308555.Teresa_J_Reasor
Pinterest: .pinterest.com/teresareasor

Sign up for my Newsletter
http://bit.ly/I7TtiC